A Sh

BODIES
AND SOLE

A Shores Mystery

BODIES AND SOLE

Hilary MacLeod

The Acorn Press
Charlottetown
2014

Other books in the *Shores Mysteries* series

Praise for *Revenge of the Lobster Lover*:

"...[an] amusing comic mystery"
– Margaret Cannon, *Globe and Mail*

"Revenge of the Lobster Lover is a good read for lovers of light-hearted mysteries."
- *Atlantic Books Today*

"Readers will find themselves hooked on this light-hearted, edgy read"
- *The Chronicle Herald*

"...readers will want to know whodunit -- and why. MacLeod's droll humour helps propel her story."
- *The Montreal Gazette*

Praise for *Mind Over Mussels*:

"...a thoroughly delightful, cosy comic crime story - a restful break from the grittier and oft times gruesome murder mysteries..."
- Cottage Lady, *Sleuth of Baker Street*

"...this country is producing a wide range of thoughtful writing in this genre - which is also often funny...Mind Over Mussels...has a lot of fun as it stretches to its rather bizarre conclusion."
- Jenni Morton, *The Star Phoenix*

Praise for *All is Clam*:

"Mountie Jane Jamison returns in this delightful Christmas confection set in The Shores, that lovely fictional spot just off the coast of Prince Edward Island...As she sifts the clues, she finds herself hoping for a Christmas miracle: that this death will turn into an accident. This one is great fun."
- Margaret Cannon, *The Globe and Mail*

"(Hilary MacLeod) manages to skillfully blend the dark side with the light, threading humour in characters and dialogue through the serious tale of human foibles and tragedy."
- Linda Wiken (aka Erika Chase), *Mystery Maven Canada*

"...her best by far...this is a complex Christmas story and mystery. MacLeod is to be congratulated."
- Elizabeth Cran, *The Guardian*

Bodies and Sole © 2014 by Hilary MacLeod

All rights reserved. No part of this publication may be reproduced, stored in a retrieval system, or transmitted, in any form or by any means, without the prior written permission of the publisher or, in case of photocopying or other reprographic copying, a licence from the Canadian Copyright Licensing Agency.

ACORNPRESS

P.O. Box 22024
Charlottetown, Prince Edward Island
C1A 9J2
acornpresscanada.com

Printed and Bound in Canada
Cover illustration and interior design by Matt Reid
Editing by Sherie Hodds

Library and Archives Canada Cataloguing in Publication

MacLeod, Hilary, author
 Bodies and sole / Hilary MacLeod.

Issued in print and electronic formats.
ISBN 978-1-927502-31-0 (pbk.).--ISBN 978-1-927502-32-7 (ebook)

 I. Title.

PS8625.L4555B63 2014   C813'.6   C2014-903532-2
                                            C2014-903533-0

Canada | Canada Council for the Arts | Conseil des Arts du Canada

The publisher acknowledges the support of the Government of Canada through the Canada Book Fund of the Department of Canadian Heritage and the Canada Council for the Arts Block Grant Program.

To Margo "Cat Lady" MacNaughton for her love and selfless devotion to cats, including Reggie, Briar, Jimmy, Curly, Baby, Hope, Gorgeous, June, Bobby, Sophie, Gray, Sarge, Paris, Lloyd, Bobby, Squirt, Drifter, Big Daddy, Laddie, Teddy Bear, Girlie, Lady Princess, Suki, Shaun, Becker, Porter, Augie, Roscoe, Rocky, Ivy and Ivy, Dagwood and Blondie, The Gang and others unnamed here, to all of whom she has given names – and a chance at life.

Hy McAllister's Facebook status:

Scientists and priests don't know where the soul lives in the body. For a long time they thought it was the liver, because it's the best-looking vital organ.

Likes: 9

Comments: If you've got soul, you don't have to be good-looking.
                    I like sole better than liver.

Chapter One

The skull washed up and slipped behind a big rock.

She had not tripped on it, thrown up on it, nor been knocked down by it.

She hadn't even seen it.

Hy McAllister was taking her usual morning run on the shore, where, a few years before, she had stumbled, literally, across a corpse.

Since then she'd had other close encounters with dead bodies, on and off the beach.

She planted wet sneaker prints in the stretch of packed sand above the surf. She splashed through the run, the outlet of water from the pond that had served up a bloated cadaver a few years back. Undisturbed, the run carved across the sand, mixed fresh with salt water, then hitchhiked to Europe on the Gulf Stream.

The sea stone rose behind her twenty feet off shore. It was the signature of The Shores, the landmark that told people they were here. Once a part of the cape, the chunk had been carved away by the wind and the waves. Each year it got smaller and changed shape. This winter's storms had sculpted it into the head of a man, staring upward in agony. A black man whose white hair had been formed by cormorant feces. The rock appeared to be screaming at the cape to which it had once been attached. The new look formed by the fierce winter gave Hy the creeps.

Her red curls bobbed on the morning air as she headed for the far cape. At low tide, she could have rounded it and continued onto the next stretch of shore, known as Mack's shore, and then on to the next and the next and the next, for miles. The capes jutted out toward the water and divided beach from beach. At high or incoming tide, it was still possible to get around them, but only by wading through water.

The tide was coming in fast. Behind her, the waves played with the skull like a soccer ball, picking it up and leaving it a bit farther up the sand each time. Then stopped. It lay, exposed on the stretch of sand, grimacing. There was no one to see.

Not even Hy.

Just as she was about to turn, a flock of gulls swooped down and began pecking and squealing and fighting. Finding nothing of interest, nothing to eat, they soon gave up, in a disruption of wing-flapping that tossed the skull about. A series of strong waves crashed up onto the sands, took it up, and deposited it in a nest of rocks, out of sight.

That was when Hy turned back.

Missed it entirely.

It would be up to someone not yet at The Shores to find it for her. Someone she didn't know, but who was already on her mind.

www.theshores200.com
There have been no murders or unusual deaths in The Shores

in almost a full calendar year. That is, if you don't count health nut Morton Sinclair who, as Gus Mack put it, "woke up dead one morning." He was always running the capes, holding his boot camp exercise sessions that no one attended, eating only organic. But he died at forty-two. Overdid it, that's what Dr. Dunn said. Too much of a good thing. Healthy living did him in. The doctor should know. He's never done a lick of exercise and his diet is fats, starch and brownies. Yet he's still alive at ninety-two.

Apart from that, everyone in The Shores has stayed alive, if not always healthy, for nearly a year.

We can't guarantee our 200th anniversary celebrations will be corpse-free, but we'll try to keep the killing at bay.

Not Big Bay.

Hy grinned, paused and highlighted what she'd written. She'd never get away with it. She hit delete. Then she stared at the blank screen.

Where to begin?

Her friend and on-again off-again boyfriend Ian Simmons had designed the web page for The Shores' 200th anniversary and she had agreed to provide the content, free of charge. *Content* was the name of her company; she provided editorial services to various websites on and off Red Island.

In the past few years, she seemed to be more in the business of stumbling on murders and helping solve them. That's what had sparked her cheeky entry.

She began typing again.

The Shores, Red Island… 200 Years and Counting

Counting…down to another murder?

She couldn't have known there was more death on its way to

the village. That it was already washing up on the shore, and would soon be rolling down The Island Way.

www.theshores200.com
As you drive into The Shores, you reach the high ground above the village.
Here at the top of the hill, the breathtaking beauty unfolds. Different every time, depending on the mood of the sky and the sea. Bright blue or brooding grey sky; the sea, dashing up on the shore, black with anger from a storm the previous day, or calm, cold. A deep navy blue.
The landscape like a patchwork quilt: fields piercing red and newly turned over in the spring; flowing gold wheat and timothy in June and July; rowed with the white blossoms and fat green leaves of the potato plants in August; dusted with pink snow in winter.

Hy shoved her chair back and pushed herself up. She needed photographs. Ian liked editing photos, but he was no good at taking them. She slung her camera bag over her shoulder and grabbed her bike from the front porch. She rode until the hill got too steep and then pushed the bicycle the rest of the way. At the top of the hill, she stopped. Turned. Feasted.

The late-spring fields were defined by rows of spruce, new crops just beginning – pale greens and the neon yellow of the canola fields, the sky and the sea in harmony, today, a cold, brilliant blue. So similar, it was hard to see which was water and which sky. The demarcation between sea and sand was much sharper, the water hugging the land as it curved in and out around the massive red capes.

Hy took photographs, although she had dozens from this

view. All beautiful. None the same. Yet all capturing the essence of The Shores.

Attaching her zoom lens, Hy brought the village closer.

www.theshores200.com
The houses all huddle in a circle, facing each other, white houses with green or black roofs. There are a few empty lots where there used to be more public buildings at the centre of the village. Only the hall stands today.

It's surprising that, until that moment, Hy hadn't noticed the streak of orange on either side of the road and the pungent smell. But now she caught a flash in the viewfinder, and followed it as it marched all the way down the hill to the hall and back up the other side of the road.

Marigolds. Along the road, someone had planted a string of marigolds, two deep, across the front of everyone's property, even the abandoned homes, even the home of the three sisters. Their house looked almost abandoned, but for the three sets of clothes hanging from the clothesline.

Monday. Washday. Hy zoomed in on the clothesline and took a photograph. She'd use it as her banner for Monday posts on the website.

The thought had hardly time to lodge in her mind when a Smart car went whizzing by her, honking.

Hy got a clear view as she walked her bicycle down the hill. Little orange soldiers, marching, two by two, all the way down The Island way. Standing ramrod straight, spiky green leaves and golden balls perched atop little hillocks of flower beds. Crossing ditches, down the length of local scumbag Jared MacPherson's house, even across the front lawns of vacant houses, they kept marching. Marching across Hy's own lawn – and all the way down to the centre of the village, where the military floral parade ended with a wraparound of the hall.

So fascinated was Hy by the marigolds that, once back on her bike, she continued riding past her house, following the Smart car that had now slowed down.

It stopped suddenly and Hy very nearly crashed into it.

Marlene Weeks, from the provincial department of tourism, had spotted an offending marigold. Some creature must have tugged it out of line, because it lay on its side, a small ball of earth and roots pointing skyward.

Marlene groped in the glove compartment for the item least likely to be found there in most cars – gloves. She slid her carefully manicured fingers into them, and got out of the car, only to find Hy shoving the plant back in place.

"That's government property."

Hy dusted off her hands, the red clay sticking to them and smearing her jeans.

"Soon to be dead government property." Hy beamed at the woman. Cheeky, thought Marlene.

She said not another word, but turned around, got back in the car, and skidded off the shoulder, spraying red dust all over Hy. Hy watched her go, then pulled out a half dozen marigolds, stuck them in her bike basket and went home, where she put them in a container on the porch.

Stolen? No. Liberated. The thought galvanized her. She got a barrel, marched it down to the road where the marigolds appeared to be guarding her property, and dug them all up.

She planted them in the barrel and stood back to survey her work. They looked cheerful. Better than the soldier formation. She dusted herself off, grabbed her bicycle and headed to see

Gus. Turning down The Shore Lane, she saw the Smart car parked at Moira's house.

Who was that woman? What did she have to do with the marigolds?

Someone must have planted them overnight because no one in The Shores had seen it happen.

Chapter Two

www.theshores200.com
Across from the hall there used to be a one-room schoolhouse and beside it was Mack's General Store. That went up in flames fifty years ago when a farmer, who will go unnamed, backed into a propane tank. Propelled by the subsequent explosion, owner Abel Mack came flying out the window, landed on his feet and went home to his wife Gus for lunch. He never rebuilt.

Gus Mack had spent sixty of her eighty-five years living at The Shores, collecting bits and pieces of history. There were photographs, press clippings and old, yellowed recipes, and letters and school copybooks spread all over her kitchen floor.

A patchwork quilt, Hy had advised her. Putting together a book was just like a patchwork quilt. It all pieced together.

Gus shook her head, and stuck a knitting needle into her shock of white hair.

She sighed and leaned forward, shoved a few items around with her hands, then leaned back and continued the job with her feet.

"You'll never get that finished in time," said Hy. "It'll have to be edited, formatted…"

"Don't 'spec so."

"What do you expect?"

Hy and Gus had gone through this over and over again during the past few years. Hy – offering to help Gus put it together; Gus – resisting all offers to sort it out.

"It" was Gus's history of The Shores – clippings, photos, handwritten anecdotes by herself and others, meant to form a book of a kind similar to those other communities had produced, all organized, typed and printed out, usually by one of the vanity presses. They were bought up, eagerly, by members of the respective communities. Everyone had to have a copy – especially of those editions that contained names and ages and family connections. They quickly became dog-eared, as locals made frequent checks of birth dates and marriage dates, all the small details of a neighbour's life a person could sometimes forget.

Gus looked up from slipping a photograph into a vinyl sleeve.

"I expect that this will be the only copy. None of that editing and formatting and printing. Just what I put together here. Always went that way in the past, and it's the past we're recording."

"Just the one book? Your book?"

"That's right. They can keep it in the hall someplace."

"Still, it would be nice if everyone in the village could have a copy. And if they bought it, it would pay for itself and maybe raise money for the hall."

"It would be nice." Gus had been trying to decide between two photographs. She chose one, and slipped it into a vinyl sleeve. "But I can't do it. That's it. Maybe if Abel were around more to help…" She shut the album. "Time enough."

Comparing this book to a quilt was all very fine, Gus thought, but she wasn't having too much luck these days with the quilts. She'd begun a traditional log cabin, because it used up lots of small pieces and she had so many of those. A back porch filled with boxes and boxes of them. Some cut and sorted, some just a thought in her eye.

This book was more like that porch. So many things, some sorted, some just a thought.

Anyway, she'd gone off the log cabin quilt, though it was meant to be a heritage project, a 200th anniversary hanging for the hall. She didn't need that. She was already immortalized in town. "In town" never meant the nearest town, Winterside. There were only two on the whole island but the designation only went to the provincial capital, Charlottetown.

Gus had a true heritage quilt there in the permanent collection of the Confederation Centre of the Arts.

"Ugly as anything," she always said. It was. She'd made it out of patches provided by her mother-in-law, patches that came from her mother and from generations of women in the family. Practically the whole two hundred years The Shores had existed. The patches weren't pretty. They were mostly from the men's work clothes – dull greys, browns and blacks, threadbare in places, but "serviceable."

The quilt went in the Charlottetown exhibition the year Gus finally buckled down and "used them up." The acquisitions curator for the Confederation Centre collection snapped it up the moment she saw it, drooling over its "authenticity."

"Welcome to it," Gus had said at the time. "Don't know what I would have done with it, home. Prob'ly have rotted out there on that back porch."

No, Gus had decided, even though it was a heritage celebration this year, there could be too much of a good thing, and she wasn't going to make "one of them dull quilts" again.

A crazy quilt. That's what she'd decided. She was finally going to get her head around a crazy quilt. She might be crazy to do it, but that would only be fitting.

It lay on the floor around her as well. Patches and bits and pieces of local history strewn around her purple rocker recliner.

She couldn't make sense of them, nor the book.

She leaned back and closed her eyes and dozed off. Hy slipped out, wondering how she was going to get the book on track for the big celebration at the end of August.

Every time Hy attempted to sort it, Gus messed it up again. It was as if she were sabotaging her own work. But Hy couldn't figure out why.

It was Hy's year to take care of the flowerbed alongside the hall. She hadn't been looking forward to the prospect until she got her bright idea.

She put a flyer in the village mailboxes, inviting all villagers to bring their marigolds to the hall, where they would be planted in a special commemorative flowerbed.

Hy knew she wasn't the only one who didn't like Marlene's landscaping. Marigolds kept popping out of line, until the straight marching lines formed a disorderly platoon.

She made it clear the villagers could keep the marigolds where they were – if they liked their flowers at attention. Gladys Fraser did. So did Olive MacLean and Estelle Joudry.

Moira Toombs also liked them just where they were. She liked the neat orderliness of them. Besides, thought Moira, shaking her doormat on the front stoop, she would be able to see the commemorative flower bed from right here, as if it were in her own garden. She'd have her cake and eat it, too.

And then there was the fact that the job was done. No extra work required, and her with another wedding to plan. The first attempt last summer had fallen through. A man had fallen off the cape right between the matrimonial couple just as they were saying their vows. Time had slid by and they hadn't set another date, but she wasn't going to let Frank get away.

Many of the other villagers found the marigolds inconvenient. They had to be watered and whipper-snipped, and the men couldn't get their mowers around them. The husbands had been threatening to mow them down.

They flocked to the hall to donate their unwanted marigolds to the cause.

By the time Marlene had any idea what was going on, it was too late for her to do anything.

Except one thing.

Mountie Jane Jamieson started every day looking out the picture window from the police house on Shipwreck Hill. She never tired of the beauty of her patch. Jamieson had been assigned to The Shores in a special arrangement with the island detachment because of the number of murders and suspicious deaths there over the past several years.

She'd started out as a tight-assed, by-the-book cop, but The Shores had worked its magic on her, transforming her soul to one that responded to the call of the most beautiful spot on the island.

Perhaps on the planet, she thought. Every morning when she stepped out of the police house, no matter how pressing her duties, she would stop and gaze down at the village, clustered in a circle of amity around the only remaining community building: the hall.

In winter, there would be smoke curling up from the hall and from all the houses that encircled it. Not from wood stoves anymore, but from furnaces, devouring oil and pumping out the heat that the village's aging population required.

Men and women who'd been born in a time when houses were not insulated – except by a bit of seaweed scattered in the attic – had become accustomed to the luxuries the modern age afforded.

Gus liked her creature comforts, too, but she was afraid of the furnace. She would not go to sleep with that monster grumbling in the basement. She'd turn it off, and swear she didn't suffer the cold at all.

People suspected that Abel turned the heat up after Gus went to sleep, and turned it down before she woke in the morning. No one could prove that, because no one ever saw Abel to ask him.

There were only two curls of smoke in the village today. Gus did like to turn on the furnace to take the chill off a spring morning. And there was the smoke billowing out of April Dewey's house, giving the May day the scent of fall.

April was the best little cook in The Shores, and insisted on cooking with her wood range. No one could dispute the results. Not Murdo Black, her partner, who suffered through the dog days of August in the baking heat of April's kitchen, with six children under twelve chasing around the room, yelling and laughing.

Welcome to it, thought Jamieson. She and Murdo had been assigned to watch over The Shores. She wasn't sure how that had happened. She didn't know it had been Murdo's persuasive tactics. He just happened to know about the extramarital affair of a senior officer, and had used it to get Jamieson and him posted together.

In part, it was loyalty to Jamieson. At the time he'd been her only friend. But it was also April. He'd fallen for her and her über domesticity, and now did hardly any police work at all.

Jamieson didn't mind. She'd stroll through the village, dazed by the beauty of the ocean or the sky, the land, or all three, taking great breaths of pleasure in the salt air. She'd pass by Murdo, mowing April's lawn, painting her front door, fixing fallen shingles, and she'd wave, sleepily, a small smile on a face not previously accustomed to that expression.

The phone rang at the police house, interrupting Jamieson's morning reverie.

"A theft. Of what?" She continued to gaze down at the shore, though the voice of the woman on the other end was high and irritating.

"Flowers? Flowers?!" Was it even possible to steal flowers? "What kind?"

A year before, the question wouldn't have occurred to Jamieson. She hadn't been able to tell the difference then between one flower and the next. Now she had a growing collection of pressed flowers stashed away in a closet – her secret hobby. Not a secret to Moira Toombs, who cleaned the police house, and snooped everywhere. She thought the less of Jamieson for having such a ridiculous hobby – when there were the flowers to be seen, in season, in the outdoors, where they belonged.

"Marigolds? Oh yes." Jamieson remembered seeing them lining The Island Way, the provincial road that ran through The Shores to just beyond Big Bay, then turned around on itself and came back.

Flashes of orange caught her eye as her gaze moved out the window from the shore to the hall, where there were several women fussing around the flowerbed. Hy, she recognized right away. With her friend, Annabelle, the glamorous farm woman who fished with her husband Ben Mack. And some of the Women's Institute ladies coming and going.

Yes, of course, Hy would be behind it. Jamieson sighed. She'd nearly charged Hy for numerous offences in the past, but had never quite been able to do it. But stealing flowers? She'd be laughed out of the village if she tried to pin that on anyone, though the screeching woman on the phone just might drive her to it.

"You're staying at Toombs's?" As if she had to ask the question. As if everybody in the village didn't know Marlene was there, when she'd arrived, how long she was staying, and who her father and grandfather were. Even though she still hadn't bothered to introduce herself to the villagers.

"Well, I suggest you look out the window, or, better yet, go over to the hall. You'll find your marigolds there. And I would say this is not a police matter, but more a matter of taste."

Jamieson had thought the marching marigolds looked ridiculous, too.

When she got off the phone with "that annoying woman," as she would henceforth refer to Marlene, Jamieson picked up her usual routine.

She would stop by Ian Simmons's house, just partway down the hill, and have a chat before she set off on her walking rounds.

Although she wouldn't admit it, even to herself, Jamieson was interested in Ian. She was well aware of his complicated connection to Hy. They were both her friends. They were both her partners, in a way, in crime-solving: Hy, curious, nosy and with odd pockets of knowledge that had been useful. Ian, analytical, a technical whiz and committed Google guy.

It wasn't for those qualities, though, that Jamieson dropped in on him practically every morning.

She told herself it was his intelligence that she found attractive, but she was interested in the man. If Hy weren't going to be bothered with him – which seemed to be the case at the moment – then she would be.

He provided her, that morning, with the perfect reason to keep dropping by.

"Look at this," he said as she came through the door. He didn't turn, just kept staring at the beautiful glowing iMac screen. He was on a page announcing a free online forensics course at a British university.

Jamieson read the page over Ian's shoulder. On his other shoulder, Jasmine, his parrot, was eyeing Jamieson warily. Other than Hy, Jasmine didn't like women, especially if she could sense they liked Ian.

"Introduction to Forensics," Jamieson read.

"For-en-sick. Gag gag sick…" Jasmine acted out throwing up as she said the words.

Too clever by half, thought Jamieson.

"Want to do it?" asked Ian.

Jamieson opened her mouth to refuse. What could it possibly tell her that she hadn't already learned in her police training?

Ian patted Jasmine's head to calm her. "Together? With me?"

That made it more appealing. Jamieson closed her mouth.

"We'd have to do it here. All the videos and everything…"

Ian had the only decent WiFi connection in the village.

Of course it would have to be here.

"Sure," said Jamieson. "It would be good to brush up my skills."

And necessary, they both thought. Forensic teams were frequently needed in The Shores, but never seemed to make it to the village.

Chapter Three

Hy and Annabelle were busy stuffing the marigolds into the hall flowerbed. In a different kind of formation. Thick twists of the orange flowers now spelled out: *The Shores,* and underneath it: *200 years.*

They stood up, backs aching from the effort, just as Marlene came out of Moira's house and in a throaty voice, demanded:

"Just what is going on here?"

In a seemingly choreographed motion, Hy and Annabelle stepped back and to the side to reveal their handiwork.

Marlene's eyes opened wide. So did her mouth. She couldn't speak. She didn't know what to say. The fact was, the planting here at the hall looked much better than the troops of marigolds descending on the village. But she didn't want to say so.

"I'd like to speak to the community liaison," she said haughtily.

"You've only to ask. I thought you might have before now." Hy pulled off a gardening glove and extended her hand to Marlene.

"Hy McAllister. Community liaison for the 200th."

Marlene sighed. A redhead and a smart Alec. She held out her hand reluctantly.

"Marlene Weeks."

They shook hands. Hy wiped hers off, before sticking it back in her glove. Marlene, always nervous, had clammy hands.

"You're a native?"

"Excuse me?"

"You were born here?"

Hy smiled and shook her curls. "No. I'm a come from away."

"Then why are you the community liaison?"

"Because no one else wanted to be."

"Hyacinth speaks for us." Gladys Fraser had been tidying up some of the plantings, and stood up straight in her capacity as President of the Women's Institute to lend weight to her pronouncement.

Hy was surprised to receive such solid support from Gladys, who never had much good to say of anyone, and had never truly welcomed Hy as a member of the community.

Hy bet Marlene was from away, too, and that Gladys knew it.

"Thank you, Gladys." There was a real thread of gratitude in Hy's voice.

"Well, you are from away. But she's from away, too. When it's our from-aways against their from-aways, well, we have to back ours, doncha see?"

"I actually think I do."

It appeared that Marlene didn't, but Gladys was right about one thing. She was from away – Nova Scotia. Marlene screwed up her face. Opened her mouth a few more times like a fish. In the end, she said nothing – just turned and left. Hy and Annabelle were left to snicker behind her back, offering up a high-five for the victory.

Marlene sneaked back to the hall when she expected most villagers would be eating their supper. She took some photographs. Returning to Moira's, she wrote a report about her landscaping triumph, galvanizing the locals into a community effort. She patted herself on the back several times in the report, just in case her supervisor didn't.

www.theshores200.com
The Sullivan house, also known as Wild Rose Cottage, was built late in the 19th century. It was what the Victorians call a cottage but it was a big house in this village – 24 rooms. The house was in the Sullivan family until early in the 20th century. Since then, it has gone into disrepair, only to be raised up again by its latest owner.

Up and over Shipwreck Hill, the road that rose from the hall, past Ian Simmons's and the police house, was the Sullivan house. Once the grandest house in the village, then fallen into deep disrepair, it had risen like a phoenix from the ashes.

Inside and outside she was scrubbed, bandaged and knocked back into shape. New foundation, roof, gutters and downspouts. New windows and doors, a new splash of paint on the exterior – trim only, black and red and white against the authentic grey cedar shingles. The wild roses in the garden were cut back, and flowerbeds with local plants carved out of the red clay. Golden Glow, Siberian Iris, Lilies, Black-Eyed Susans, Dahlias. They would all have their day in the sun as spring and summer plunged along toward the heritage day celebrations.

Behind it all was a woman rumoured to have had three husbands. Vera Gloom. She'd bought the place in the fall, given her orders to the contractor, and returned to the revived house in the spring. With not a husband to be seen, except, perhaps, in the glint of blue diamonds on her fingers. The villagers were curious, about the diamonds and the house. They wanted information. The carpenter, Harold MacLean, was the only villager who'd been inside. He'd done the finishing work, so he'd seen the whole thing just before it was, well, finished.

But Harold, everyone agreed, was worse than useless. They liked him, and he was a great carpenter, but he spoke, if at all, in one-word sentences.

"What's it like?" people would ask.

"Nice," he'd say, and, if he were feeling chatty he'd add, on a long intake of breath, "Heyup. Nice."

"Of course it's nice," Hy had complained to Gus one afternoon shortly after Vera had moved in. "It's bound to be nice. We saw all the right trucks from all the right stores going in and out of there. High-end stores. Stuff from Halifax, Boston." *That great New England touch.* "How could it not be nice?"

"Well, then, and it might not be." Gus had surveyed with satisfaction her forty-year-old linoleum floor that extended from the pantry, through the kitchen, laundry room and mud room. Real, genuine, one hundred per cent linoleum. You couldn't get that anymore. This vinyl flooring was all very fine, but she wouldn't have it in her house. Wouldn't last a week, with all the comings and goings.

Hy followed her gaze. The linoleum was in great shape. It shone from weekly scrubbing and seasonal polishing. No need to replace it with what Hy agreed would be an inferior product.

"Tile. She'll have tile, no question." Hy had gazed out the window, as if she could see all the way to the Sullivan house, on the other side of Shipwreck Hill. But all she could see was Ian's house, and she turned her eyes away. Ian, and his house, held less interest for her than usual. Their on-and-off relationship was off at the moment and Hy knew she was to blame. She'd become indifferent to Ian, other than as a friend, because she had a new interest. An interest she hadn't told anyone about. Truth was, she found it a bit embarrassing.

Vera Gloom was rattling around in the big old Sullivan house. Twenty-four rooms, and she was using only two or three, if you counted the bathroom. Three more when the boys came. She placed her teacup and saucer in the kitchen sink – a newly gleaming addition to the old house, double cast-iron, with a thick layer of white enamel, and porcelain handles on the old-fashioned-style faucets. It was an ultramodern nod to the past.

Vera touched the smooth enamel with hands encrusted with rings that appeared to be a series of engagement and wedding rings, collected on her ring finger and all the others, except for the pinkies. Gold and platinum settings, sparkling with white and blue diamonds. Unconsciously, she caressed the rings on hands otherwise unattractive, so thin and thin-skinned, the veins popping up in a purple-blue march across her knuckles.

She turned and left the room, admiring the new features in the old house, the gleaming wood floors – not replaced by laminate as had been suggested by the contractor. She slid slippered feet across the shiny surface. The original wide pine, sanded down and waxed up, showed the marks of its age and wore them well.

She drew a hand across the tongue-and-groove wainscoting that lined the hallway. Original, too – except for the parts that had had to be fixed, a job done so expertly by carpenter Harold

MacLean that you couldn't tell what was old and what was new.

Strange man, Vera thought, as she looked up to the ceiling to admire the tongue-and-groove there, now painted a brilliant white. He was a carpenter, yet each of his fingers was different, as if each belonged to someone else. You wouldn't have imagined he'd have any dexterity. But he did. He did.

It was a pity that the chair lift had to be installed up the beautiful, generous staircase with its milled banister, but that was the price she had to pay for having the family here. Once they were settled in, they'd be up and down. She was fooling herself, of course. Vera sighed. Once in their rooms, that's where they seemed to want to stay. It was she who used the lift to bring their meals up and down.

The family. She smiled as she hauled herself up the stairs, needing the banister to be able to ascend herself. It hadn't been necessary a year ago.

She was getting old. Who would take care of her when her time came? As she had taken care of them? They certainly wouldn't do anything for her. The men.

The family. Soon they would be here. And the house was prepared for them. Each one of them. She opened the first bedroom door.

Blair would love the mahogany desk. She could see him now, sitting behind it, pen in hand. He wouldn't use a computer. Blair was strictly a pen and ink man. Fountain pen. It was one of the things she admired about him.

He hadn't written anything in a long time. To inspire him, she had left some pages on the desk, a long love poem he had once written for her. Perhaps it might inspire, not only a desire to write but a renewed desire for her. He would become her husband again, not just in name.

But that wasn't what she really wanted. She wanted someone new. A fresh face – and funding. She got these feelings sometimes, because their divorce had been such a success. They all had been. She prided herself on that.

Blair's only interest now was in his books. He would love that big chintz armchair. The wall-to-ceiling glassed-in cases filled with his library. New books were arriving every day as she ordered them.

She could see him already, sitting there, chewing on a pipe, his reading glasses perched on his nose, hardly noticing her come into the room.

The door to the next room was already open. She'd been in there earlier in the morning, setting things up. The easel placed just so in front of the window, to catch the morning light, when Charlie liked to paint. Propped on it, the watercolour he'd been working on most recently, taken from a photograph of Sullivan house, with a man who appeared to be waving from an upstairs window.

She made her way to the next room.

There was the new wine silk bathrobe she'd bought for Hank. It was draped artistically over the end of the bed, a beautiful four-poster, made up with crisp white linen sheets, a fat white wool blanket, and paisley bedcover – in wine and cream.

She walked over to the bed, smoothed the linens, plumped up a pillow, and stepped back.

Not that Hank would ever get under the sheets. He'd spend his days on it. That was just as well. Saved the making of it. A considerate man.

She left the door of the room slightly ajar. She expected Hank would be the first to arrive. He usually was, she wasn't sure why.

People seemed to find it odd that she housed her former

husbands and her current one – and that they all seemed to get along.

Satisfied that all was ready for the family, Vera retreated downstairs. The boys would be comfortable. It was surprising how much each depended on her, how they put up with each other and got along so well. Never an argument. She was fond of all of them, but she wasn't a one-man woman. One at a time, yes.

Now it was time for another one.

The room off the kitchen that used to be the pantry was her office: iMac computer, printer and phone.

She sat down and got online. She began to scour through local nursing homes and recent obituaries. She bent intently over the keyboard, clicking and scrolling with her mouse, her search spanning numerous websites, until the Internet connection, inevitably, died on her.

None.

No. None today.

Widowers were a lot harder to come by than widows.

Too bad she wasn't a man. She'd seen many women that she bet would be ripe for the plucking.

She called what she was doing research, but it was really her own form of online dating.

Chapter Four

Am I computer dating?

Hy had begun asking herself that since she'd become involved in an online back-and-forth with an intriguing keyboard pal several weeks before. She'd tired of her work on the village website and had slipped onto Facebook.

Over the winter, she'd discovered Facebook in a dull moment when the weather had raged outside, the snow suggesting a glass of wine and a virtual tour of sunnier places where she might escape for a week or two.

Before she knew it, she'd clicked on Facebook, established a page, and become hooked. That is, she checked into the site first thing in the morning and once at night. She posted occasionally. Friends trickled in, including some very old pals she'd lost track of. And, since she knew the site could be good for business, she'd posted and shared a link to her late mother's back-to-the-woods bestseller, *A Life on the Land*. It was written in ink made from nature and the drawings sketched with charcoal from the woodstove. Life in the woods had cost Hy's mother, father and grandfather their lives. It had nearly killed the infant Hy when a bush plane her grandfather flew in to rescue his daughter and granddaughter crashed on a remote and frozen lake. Her mother's manuscript had been strapped to the infant Hy's life jacket.

The book hardly needed promoting. A coffee table edition some years back had brought on a resurgence of popularity and provided a steady flow of income to Hy's nest egg.

There was a steady flow of friend requests from people who knew, or wished they'd known, her mother. More came from others who'd put two and two together and identified Hy as the woman connected with the series of murders at The Shores, now world-famous, not for its beaches, but for its air of mystery.

Hy found it fairly easy to sort out the weirdos from the genuine friends.

But she wasn't quite sure how to categorize him.

He'd popped up after *A Life on the Land* had gone into another new edition.

"I'm a great admirer of your mother's book and work. If she had lived, I'm sure she would have been an inspiring advocate for the environment. I was only a few months old when she died – hardly in a position to form opinions about the woman and her work. What I know, I know from later, when I read her book and understood the depth of her experience."

Though he was a bit cagey about his own background and current situation – his Facebook site didn't tell much – Hy considered him genuine enough and accepted his friend request. She now listed "Finn" Finnegan among her friends, one of about forty Americans. To her surprise, she and Finn had begun corresponding regularly, sending messages nearly every day.

One thing Hy did know about Finn. He was good-looking. A shock of thick black hair. Burning blue eyes. And he was single.

Or so it said in his stats.

Am I online dating?

Chapter Five

Frank Webster was driving across the causeway behind a moving truck. Frank himself had just a modest van, with which he made deliveries around this end of the island. He wondered where the truck was headed. It had to be The Shores – there was no other community around. But a moving truck? There wasn't much cause for those here – unless it was some wealthy new tourist on the capes. He went through a mental list, but couldn't come up with anyone who'd need a truck that big.

That woman at the Sullivan house? But all her stuff had been delivered a month ago, hadn't it? There had been two huge moving trucks. Surely enough to fill that big old place.

When he got to the village, he didn't stop at his fiancée Moira's house, but continued following the truck, taking the turn at Shipwreck Hill, up and over the rise, and down toward the Sullivan house.

The truck turned into the driveway ahead of him. He pulled over to the side of the road, jumped out of his vehicle, and flipped open the hood, pretending to be occupied with some trouble, positioned so that he could see what was going on.

She came out of the house to inspect the contents when the driver opened the back of the truck. Frank knew who he was.

Bernie Stubbs. Not just the driver. Son-in-law of the company owner. Frank thought of the woman as that "hard old bitch" Vera Gloom, though he'd had little to do with her. A few small parcel deliveries. No tips.

Bernie released the ramp and jumped into the truck. He came out with a square box on a trolley. Big box. The double front doors of the house had to be opened to get it in.

Not too heavy in spite of its size, Frank thought. He had experience with that sort of thing, would have noticed the degree of pressure on the ramp.

Vera and the driver emerged from the house, she still talking and gesturing in every direction. Bernie, head down, plowed forward, every bit of his body language concentrated on silencing her sounds and movements.

He just wanted to get the job done and get gone.

Frank continued tinkering under the hood of his vehicle, keeping a sly eye on the proceedings.

The next box to emerge was oblong. It had to be tilted on the trolley to clear the roof of the van. About seven feet long, Frank estimated. Maybe three feet on all sides. If he could only touch it, he'd be able to guess its weight within a few pounds. A skill he'd picked up in the business. He could do it with women, too. Estimate the weight of them from just a touch. They didn't like it when he'd say, "130. 140. 150…," even though he made sure to round it down.

His fiancée had only noticed this annoying habit after they were engaged. Like most brides, she'd lost weight before her wedding, even though she was thin as a dried spaghetti noodle to begin with. With a second wedding attempt in the wings, Moira was hardly eating and when Frank touched her, he was constantly making downward estimates. "140… 135… 130…

now, Moira, that's way too thin."

Moira had smiled at that. Too thin? Not possible according to what the secret stash of *Cosmo* magazines under her bed told her.

Again the panicked gesturing from the woman as Bernie rolled the second package down the ramp, the word FRAGILE in bold black down the full length of it.

She followed him into the house. Just the hallway, Frank guessed, because out they came again quite quickly. Bernie into the truck. Vera Gloom and her unpleasant face remaining at the bottom of the ramp.

Suddenly, she let out a squawk. Bernie halted at the top of the ramp, another oblong box, but this one shorter and fatter, perched on the wheels of the trolley.

She was gesturing wildly. It seemed to Frank that she wanted the box upended. It also seemed to Frank that Bernie had no idea what she wanted.

"The other way. The other way," she screamed.

Horizontal?

"My creations!"

Maybe he should offer to help?

Frank slammed the hood shut, and went to investigate.

Relief washed over her face when he strode over.

"Thank God. The two of you can do this properly." She turned to Bernie. "Forget the trolley. You can pick it up together. And be careful. This is art. These are works of art."

Bernie looked dubious. Picking up was in the contract. Picking up and carrying was not. That's what the trolley was for. Still, he was anxious to get the job over with.

He and Frank hoisted it together. Hoisted it too high at first. It was much lighter than its size would suggest. About twenty or thirty pounds, Frank would guess.

It was deceptively light, but awkwardly shaped. They carried the box into the front entrance, now crowded with the three boxes.

"Anywhere we can take these for you? Clear the road, like?"

Bernie frowned at Frank. The job was done, as far as he was concerned. He wanted his dinner.

She assumed her only smile. It was much more of a go hence than a come hither.

And so the two men muscled the boxes upstairs. They weren't heavy, as Frank had observed, but they were unwieldy and had to be carried above the level of the banister. That made it heart attack work.

One by one, they got them to the upstairs hallway.

"Perfect," she said.

"Any help with the unpacking?" Frank dusted off his hands after they shoved the last box into place beside the others.

This time, her standard, unsatisfactory smile turned almost soft.

"No, no." She combed her diamond-encrusted fingers lightly through her hair and fluffed it up.

"No," she repeated. "I'll do that myself. At leisure."

Bernie was ready to join his cronies for dinner at their watering hole in Winterside, and, making a hand available for a potential tip, started down the stairs.

He left empty-handed.

So did Frank, who didn't expect one. Often, his lady customers were generous in other ways, and he accepted, even though he was engaged to be married to Moira Toombs. The wedding had been put off too long. And Moira wasn't generous with what little she had to give a man.

No, in spite of his premarital starvation diet, Frank didn't want a tip from Vera Gloom – of any kind.

He wanted to be in her good graces though. She was a rich woman. And it never hurts to court their favour, if not their charms. She'd be buying all sorts online, he could tell the type. And UPS wouldn't deliver out here, not with the unreliability of the causeway. So they threw all their work his way, and would keep on doing it as long as the customers were happy.

No one had any idea of who Vera Gloom was, so they made it up.

She was the main topic of conversation at the annual lobster feed at the hall the next Saturday night.

"I heard she was a realtor, going to fix that house and flip it," said Ben Mack, Abel's much younger brother.

"Not with two van loads of furniture moved in there, she isn't." Frank was talking and eating at the same time. Moira was frowning at him from across the table.

He swallowed and wiped a sleeve across his mouth. "And all that art."

"Three husbands, I heard." Gladys Fraser put a final plate on the table and sat her bulldog body down beside Wally. "All of them livin' and all of them here."

"When did they come?" Ben had just stolen one of Annabelle's lobster claws and cracked it open. She snatched it back.

"Swear I saw a car drive up there the other night, three gents in it." Wally Fraser fished a napkin off the table and tucked it into his shirt. "You saw it, Germaine."

"Three gents and a driver." Germaine Joudry looked disappointedly as his wife, Estelle, removed a pat of butter from his plate. He'd had heart surgery the year previous.

"Looked like a limo to me." A fat piece of lobster fell off Wally's fork, poised to make his point. "Idled a while outside Sullivan house, then came back."

"Empty," said Germaine. "Lights on up there for a while after that. Past the usual time she goes to bed."

Germaine and Wally knew exactly when Vera retired because they spent most nights outside Wally's shed, drinking and smoking and hiding from their wives. Some nights they drank more than others, their imaginations and tongues running wild.

Ben nudged Annabelle and winked. "Truth or fiction?"

"That art, Frank. Did you see it?" Ian's place was just up the hill from the Sullivan house. He'd seen the truck pass by the day that Frank helped take the boxes in.

Frank chewed on his food for a moment.

"I been up close," he said.

Frank had eaten and imbibed several times already on his brush with Vera and the information that she was an artist, with huge but lightweight sculptural creations, most likely made out of balsawood, or something very, very light.

Had he seen the art? No, but he began to imagine that he had, and, a few glasses in, would begin to describe alien insects, oversized cockroaches and grasshoppers that had mated with dinosaurs.

"Yeah, I seen it."

Moira kicked his leg under the table.

"As good as," he whispered to her. He'd touched those boxes. He knew what they weighed. She'd said: "My creations." If it was art, it had to be balsawood, or maybe plastic.

"Insects, you said?" Ian wasn't looking at Frank. He was hoping for a glance from Hy. None came.

"Insecks or airplanes. Hard to tell." There, thought Frank, that should satisfy Moira. Hard to tell. Wasn't that the truth?

"Luftwaffe mebbe. I hear she was a tabletop dancer in Poland before the war." Jared MacPherson had slipped into the dinner and was somehow eating lobster without paying.

"Which war?" Ben challenged.

"Second, of course."

"Do your math, Jared."

Jared looked up, eyes blank. He couldn't do math.

"No, no, no." Frank slurred his words a bit. He'd been nipping at a flask he kept in his pocket for what otherwise would be a dull occasion.

"She's an artist, like I been telling you all. Big balsa wood insecks."

There followed the usual mumbles and grumbles:

"She won't find balsa wood here."

"Plenty of insecks, though."

The most silent person in the hall was Marlene. She talked to no one and no one talked to her. She had, not for a moment, taken her eyes, mouth or concentration off the food in front of her. She ate every single bite the lobster could offer – chewing on its legs and the fan of its tail. When she'd finished, the last to do so, she looked around the dishes lining the table. She hadn't been lucky enough to get any tomalley or lobster caviar – the red roe of the female crustacean. Others had and they hadn't all eaten it. Marlene's eyes gleamed with envy and she began to plan an escape from the hall that would allow her to scoop up some on her way out. She slid a few napkins into her purse.

To the villagers' disappointment, neither Vera nor her three husbands showed up for the "feed."

Chapter Six

www.theshores200.com
The Sullivan house was pieced together like a quilt. It was built over time and generations until Daniel Sullivan completed it. He later became a respected architect of upper-crust homes in Winterside. When he finished the work of his ancestors to perfect his Victorian "cottage," he had no money. He had used fish crates instead of lath. He and his bride never lived in it. She died tragically before they could.

Hy had known some of the history of the Sullivan house before, but she was finding more for the website in the provincial archives. Her interest was personal as well as professional. A couple of years before, a family had lived in the house when it was almost uninhabitable. They'd pitched a tent in the kitchen in winter because the roof leaked. There had been many more rodents than humans in the place. There had been a murder, a miscarriage, the exposure of a hidden identity, all tied to a family secret.

This Vera Gloom was bound to be less interesting than that.

Hy wheeled her bicycle up Shipwreck Hill, deciding she would introduce herself on the pretext of wanting to write an article about her. About having restored this magnificent house to its former beauty.

Maybe also about her art.

Thanks to Frank, it was all around the village that Vera Gloom was an artist. Hy had Googled her, but came up blank. Must be just an amateur, with money to spend on materials.

A doorbell. It was the first thing Hy noticed. Probably the only one in the Shores, certainly of its kind. It was the closest up she'd been to such a thing. A Victorian doorbell. Mechanical twist. Solid brass.

Hy gave it a turn. It gave a strangled ring, like a bicycle bell, only bigger. She waited. Gave it another turn. Still nothing.

Perhaps it couldn't be heard, deeper into the house. The days of servants who might be close at hand to answer were long past.

She twisted one more time. Waited a minute or two. Backed away from the door. Looked up at the windows.

The house stood silent. Dark as a tomb. She shivered at the thought. The Sullivan house might have been restored, but it was still gloomy. She walked around to the side. Shoved her face at a downstairs window. The curtains shut suddenly, dragged on a pulley.

Had she been seen? Was she purposely being excluded?

She backed off. Looked at the upstairs windows.

There was a man in one of them.

Waving at her.

She waved back.

He kept on waving.

Feeling foolish, she waved again, and backed around the

front of the house, still waving, because he was. Still backing up. Right into Vera Gloom.

"Ah, there you are."

Hy turned and looked straight into the unwelcoming face of The Shores' newest resident.

"Oh, hi. I'm Hy…"

"Hello. I'm Vera Gloom. And you are?"

"Hy…"

"Yes, I know. We've said our hellos."

"Hy…that is… Hyacinth McAllister."

"That's more like it. What can I do for you?"

"I…uh… I'm a writer, and I'd be interested in writing about your restoration of the cottage."

"You're certainly not alone."

"I'm sure, but I'm the one with the most intimate knowledge of this house and its history."

"I'm not sure I want it talked about."

"Well, it's being talked about in the village, so you might as well set the record straight."

"And what is the record?"

"Among other things, that you're an artist and you've been married three times." Hy looked down at Vera's hands. Blue diamonds. Unusually blue. Vera clasped her hands, hiding some of the glitter.

"Some even say you plan to run a Bed and Breakfast here."

Vera raised her eyes. "Spare me. The house is for my family."

"Family?"

"My boys."

"Sons?"

"Not exactly." They were like little children, though. So helpless. So in need of her care.

Hy darted a quick look up.
The man in the window – one of the boys?

Hy didn't get her interview, and, disappointed, cycled down to Gus with the fresh gossip.

"Did you see the big insects?" Gus asked immediately.

Hy shook her head and sat down.

"I didn't see anything – except a man waving from an upstairs window."

"One of the husbands?"

"I guess so."

"Imagine." Gus shook her head several times. "A woman of her age, living with all those husbands."

"Ex-husbands, I think it is." Hy wasn't sure what was true about Vera and what wasn't.

"Is it legal?"

"I think so."

"It may be, but I've never heard anything so foolish. One husband is quite enough, thank you."

Especially when you never see him. Hy wondered if Abel Mack would show at the 200th anniversary celebrations.

Hy quickly scotched the rumours that Mrs. Gloom was going to run Sullivan house as a Bed and Breakfast, much to Moira's relief. Hers was the only B&B in the village, and she had only Marlene staying there.

Moira never had any visitors, in spite of her ads on the Internet. It may have been because of her ads on the Internet. They showed her rooms for what they were: grim, Spartan cells.

It was in one of these that Marlene Weeks was staying – with an eye to being economical with public money. The bed was hard, the linens well-used and starched, the house cold on a cool morning, no rug in the room and newspapers covering the floor everywhere else.

Marlene woke, satisfied with the way things had turned out over the flowerbed. Eagerly, she opened her laptop, before even getting out of bed, to see if there had been any effect on the Internet. She clicked first to The Shores website.

Ian Simmons had spent hours designing it, and Marlene was gratified to see he had used one of her photographs of the community garden as a cover photo for the page. Her selective memory had by now convinced her that she had not only taken the photograph, but also created the flowerbed. She silenced that niggling voice in her mind. She'd as good as done it. She'd inspired it with her marigolds.

She also considered herself the designer of the website. Or as good as. The technology types in the department of tourism had hooked her up with Ian. The tech community on Red Island was quite small and Ian was well-known. Before she even came to The Shores, Marlene had connected with him, and, to her delight, he had agreed to create a website for the big event. For free.

He was scanning old photos and old documents, changing the site every day. He wanted to get his hands on the mountain of material Gus had – from a lifetime of pack-ratting local history.

"You can't have it," Gus had told him more than once. "It's going in a book, a proper book, not on that inter thing."

"You like the Web well enough to speak to your daughter and granddaughter on Skype," he'd replied more than once. He was annoyed because he'd given her a computer so she could do that. One of his old ones. An iMac, just two years old.

"That's one thing. You can't do that any other way…see them and hear them. This you can. In a book." She hugged her fat folder to her, as if he might steal it. Sometimes he was tempted to.

"I would just borrow it. Bring it right back."

"How do I know that scan thing wouldn't destroy the papers and photographs?"

"You have my word that it wouldn't."

"Still, the answer's no."

Ian found it frustrating. It seemed that Gus was the guardian of the village memory, that it resided nowhere else. Everyone had a few papers, a few photos, but Gus had the mother lode. And what would she ever do with it?

"Maybe nothing," said Hy, after one of Ian's sessions with Gus. "She hasn't done anything with it that I can see in years. I think she's overwhelmed."

"Well, maybe you could convince her."

"Oh, no. You're not going to haul me into it. She won't let me help put a book together. I doubt I can get her to give in for that Internet thing, as she calls it."

The truth was that Hy, as well as Gus, felt somewhat possessive about the material Gus had amassed. Hy still had hopes of putting together a book for the bicentennial, and didn't want it watered down by publication on the net. She was selecting her own material for the website to avoid that.

Chapter Seven

The Shores. 200 Years. The flowerbed shone the message as loud and clear as the sandwich board sign outside the hall. It was usually devoted to ceilidhs and strawberry socials, but was now one of dozens of signs around the village that proclaimed the bicentenary:

200 years and Counting

"And counting…down," thought Marlene. It was touch and go if this village would last long enough to make the two hundred mark – one reason maybe that the tourism department wasn't putting a lot of money into it.

There was no sign of modern life at all. Not a satellite dish… not a hot tub…pool…or golf course. How could it survive? And why were they celebrating this…this backwater at all?

As it happened, it was the minister of tourism's birthplace. He hadn't set foot in it in forty years, but, in a weak moment, had given into his mother's nagging to do something for the place their family came from. She hadn't set foot there in forty years either.

Marlene grabbed a coat and scarf. It was fall weather, though it was May. Maybe she could get an idea of what to do if she took a walk around the neighbourhood. Consulting the villagers was an idea still not on her radar. And she had no real desire to liaise with that cheeky community liaison person.

Uppity local. Hy would have been pleased to be considered local, instead of always from away.

Marlene saw Gus hanging out a patchwork quilt on the line. Her neighbour Estelle Joudry was bustling from a shed with a huge canning pot, her husband Germaine struggling behind her with a box full of glass canning jars. Both women were wearing housedresses, a piece of clothing not seen anywhere else. By contrast, ladies' pants were rarely seen in the village, except on tourists or people from town, like Marlene. She'd heard them called slacks here. Who used that word anymore? Capris, skinny jeans, low rise, boot leg, dozens of names, but never slacks. These people were from another century. Only the flowerbed women wore jeans. Hy and Annabelle. Named like the clowns they were.

Marlene sighed. No raw material to work with.

That's when it struck her. Of course. Two hundred years. A Heritage Village. A Living Village. The Village that Time Forgot. They were all good, all bound to attract tourist attention.

She would have to wipe the village clean of any signs of modern life. No cars. No trucks. Excited, she stopped at Gus's house. Gus was now hanging clothes on the line. They'd never met, but that didn't stop Marlene from barging in to test her idea on the grande dame of the village.

Marlene introduced herself and explained her idea for the bicentenary.

Gus sliced it apart without taking the clothespin from her mouth.

"A Living Village? And so what is it now? Dead?"

Marlene privately thought so, but didn't say.

Disappointed, she returned to Moira's and tried "The Village that Time Forgot" on her. She got no better reception.

"Well, my father would not like to hear that. He was a man for timeliness." Moira looked up at the face of the grandfather clock in the hall. It was the family's prized possession. Her father, a "waste management supervisor," as she liked to call him, had pulled it out of the dump. It told time faithfully – twice a day – at six-thirty in the morning and six-thirty at night.

Chagrined, Marlene left the house again and got in the Smart car – another tourism department economy. She drove around the village to assess how hard it would be to turn time back. She was delighted to see that it wouldn't be difficult at all. Just get rid of the vehicles and barbecues. She frowned.

And ride-ons.

She drove to Big Bay Harbour, and there her imagination took off. The fishing shacks were sad-looking affairs. All grey cedar shingle, probably looking very much as they had two hundred years before. But they wouldn't do. They simply wouldn't do. A splash of paint – each a different colour, turn one into a café, others into little shops. Just what the tourists would like.

Hy was discouraged to see Gus's historical ephemera all over the kitchen floor. Gus was a doer, she liked to get things done, but she wasn't doing anything with this, other than shuffling it around the floor with her feet.

Something was stopping her.

Hy slumped down in the recliner opposite Gus.

"What is it? What's got you blocked?"

Gus said nothing. She continued to rock and knit.

"There must be something. There must be some way I can help."

Gus darted a quick hopeful look at her, soon extinguished.

"Come on. We can do this together."

Gus squared her shoulders, as if resolving on something. Then they drooped, and she shook her head sadly.

"She's allus looking over my shoulder."

"Who's she?"

"Me Ma. There." Gus pointed to a schoolhouse photograph, lying close to Hy's feet. Hy picked it up.

"Around 1921, I think. That's me ma. In the middle."

"The schoolteacher?"

Gus nodded and rocked.

"Thought everyone knew that."

That was the trouble with The Shores, thought Hy. People were born knowing everything, or very quickly acquiring it so it was as if they'd always known it. It could leave information gaps for people from away like her.

"Yes, she were a schoolteacher. She were also a writer. Wrote poems and such. Wrote a book once."

"Really?"

"Yup. Sent it to a publisher and all."

"And?" She hardly need ask. The answer was written on Gus's face.

"Sent back."

"And?"

"She burned it. In the wood range. Leastwise, she said, it

could feed us supper. Never wrote again that I know of. Had ambitions, but she also knew how to take no for an answer."

"She never wrote again?"

"Nope. She said she must not be good enough."

"That's very sad."

"Reckon it is."

"But this is different. And it shouldn't stop you."

"Happen it is different. But it is stoppin' me. She were smarter than me, and she couldn't do it. I can't do any more with this than I have, not with her lookin' over my shoulder."

Hy let out a big sigh.

"Then let me, Gus. I've asked you before, and I'm asking you again."

"You don't want to be bothered."

"But I do. Very much. I'd be thrilled. And I can tell you that your Ma is not looking over my shoulder."

Gus smiled. "Don't be so sure. No. Leave it. I'll get around to it."

"Well, let me clear it up a bit for you."

Hy began putting it in organized piles by subject matter, by whether it was a newspaper article, photo or handwritten note. She soon gave up, and began lumping it all together, just to get it off the floor.

She uncovered, stuck to a wad of bills from Macks' General Store, a sealed envelope, marked "Toombs" in a spidery handwriting.

She held it up.

"What's this?"

Gus craned forward and peered at it.

"Don't know. Can't say as I've ever seen it. Not my handwriting. Open it."

Hy carefully slit the brittle envelope open, the old dry gum giving way easily. Inside were several pages of a letter. She began to scan it. Her eyes widened.

"Well, what does it say?" Gus, impatient.

"You'll never believe it."

"I can't believe it if I don't know what it is."

So Hy told her. Gus's mouth shaped into a fat round "o" of disbelief.

"Can I take this?"

"I 'spose. What are you going to do with it?"

"I'm going to tell Moira. She should know."

"Rather you than me." Gus rocked to the words and repeated them. "Rather you than me."

Chapter Eight

Marlene watched the fishermen bring in their lobster catch and sell it to suppliers on the wharf. When they were finished, she launched into her attack – to cajole them into sprucing up their fish shacks.

Above them, gulls were circling and diving down for scraps of bait and broken lobster parts. On their way back up, they were squawking at each other and defecating. One fisherman earned a glare from Marlene when he shoved her out of the way of a descending deposit. Until she realized what he'd done. Then she gave him a weak smile. Miss Manners had no guide for such a social situation.

A real, working harbour, Big Bay was picturesque, but not the kind of picturesque Marlene was looking for. She wanted the fishing shacks painted bright colours – red, yellow, blue with pots of flowers lined along the dock and window boxes with trailing ivy and lobelia. Pretty and fragrant. Not damp, grey, smelling of salt water and fish, and covered in gull poo.

She'd brought sample colour swatches with her to tempt the fishermen. She'd brought pots of paint as well. A few fishermen had gathered round at the prospect of something for nothing.

"Free," she said. "No charge. It's on the province. If you agree to paint your shacks, the paint's free."

"And the labour?"

She shrugged her shoulders.

"As for that, it's up to you."

Some accepted the bribe of paint, although they weren't too fussy about the colours. Pink. Purple. Marigold. Lime green. What kind of colours were those for a serious working harbour?

Encouraged by her success with the paint, Marlene floated her next idea. She wanted the fishermen to lease their shacks for the season to retailers who would open a string of crafty boutiques.

"And where does that put us?" Andy Gallant growled through the pipe perpetually dangling from his lips. "We gotta livin' to make."

"Surely you can let it go for one year." Marlene didn't get it. She didn't have to work. She had a private income, left by her father. This tourism job was her public duty. That there was money attached to it, she supposed was nice, but she never saw it. It went straight into the bank. She knew many people had to work for a living, but surely they didn't spend it all. They, too, must have some in the bank for occasions like this.

A couple of fishermen decided to go fish out of another harbor and put their shacks up for rent, and took the free paint. Marlene held them up as an example of entrepreneurship and civic duty.

The rest shuffled off, grumbling about how the government chose to spend their taxpayer dollars.

Paint.

Pink and lime green.

Chapter Nine

Before she left Gus, Hy reread the pages, more carefully this time. It was several pages, handwritten, a century before, by Marie Toombs, who must have been Moira's great-great grandmother. A Frenchwoman. That would come as a shock to Moira, and so would her story.

Hy found Moira outside, washing her downstairs windows.

"I've got something to show you." Hy held up the envelope. Moira looked at it with distaste. A dirty yellowed envelope.

"I haven't got my glasses." Moira wanted to get the windows finished before the sun moved around the house and caused streaking.

"Come. It's important." Hy went ahead of Moira into the house. Moira picked up her glasses off the hall table, and headed for the kitchen, the two stepping over newspapers laid out neatly over the floor. Moira washed her floors once a week and, as soon as they had dried, laid several layers of newspaper down to keep them clean.

To lend the occasion the recognition it deserved, Hy steered Moira away from the kitchen and into the front room, where the furniture had once been protected by that upholstery condom – draped in plastic, until it became yellow and brittle and too expensive to replace. The chairs and love seat still looked unused.

Hy sat Moira down in one of the needlepoint chairs, and handed her the letter.

Moira read the pages, frowning more deeply the more she absorbed. It took her a long time, so much time that Hy became agitated with waiting. She curbed her impatience because she knew Moira was a slow reader and there was a lot to digest.

Or not.

"It's not true." Moira looked over at Hy, firm conviction etched on her face. Just as firmly, Hy responded.

"She was your ancestor." This was not going to be easy. But she had known that.

"Marie?" Moira looked down. "Yes. She was. I never knew she was a Frenchwoman, though." She said "Frenchwoman" as if it were a dirty word.

"Not with a name like Marie?"

"Well, we never said it that way. We said it like Mary. The way it's meant to be said."

"Meant to be said?" No, this was not going to be easy.

"Like in the good book."

"The good book…" Puzzlement on Hy's face, then sudden clarity. "Oh, the Bible. Of course."

"Of course."

"Anyway, she knew the story well, and gives proof. For one thing, that your ancestor was shipwrecked on the *Annabella*."

Moira's spine stiffened with pride at being so connected to early island origins.

"And he survived that first winter, as many islanders did, with the help of the Mi'kmaq."

Moira nodded, less confidently.

"And he married a Mi'kmaw woman."

Moira stood up, the fragile letter crushed in her hand.

"No," she said.

"Yes," said Hy.

Moira slumped down again. Combed through the pages one more time. Looked up, disgust in her eyes.

"A Mi'kmaw?"

"Yes." Hy was torn between keeping silent – what would be the point? – and ripping a strip off Moira. She chose the middle ground.

"You should feel privileged."

"Privileged?" Confusion mixed with the disgust in Moira's eyes. Not diluting it, but turning it into a different kind of ugly emotion.

"Yes. To be part of the people who owned this land to begin with. If any humans ever did, they did. The originals."

"The aboriginals." Moira didn't exactly spit it out, but her tone held all the contempt of a spit.

"You can't hate your own people. You're one of them."

"Partly."

Hy could see it pained Moira to say it, to admit the possibility.

"It's in the blood, Moira. Your blood."

Moira looked as if Hy had struck her. That's just what Hy wanted to do. Give her a good slap. Shake some sense into her.

"It's your heritage."

Moira bit her lip.

Biting back words? Maybe a start.

"My heritage is this." Moira looked around her at the cheap, tired late Victorian furnishings, love seats, hard and lumpy, armchairs stuffed with horsehair, occasional tables of more recent vintage with brown veneer surfaces. Her glance grazed over the china cabinet, her mother's pride. Her eyes fixed, finally, on the grandfather clock, her father's pride, which told its bang-on perfect time twice a day.

"This?" Hy's tone now seeped with contempt.

Moira straightened, stiff with pride.

"It is a perfectly respectable heritage."

"If you like that sort of thing." Hy mumbled, so that Moira did not hear clearly.

"Sure, a part of your heritage is here, within these four walls. There's no denying that. But what about that?" Hy jabbed a finger at the front window.

"The village?"

"Well, yes, the village, too. But I meant outside. All of outside. Your inheritance. Your legitimate inheritance, as a daughter of the island."

She had struck a chord. *Daughter of the island.* It resonated with Moira. She sat up even straighter for a moment. Then lost hold of what had inspired her.

"I don't like outside. And I don't want to be Mi'kmaq. Mi'kmaq." Moira shook her head, then buried it in her hands. She was responding as if someone had died. Perhaps someone had. Her idea of herself.

"Yes, Moira, Mi'kmaq. And European. A blend of the cultures that makes Red Island what it is. If you hate that, you hate yourself."

Moira looked up. Despair flooded her eyes.

My God, she does. She hates herself. Mi'kmaq or white. It doesn't matter.

It was a revelation to Hy. She'd never liked Moira, but had never given the woman a lot of thought. Moira had always seemed mean-spirited and even a bit vicious to her. Underhanded. Sneaky. Now, looking at her lips trembling and her chin buckling – even though it was for all the wrong reasons – Hy felt sorry for her. Sorry for Moira's limited scope and imagination, the smallness, in every way, of her world. The newspapers guarding her floor. The fiancé who was marrying her tidy life, not her. The sister who feared her, whose affection was only dutiful.

Moira slumped, looking at the floor. "What will I tell people? The women of the Institute? This can't go in the book."

Hy was determined that it would go in the book, if there ever were a book, but that would be a battle for another day. If she could only get Moira to reconcile herself in some small way, to begin to embrace a connection, a heritage of which the orphan in Hy was envious.

That's it. Envy. Moira understands envy.

"I envy you."

A spark of light appeared in Moira's eyes.

"Envy? You do? Why?"

"It makes you more of an islander. A true original. A heritage princess."

That was going over the top a bit, Hy thought, but she couldn't think of another way at the moment to get Moira to accept her very interesting ancestry.

So she repeated what she'd said, hoping to get through to Moira's pride.

"Moira, listen. This makes you the oldest family in The Shores, bar none."

A glimmer joined the light in Moira's eyes.

"The oldest family on this side of the causeway. This part of the island. As old as anyone anywhere else. A founding daughter."

Moira straightened. The Toombs had only ever been ordinary. Commonplace. Never the first. The only. And now – the originals? Moira read the letter again. She folded it carefully, stood up and opened the locked china cabinet that contained a few tea cups and saucers, valued because they were Royal Doulton, but chipped or cracked or desperately yellowed with age.

There was a silver cigarette box in the cabinet, polished to a shine but with a dent in it, and she reverently placed the letter in that, closed it, held her touch on it for a moment and then locked the cabinet again.

Hy could tell this was going to be a much bigger deal than the grandfather clock.

Chapter Ten

Marlene was so excited by her idea – in spite of the immediate opposition from Gus and Moira – that she swallowed her pride and her dislike and phoned Hy.

"Hy? Marlene."

Marlene? Marlene who? thought Hy.

A long pause.

"Marlene Weeks."

Still no lights went on. Hy was on the point of hanging up.

"…Ministry of Tourism."

"Oh… Hi, Marlene." No enthusiasm.

"Look, I have a great idea for the bicentenary."

"Does it involve marigolds?"

Now Marlene was on the point of hanging up, but she needed Hy to move her plans forward. She squeezed out a weak laugh as a peace offering.

Marlene decided it was worth a small piece of her tiny budget to bring Hy on side.

"Why don't we meet at that seafood restaurant at Big Bay. My treat. I'd appreciate your suggestions for my overall plan." Marlene chose her wording carefully to hold onto ownership of her idea.

"Okay. When?"

"No time like the present." Marlene's tone was overly cheerful now that she'd got her way. "Say tomorrow…at noon?"

"Sure. Fine."

Hy was preoccupied with what Moira was going to wear to her wedding – and where it would take place. Not on the beach. The first attempt there had been a disaster.

Helluva mess. Moira had been furious. This time, Moira had chosen the conventional safety of the hall.

"Where she shoulda done it in the first place," said Gladys Fraser, President of the Women's Institute.

"The never-ending bridesmaid." Hy sighed as she checked another e-mail from Moira, who'd been issuing online instructions of various kinds since before the aborted wedding last summer. Most of them lately revolved around the dress. Moira still didn't have one, and she was panicking. Her original dress, her mother's, had, like the wedding, been ruined. The Sears catalogue had failed to produce anything suitable.

So had her reluctant bridesmaid.

Hy had no idea what to suggest.

Marlene showed up before Hy for their lunch meeting, and was gratified to see that a couple of the shacks had been painted, and that one appeared to have been leased.

Hy rolled in on her bicycle, as Marlene was squinting through nearsighted eyes at a rather strange sign overhanging the door: *Do Tell a Sole. Fish Skin Clothing.* On a sandwich board beside the door, it read: Wear a trout when you go out. A sign in the window invited potential customers to *Slip into some sole.*

What the…?

This was not the crafty kind of store she'd had in mind. It

was weird, definitely weird.

Hy had a big grin on her face as Marlene marched along the wharf, heading straight for the offending storefront. She followed at a discreet distance, waving at a few fishermen who were loafing around, the day's catch taken in and taken care of.

They smiled and winked. No one liked the tourism woman.

At the door of the fish skin clothing store stood a strange little man with bowed legs and dark, slicked-back hair.

"Mornin', ma'am." He held out a hand as Marlene strode up to him. She ignored it. Instead she looked with distaste at his sign – and him. She ventured a peek inside the store, full of what appeared to be leather jackets.

"Salmon," he said. "You won't find finer. I sell to a couture house in Paris." He motioned her inside the store, and, in spite of herself, she entered. She kept her distance from the merchandise.

"But who…who would buy these?"

"Not everyone. I agree with you there, ma'am. You gotta have money. They don't come cheap."

"What are you doing here?"

"Free country, I guess. Save on supply and delivery bills. A bit of PR…advertising, connecting myself to this here village celebrating two hundred years."

Hy slipped into the shack. It was dark and a bit damp inside. It smelled fishy, and…something else…

Up front was a rack of jackets. They looked like the skin on the salmon filet she'd had last night.

"Made out of salmon? For real?"

"Yup. Go ahead. Touch one. It won't fall apart."

It felt just like leather.

"Try it on."

Hy slipped into it. It felt like any leather jacket. It looked like fish.

Marlene entered the shop and looked around with disapproval, resisting holding her nose. The jackets looked like fish. Smelled like fish.

"I'm Catfish Cloutier. Friends call me Cat. Funny, when I'm in the fish business. Used to be for real, you know. Then I got looking at them skins. Well, here, let me show you."

He scurried, ungainly, to a counter at the back of the shack, and returned with a tray of fish skins, all neatly labeled.

He set it down on a display counter at the front of the store. Hy leaned forward to have a look. Marlene stepped back.

"Now this'd be your tuna." He pointed to a thick, dark grey slab of skin.

"Call it the denim of fish skin. Rough. Tough. Gotta be, to hold in five hundred pounds of fish."

He jabbed a finger at a salmon skin sample. "This you seen. In demand this one. Dries faster than the tuna. And more elegant. That's why it's in demand."

Hy caught Marlene mouthing the word "elegant?" in disbelief. Cat skipped by the next, with a brief comment.

"Pike, now there's a lovely fish. Skin so soft." Hy wondered if it repelled mosquitoes.

"And here's the charmer." He stroked a delicate thin skin.

"Sole. It's the silk of the fish skin line. Not easy to do. Lose as much as you produce. Very, very fragile. Nobody does the sole but me. That's my specialty. There are others, but them's my top ones.

"Got a lovely outfit right here. Salmon skirt. Sole blouse. Both wraparound."

The skirt shimmered, iridescent shades of grey and pink

and green, and fell in a fetching shape to the floor. The blouse was soft and flowing. They were beautifully crafted. Hy fell in love with them.

"Who made these?"

"My wife, when she was alive. Skilled seamstress."

"I'll take them." Hy grabbed the two pieces of clothing as Marlene looked on in horror.

"Won't you try them?"

Hy grinned. Shrugged. "Not here. Not now. Pretty sure they'll fit – wraparound. If not, I assume you'll take them back."

"How'd you get the idea?" Hy asked as she paid and he wrapped the items.

"It's been around a long time. That's why I thought it'd fit your bicentennial."

Marlene gave a "not if I can help it" face.

"It's heritage." Cat lifted the tray and took it back to the counter. He gestured to the first of a series of wall mountings, each illuminated by a pool of light.

"The native people of North America…probably the world, them that lived by the ocean, they made all kinds of things from fish."

The wall mounting had graphics of parkas, mittens, boots, headgear – all made of fish skin.

"Waterproof, that's the thing. Waterproof and flexible."

Cat moved to the next mounting.

"They'd smoke the fish, see…"

That was it. The other smell.

"…I do that right here…in back. You smoke 'em so's they dry nice and slow and stay flexible. Keeps the oils in and bacteria out."

Marlene let out a heavy sigh. She was imagining bugs crawling all over the clothes. She kept her distance from the bag in Hy's hand.

"I don't see what that has to do…"

"Like I said. Heritage."

Marlene's lip curled.

"Native heritage. Not European."

Cat's eyes popped open in wide disbelief as he darted a look at Hy.

"I expect if you checked out your genes, you'd find a Mi'kmaw in your closet."

Marlene took a sharp breath.

It was perhaps because of that, that Cat brought up the next item with more than usual pleasure.

"Piss, they used."

"What?" Marlene looked even more disgusted. Hy had to stifle a laugh.

"Piss. Men's piss. The good stuff. Strong as detergent. Used it as a cleanser before they smoked 'em."

Marlene turned her back on him. That just got him going. He pointed to a pair of moccasin-style boots.

"Don't want to step in any kind of poo in them boots. They'll just disintegrate. Fast. Sum'pn to do with proteins and enzymes and collagen."

Hy continued to look at the wall mountings – photographs of artifacts of clothing made from fish skin and bird skin.

"Birds?"

"Oh, yes. Me, I wouldn't use birds. Gulls mebbe. Nasty dirty scat-throwing scum. But I do have some other species here."

He led her to a display case.

Belts and trinkets of various kinds made with snakeskin.

"You have to have the small items some folks will buy as a

thank you for the entertainment. More snakes than I expected around here."

"Only two species, though." Hy looked closer into the cabinet. "Not all the ones here."

"Oh, yep, those are all island snakes."

"They can't be island snakes. There are only two kinds here. They must be from away."

"Caught 'em and skinned them myself."

And then it came to her. The snakes were from away – and from the island. The bizarre fall of snakes from the sky last summer. An unexplained phenomenon that had chosen The Shores as it target. There'd been no official recording of them by species. They fell too fast and slithered away just as quickly. Truth was, Ian, the self-styled scientist, was terrified of snakes, and hadn't pursued even one.

As they left Big Bay, the idea began to unfold in Hy's mind about Moira's wedding dress.

But would she go for it?

Chapter Eleven

The boys were settled, her art in place.

Vera took turns spending evenings with them. She'd never been that handy but she'd learned that elderly gentlemen liked a woman knitting or crocheting or engaging in some form of feminine art, sitting with them in the evening. She'd taken the habit of making crocheted covers for toilet paper in pastel Phentex yarn. She'd expanded from there to making antimacassars to keep natural oils off the backs of armchairs. Only one of her boys used an armchair, and he was not the least bit oily, but she had to do something to while away the hours.

None of them were great conversationalists, or was it just that they had run out of conversation with her?

"What are you reading, dear?"

The most she got was a grunt. Or at least it sounded like a grunt. Blair's eyes were, as usual, glued to his latest book.

She looked at the walls around them. In fact, she couldn't see any walls. They were all covered, floor to ceiling, wall to wall, in bookshelves jammed with books.

He'd read every single one of them and Frank delivered more every day.

She was surprised Blair could even keep up with them. He was having a hard time. They were stacked in piles at his feet, tomes as yet unread.

He was plowing – chronologically – through every work of fiction ever written, she thought. Certainly all the main stuff. He was now well into the nineteenth century – terrain that was more familiar and palatable to her than Beowulf and Chaucer's incomprehensible early English. But she never read herself, just crocheted at his side every third evening and anticipated when he'd come to the last page.

Even then he rarely uttered a word, not one that she could remember in recent history. He just held up that book in a certain way, and she knew. He was finished. She'd slip it out of his hands, find it a place in the bookshelves, arranged alphabetically by author, and then pick up one of the ones at his feet and slip it into his waiting hands. It didn't usually matter which one. He always seemed content with her selection. He certainly never objected. The smile on his face was her reward.

Each of her ex-husbands got two evenings a week of her company, and all three appeared satisfied with the arrangement.

The truth was that Vera was an incredibly boring woman, and so they were probably happy to be left mostly to themselves.

Charlie, the artist, would not even turn from his easel to greet her when she came in. He was a slow and meticulous painter, and the same work could sit on that easel night after night, week after week, month after month. He always returned, though, to the same unfinished painting. The painting of her. There it would be, suddenly produced and propped up on the easel. There would be no crocheting then. She would have to stand and pose for him. Sometimes she felt his eyes were hinting at more – at a renewal of their marital relations. But he'd never been any good at it, and the thought of him pawing her body made her shudder. You would have thought his artist's hands would have been more sensitive, but no. It was as if he were a potter, not a painter, and had been digging into her flesh in hopes of entirely reshaping the clay.

On the nights when she saw the lust in his eyes, she cut their evening short. After all, she had to be fair to all of her boys. What she gave to one she must give to another and she would not turn her house into a bordello. Besides, at her age, sex was ridiculous. She hoped that her next husband would agree.

She didn't have to worry about Hank. His eyes barely grazed her when she came into the room. They were fixed on the television, the remote control gripped in his right hand. It was hard to say what he was taking in. He, poor lamb, had had a stroke, and though he was left physically able, with no apparent damage to his body, his mind was gone. She doubted he even knew who she was. She often cheated on him, leaving him alone before nine o'clock, because she was convinced that it made no difference to him.

Those were her dutiful six nights of the week, two nights apiece spent with each of her ex-husbands. It was the least she could do. They were really not much bother, not at all demanding. Even so, she treasured the seventh evening, her evening of rest.

She would go upstairs and call out from the hall:

"Good night."

And they would chorus back in a charming harmony of male vocal power:

"Good night."

She'd toss the crochet hook aside, kick off her lambskin slippers, roll down her support hose and relax. No reading, no television, no arts and crafts. Just time for Vera. Time alone. Time to think up her next move on the marry-go-round.

Today, she thought she'd hooked a live one.

Chapter Twelve

"It'll never work. You can't keep all signs of modern life out of the village."

"There's not much in it now," Marlene mumbled, as she slipped a tender mussel out of its shell.

"Granted. But the men must have their trucks and ride-ons and the tourists their laptops. There's Wifi Wednesday at the hall. We can't do away with that."

A drop of garlic butter sauce dribbled down Marlene's chin when she opened her mouth to protest. She dabbed at it with a napkin and looked out the large arched window that formed most of the back wall of the restaurant. The view of the dunes and the sand bar that stretched across the bay was magnificent. But the dull grey shingle shacks were pulling it down.

She turned her gaze to the restaurant interior. A medley of blues. Fresh paint job. Nice enough. Solid tables and very solid chairs – recycled from a schoolroom, she had no doubt. They'd do, but –

Her imagination hazed over the solid reality of the room, and turned it into a whimsical Paris café, with pretty little unstable wrought iron tables and chairs with checkered tablecloths. She saw not the stolid waitresses who had served them and called them "yous guys," but undernourished French boys with thin reedy voices to match, bowing and scraping at the clientele. That would be more like it.

"Who owns this place?"

"Andy. The grumpiest fisherman on the wharf."

"Oh, dear."

They ate in silence for a few moments.

"I think I'll have to call a public meeting. Can you help me with that?"

"Yes, of course…"

"And of course, you'll back me up on my ideas."

"Well, I – "

What had she got herself into? Hy had thought this community liaison thing would be a piece of cake.

She hadn't reckoned on Marlene Weeks.

Following their lunch, Marlene shoved flyers in Hy's leaky mailbox on a rainy day. They were calling for a community meeting and came with a note: *To be distributed*. Hy hauled the sodden mass out and dumped them onto her harvest table to dry.

They lay there like an accusation.

Resentment built in Hy.

I'm not her dogsbody, she thought. The sooner she knows that, the better.

She gathered them up and stuffed them into the recycling.

But the village women did show up, even though they didn't

know about the meeting. Marlene had scheduled it right after the monthly Institute get-together, where Moira had just announced a change of venue for her second stab at a wedding. It wouldn't be at the hall after all.

She'd read an article in *Cosmo* about a wedding on a pier in California, with a beautiful glassed-in gazebo at the end of it. It stirred her romantic imagination. She thought Big Bay would be an ideal setting for their vows.

She'd decided on the wharf. It wasn't quite like having a Mexican beach ceremony as she'd tried the first time.

"This will be more traditional," she explained to the Institute. Most of the women thought it was foolishness. Some were wondering if they'd be required to produce a second wedding present. Moira had not sent the first ones back.

Gladys Fraser looked at Olive MacLean. Olive looked at Rose Rose, the minister's wife. She tried to look noncommittal. But they were all thinking: What was traditional about getting married on the wharf? To their knowledge, no one ever had. It was going to be a very new tradition.

Moira misunderstood the skeptical glances around the table.

"Well, with my family background on the sea."

The looks became more puzzled. The Toombs's occupational history had been in garbage collection, as long as anyone living knew.

"The *Annabella*." There was a great deal of skepticism about Moira's claim to having an ancestor who had landed on the island when the *Annabella* sank in Big Bay. No one but Hy and Gus knew yet Moira's legitimate claim to the *Annabella*. She was keeping the secret close so far. There was no rush to reveal it. Gus showed no signs of producing the heritage book.

It was certainly not an auspicious arrival of the Toombs

clan on Red Island, and perhaps didn't bode well for Moira's second attempt to marry Frank.

Marlene barged in just as the Institute meeting was breaking up. She charged up on stage and sat the women down again.

"So glad you could all come." Then she looked around the room, puzzled.

"But where are the men?"

Even if the men had known about the meeting, they wouldn't have come. A meeting called by a woman must be women's business, nothing to do with them.

So the women stared, puzzled, at Marlene.

"The men are…well the men are where they're s'posed to be." Gladys Fraser jerked her head in the direction of the outdoors. It focused attention on a hum coming from behind the hall. The hum became a buzz. The buzz became a roar as Billy Pride circled the hall on his ancient ride-on, a lawn-mower-cum-car. Billy used it to transport himself around the village.

The roar became a clang.

The clang became a clunk.

A pop.

A hiss.

A swear word that made Gladys, Rose and Olive cover their ears, and the pasty-skinned Moira turn bright red.

Billy came dashing into the hall, slammed the bathroom door open, left with a bowl of water and the tap gushing behind him. He repeated the performance several times. Hy had gone to the window to see what he was up to.

"Overheating," she said, finally.

"We'll have none of that for the 200th." Marlene looked smug.

"None of what?" Hy challenged.

"Those ride-ons. Ladies, that's what I'm here to talk about. We had such a wonderful collaboration on the commemorative flowerbed, but that's just the beginning. There's so much more to be done. I have a dream…"

Hy groaned.

Marlene outlined her idea to turn The Shores into another world. The women, who were always saying things had been better in days gone by, didn't like the idea at all when actually presented with the possibility.

"Hide our vehicles? And just how are we supposed to do that?"

"Why, drive them around the back of the house." Marlene said it as if it were the most reasonable suggestion.

"Over the grass?"

"Oh, yes." Marlene was reminded. "The grass. There would be no grass cutting, of course. For at least two, maybe three months. After all, we want authenticity, don't we?"

A cry of outrage arose, peppered by:

"No cutting the grass?"

"I'd be ashamed for my family to come visit."

"Never mind that, what about the minister?"

"Our husbands would have nothing to do. They'd get up to all sorts."

And so on. Hy finally raised her arms and called for silence.

"I don't believe Ms. Weeks means it."

"I most certainly do."

"Then I think the husbands must come to the next meeting. This concerns them most of all."

When the village women had left, grumbling and complaining their way out the door, Hy turned to Marlene.

"You can't be serious," she said.

"Deadly serious," said Marlene.

71

Hy thought that might be too close to the truth. She was sure she wasn't the only one who wanted to wring Marlene's neck.

It was the ride-ons. They were the deal breaker. No one wanted to let the grass grow for authenticity, the way it used to be. Tidy farmers and homemakers, they couldn't bear the sight of unruly growth, so used were they to the neat rows of potato plants, fields of wheat, timothy and canola, growing in well-corralled order around them. To let it all fall apart at their doorsteps was unthinkable.

They were proud of their lawns in The Shores. The whole island boasted neatly trimmed acreage, clipped right down into the ditches and back up, meeting with the provincial government clippers that took care of the roadsides. Some complained that this was killing off the lupins, the tall spikey, multi-bloomed flowers that grew like pink and purple weeds all along the island roadsides in late June.

Certainly there were fewer of them now the mowing machines sheared their long blades beyond the grassy shoulder. They'd joined snowplows as the scourge of mailboxes and laneways.

Marlene could do nothing about them, but she wanted the authentic look for the village. How could she ever bring the villagers under control? Invite the men, Hy had said. Marlene suspected that Hy had never delivered her previous flyer. So many told her they'd never received one.

She would organize another village meeting at the hall. This time, she would deliver the flyers herself.

She spent most of the morning working on them, nose pressed to the computer screen. She needed glasses but was too vain to wear them, even when alone. So it was no surprise that the flyer had two proofing errors. She stuffed the mistakes into mailbox after mailbox, the Smart car starting and stopping, starting and stopping, and she having to get out each time.

The Sores Re-enactment Village
Pubic Meeting
Saturday May 30 6 pm

No one came.

That was no surprise. Even without the proofing errors, and very few actually noticed them, no one was interested in what Marlene had to say. They assumed that it was more of the same – about not cutting their lawns. Outrageous.

Marlene leaned up against the hall stage, waiting for people to come and sit on the chairs she had neatly arranged.

Still no one came.

Slowly, she gathered up the information sheets she had placed on each chair, and, reluctantly, began to stack the chairs and put them back along the walls of the hall, hoping that someone, anyone would come.

As she popped the last stack into place, finally someone arrived.

It was Olive MacLean, Women's Institute treasurer and the member on clean-up duty that week.

With a smile, Marlene descended, grabbing one of the information sheets and brandishing it at her.

Olive reeled back in horror, as if she were at the wrong end of a knife.

Marlene kept coming forward.

Olive kept backing away.

"No, no." She couldn't back away any farther, so she had to speak. "I'm not here for that." She pointed at the paper as if it were something disgusting.

Marlene dropped her arm down in disappointment.

"I'm here to clean up." It was Olive's turn to look disappointed. The place was perfectly tidy.

The two women left the hall together, each hugging her own defeat. Olive at least had the satisfaction of locking the door. That needed to be done, and was, with a flourish of importance.

It was pouring. Marlene hadn't brought a jacket.

Dejected, she dragged herself "home" to Moira's unwelcoming abode.

Chapter Thirteen

Hy pushed the door open and flew into the house. It was lucky the mudroom was small, so that she was able to fling her arms forward and stop the fall on the opposite wall. She steadied herself, pushed upright and searched for what had tripped her. Hy was so naturally clumsy, there didn't always have to be a reason.

But this time there was.

"Could you use a cat?" Gus called out from the kitchen.

Hy scrunched up her face. "A wha…?"

There, at her feet, was a small bit of fluff. A black cat. *Don't let a black cat cross your path.* She saw the meaning of that now. Not a superstition at all.

A black cat. Sniffing at her shoes as if it were a dog. Hy reached down and patted it. It rolled over.

A white cat. Everything under was white, belly and all. Everything on top was black. Even the legs divided black and white. Black down the outside; white inside. Hy tickled the cat's stomach and it began playing with her hand, softly, claws pulled in, kneading her hands.

"It likes you." Gus came into the room carrying a tray with cookies and cheese, cups and saucers. The Pyrex pot was boiling three tea bags a thick dark brown on the stove.

Hy kept tickling, the cat rolled around in delight, and sunk its claws right into her hand.

"Ouch!" Hy pulled her hand away.

The cat skittered off.

"It does like you. Better take it home."

"Gus – a cat. You? You don't like cats."

"It's not my cat." Gus sat down, worked a few more stitches onto the sock she was knitting, but the cat was tugging at the ball of wool on the floor. It went chasing after it, batting it around, turning the room into a giant cat's cradle. There was a reason Gus didn't like cats.

Nursing her hand, Hy slumped into the reclining chair by the window. She could see through into the pantry, where there were two little dishes set down beside the big white plastic garbage and recycling bin.

Cat dishes.

"If you're feeding it, it's yours."

Gus looked, guilty, at the bin.

"More Abel's."

Abel's. Hy snorted. That was even more preposterous.

The cat jumped onto Hy's knee, its tiny sharp claws digging in. She winced and tried to pull it off, but when a cat doesn't want to move, it doesn't.

"I reckon she'll be company for Abel when I'm not here."

Hy opened her mouth to say something and then shut it. Shook her head.

The little feline kneaded Hy's lap, circled a few times, gathered itself into a comma and fell asleep, its purring as loud as a whipper snipper.

"Where did it come from?"

Gus shrugged. "Reckon it came from somewhere handy. Not a thing wrong with her. Not starvin'. Not wild. Mebbe a barn cat from Frasers', looking for a better life."

The Frasers had more barn cats than anyone in The Shores. The irony was that mean-spirited Gladys Fraser, president of the Women's Institute, fed them and fed them well. She wouldn't have one in the house, but didn't care how many there were in the barn. Fed them on the good stuff, top-of-the-line cat crunchies, was the word in the village.

Hy stroked the purring cat softly and it jumped up, jumped off and showed her the back of its tail before it hopped up on Gus and stopped her from knitting.

"What's its name?"

"It's a she, and I call her Blacky. What else?"

"Whitey, maybe. Anyway, Gus, if you've chosen a name for her, she must be yours."

"Mebbe, but she's not here all the time, you know. She eats here, of course she eats here. My good food. Fish cakes and potato salad and biscuits. Them biscuits are made with cream."

Gus quit trying to knit with the cat on her lap, and put down her needles. Mission accomplished, the cat jumped down, and, with one meow, had Gus up out of her chair and spooning tuna fish into her dish.

"Abel won't eat leftovers, but she will."

No doubt whose cat it was.

But when Hy left, the cat bounced off Gus and tore out the door the moment it was open just a crack. Blacky waited while Hy got on her bicycle and skittered along beside her as she made her way up Shipwreck Hill. Hy was planning to stop at Ian's, but as she turned into his driveway, the little cat kept going. Stopped. Turned and looked at Hy. Started up again.

Stopped. Looked back at Hy. She clearly wanted Hy to follow. Curious, Hy followed.

Blacky went all the way to the police house, where she turned in and started scratching at the door and meowing.

Jamieson came to the door.

Hy ducked behind the lilac hedge. It was redolent of that lovely spring smell, although the blossoms weren't quite out yet.

The cat rolled over and showed Jamieson its belly. Jamieson leaned down and rubbed it. It sounded like two cats purring.

"C'mon, Whitey," said Jamieson. "Come in." The cat sauntered into the house as if she owned the place.

Jamieson shot a look in either direction, and closed the door quickly.

Hy grinned. Jamieson had become a real softy. Alice, April Dewey's five-year-old hero-worshipped Jamieson for saving her life when a wind turbine collapsed on the cape last year. That Alice had captured Jamieson's heart, too, had been obvious. She allowed the kid to follow her on her rounds, holding her hand and sometimes holding her grubby stuffed bunny, too.

And now this, this kitten.

A kitten who appeared to have two, somewhat reluctant, homes. And two names. No, not two. Three.

Whacky, thought Hy.

That's what I'll call her.

Hy was about to leave when she thought she'd like to tease Jamieson about the cat and maybe talk to her about Vera Gloom. She marched up to the door. She knocked, as Jamieson had instructed everyone to do, though it was not the village custom. When Jamieson answered, Hy pointed at the feline stretched out on the couch, depositing white fur on the black fabric.

"Caught in the act."

As Hy had expected, Jamieson looked immediately guilty.

"It's not my cat," she said defensively.

"Looks pretty much at home."

There were catnip toys scattered all over the floor. Hy eyed them.

"Busted," she said. "By the way, have you spoken to your new neighbour?"

"I've hardly seen her. A glimpse now and then."

"Maybe you should pay her a visit."

"Why?"

"Oh, I dunno. Official welcome to the village, something like that."

Curiosity, thought Jamieson. *Snooping again. And trying to get me to do it for her.*

"It's just that…oh, never mind." Hy turned to leave. Now she'd piqued Jamieson's interest.

"Just that what?"

Hy turned back.

"Just that…is she living there alone?"

"I presume so, but I can't say yes or no."

"No. No one can. It's just that…"

Jamieson was now impatient.

"Just that I saw a man waving from an upstairs window."

"And?"

"I'm not sure. He just kept standing there, waving."

"Doesn't sound like a police matter to me."

"No, but – "

Hy had accomplished what she'd set out to do – rouse Jamieson's curiosity. Jamieson had come to trust Hy's hunches, though she'd never let her know. The woman next door was quiet and kept to herself. Only in The Shores could that be considered suspicious.

Blair was reading *The History of the Decline and Fall of the Roman Empire*. He always insisted on calling it by its full name, to Vera's irritation.

"Finally getting around to it," he told Vera when she carried his breakfast tray to him in the morning. She put the tray down on the occasional table by his side and looked with disapproval at the six volumes stacked at his feet. He could kick them over so easily. She moved them away, picked up the top one, Volume One, and handed it to him.

He didn't even say thank you. Not for the book. Not for the breakfast. He was already completely absorbed in his reading, and probably wouldn't eat a thing.

He really was getting too thin.

She went back down to the kitchen and got the second breakfast tray.

Charlie was up and active, working on a new painting, this one set in the woods outside his window, with the sun, low down, glancing through the trees as it set.

"Beautiful colour, doncha think?" He didn't even turn toward her. She had to dodge his arm, upraised and targeting a new piece of the canvas with his brush.

"Yes, Charlie, lovely." She set the tray down on a small table behind him, expecting that she would not be rewarded for her efforts with Charlie either. He was in another world, his own world of colour and light, canvas and imagination, the palette of his life.

He rarely ate his breakfast either.

He, too, was getting thin, she thought.

Another kitchen trip for Hank's tray. He never noticed when she came in, if she came in or not. But he had to be fed.

"Good morning, Hank," she said as she pushed through the door. Was that a grunt coming from the bed? If so, it was more than she usually got from him.

There he was, neat and tidy, in his striped pyjamas and the blue velvet robe today, leather slip-on slippers. She had tried to keep him from wearing his slippers on the bed, but with no luck. What did it matter, anyway? He never left the room. The soles of the slippers were perfectly clean.

Hank was watching his favourite morning program: *Good Morning America.*

From there, through the day, he would be channel surfing for a variety of programs he liked, recording others on his PVR if they coincided with shows he also wanted to watch.

Vera slid the tray onto his nightstand. His eyes remained riveted to the TV.

She went back downstairs and sorted through the mail on the kitchen table. A lime green flyer stood out from the batch:

Men of The Shores,
Throw off your Chains!
What you can do for the Bicentenary
By doing nothing!

Chapter Fourteen

Marlene was taking another stab at a meeting with a direct appeal to the men this time. It was an appeal that spoke to Vera, with one word.

Men.

Hers would not be going. But she would. Perhaps she'd find one there. Right at her doorstep. She had a few days to glam up. Not that glamour was what Vera was selling. She was selling handmaiden. Matron. Nurse. Rich widow?

As it turned out, there was no suitable man at the meeting. Those of the right age were married or poor or both. Not one of them attracted Vera's interest.

But she certainly attracted it. Almost no one had seen her close up. When she entered the hall, the villagers were grumbling and complaining and working up their arguments against the "tourism woman."

But when they saw Vera, there was silence. Absolute. Total. Silence. Mouths dropped open or set in firm lines. Eyes scraped her couture clothing, soft slinky silk, completely out of place on a cool June morning in The Shores. The click click of her four-inch heels resounding off the dance floor, and totally out of place. The hands, covered in rings, engagement rings and wedding rings. Blue diamonds and white gold.

So it was true that she'd had three husbands?

The men and women had been sitting on different sides of the room, as was their custom. The women, reading Vera as predatory, began to gravitate toward their men, clutching them by the arms, taking ownership. Wally Fraser, Harold MacLean, Germaine Joudry and the rest of them might be no prizes, but, as the village wives would say, "we're used to them."

Vera's arrival took the stuffing out of Marlene's meeting.

With all eyes on her, no one was paying attention to what Marlene said.

"I'm looking for ideas. From you. This is your celebration. It should be what you want it to be."

"A yard sale. Let's have a yard sale," offered April Dewey. It was her answer to every celebration or statutory holiday. When you have six kids, there's a lot of clothing and toys to be recycled.

"A yard sale." Marlene looked doubtful, but she wrote it down. Her notebook was otherwise blank.

"A ride-on race, around the village," Billy Pride suggested. "With prize money." He squeezed Madeline, Moira's little sister. He was saving up for a car and an engagement ring.

Marlene looked even more doubtful, but she jotted it down.

"A quilt competition," Rose Rose, the minister's wife, said on behalf of Gus, who'd quietly suggested it, knowing she would win. None of the other Institute women pieced any more. They quilted, but they didn't piece.

"A costume party," piped up Millie Fraser, teenage granddaughter of Gladys and Wally. Marlene rewarded her with a smile. Good to have the young people involved. She sketched a star beside that idea.

"A historical re-enactment," Hy suggested.

"Great idea. I'm in." Ian backed her up, safe in the knowledge that it would never happen, and, if it did, might at least bring them closer again. She did glance his way. She appeared grateful for his support.

Marlene was pleased, too, at the quantity of suggestions, if not their quality.

There was a brief, a very brief discussion about the ban on lawn mowing.

When Marlene brought it up – it was, after all, her main reason for the meeting – everyone in the hall, in unison, said: "No."

In the end, she said she'd send around a flyer and they could vote on the items they were willing or not willing to do.

Her big mistake was allowing "none of the above" as an answer in each category.

That's what everyone ticked. About almost everything. Most definitely the lawn mowing ban. The yard sale and the costumes squeaked through. In the first case, April tipped the balance by having all of her children vote. In the second, Millie Fraser, the only teenager at the event, sent messages on Facebook to all her friends to vote.

Apart from those two items, Marlene was back to square one.

But not Vera. She'd picked herself up and moved on. Going forward, as people were fond of saying these days. Forward. Back from the hall and a return to the computer, and bingo! Husband number four would soon be knocking on the door.

Except that husband number four wasn't capable of knocking on the door. He had to be brought in by ambulance – or what passed for an ambulance in The Shores. Volunteer paramedic

Nathan Mack's beat-up old van.

Nathan lived just down Shipwreck Hill from Vera, with his beloved Lili, the local yogi and flower farmer. Nathan was the son of Ben and Annabelle Mack.

That's about as concisely as it can be said. The thread of relationships and family connections in the village got a lot more tangled than that. It was hard for an outsider like Vera to keep them straight.

But she knew what she wanted, and how to get it. Combing through the online obits she'd found a man who had everything she wanted in a husband: a dead wife. Cyril Boomhauser needed a live one, someone to take care of him, and he was quickly enraptured by Vera, in a flurry of online correspondence. He had a few rental properties in town and a comfortable government pension, as a veteran who'd not only served his country, but been injured for it, in the worst place a man can be. He had mobility problems as well, but neither bothered Vera. She was used to taking care of people.

She didn't mention the three ex-husbands upstairs. Time enough for that. After they were married.

They were married in haste, by a justice of the peace in the gloomy living room of Cyril's Victorian in Charlottetown. Heavy velvet curtains framed tall windows that let in very little light because of the trees outside and buildings opposite. The groom was in a wheelchair, and the bride was in a plain dark housedress, a muddy brown, the kind of brown that seems practical because it won't show the dirt. There were no flowers, except the small bouquet in the bride's hands. There were no attendants. The housecleaner and Nathan signed as witnesses.

It was the kind of wedding a witness should perhaps be leery of putting a signature to. Isn't that what witnesses are for: to say it was all above board and everything was done correctly?

And maybe it was. Vera got what she wanted. Cyril. Cyril got what he wanted: not so much a wife as a caregiver.

It looked as if it were going to be another bad summer for Moira's Bed and Breakfast business. With the exception of Marlene, who at least was long-term, she had no guests booked this year. It meant she had to continue cleaning cottages on the cape.

It was with mixed feelings that she had taken on a new customer – Vera had answered her online ad for "discreet, quality cleaning services."

"You'll not need to do all twenty-four rooms every week of course." Vera had poured tea in the front room of the house, soon to become a sickroom, while Moira had memorized every detail of the woodwork, wainscoting and tin ceiling.

"In fact, you'll confine yourself to downstairs. This is where I live. I can worry about dusting and do the occasional vacuuming upstairs."

They had agreed on a day and a price, and Moira had left with a mouthful of gossip for those curious about what the place looked like inside.

Moira had been working for Vera for just a week when Nathan's ambulance transporting bride and groom arrived. Vera had been out when Moira got there, but now she stepped out of the back of the ambulance, a bouquet of flowers in her hand and wearing a smart little hat with a veil.

Nathan wheeled an elderly man into the front room. He looked pleased, but a bit confused, and he was drooling.

Vera saw that he was comfortably set up in a rental hospital bed, and slipped through into the kitchen, where Moira was aching with curiosity.

"My husband," Vera said, with her closest approximation of a smile. "We were just married today."

Moira's hands flew up to her mouth to stifle a squeal.

"Come, come and meet him."

Moira followed Vera into the front room.

The old man showed a spark of interest when the two women came in, but his eyes quickly dulled and the drool resumed sliding down his chin.

Leaving the house, Moira reflected on her own marital situation. Non-marital situation.

She'd decided on the venue, a word she loved to use. Now it was just a question of when, and what to wear.

Hy popped her head into Ian's. She didn't just stride in as she'd been in the habit of doing. The recent distance between them had got in the way of their old, easy style with one another.

"Hello," she called out. Something she'd never have done in the past. Was it just she feeling this uneasiness or did it go both ways? She wasn't sure.

"We're in here."

Jamieson would be there, then.

Hy joined them at the heart of Ian's home – his computer desk. He and Jamieson were side by side, shoulders touching. Cozy.

On the screen, in living iMac colour, was a woman slumped in a car seat with a bullet hole through her temple, dripping blood.

"Lovely."

"Interesting." Ian looked up at Hy. "It's the case study in our online forensics course."

"For-en-sick…sick…sick." Jasmine the parrot chimed in

as she always did when she heard the word. Then she made repeated gagging sounds. Ian and Jamieson had tried to avoid saying it, referring to it as "the f word."

"Learning anything?"

"Quite a bit, actually. Every contact leaves a trace."

"And that nothing is a given." Jamieson pushed her chair back and stood up. "Can you download today's material for me?" She handed Ian a shocking pink USB drive.

Odd. Girly. Not at all like Jamieson. Trying to show Ian her feminine side? What feminine side?

The jump drive loaded, Jamieson left. As soon as she had shut the door, Hy turned to Ian.

"Will you do me a favour?"

"If it's in my power." He smiled, a smile that appeared to have a conciliatory message in it. "What is it?"

"Just come down to Moira's in an hour."

"That's it?"

"That's it."

Chapter Fifteen

Knowing Moira would object, Hy had devised a scheme to sell her on the fish wear as wedding garb. She brought the blouse and skirt to Moira's and changed into them in a spare room. She told Moira to wait in the front room – a signal that what was going on was significant. It was the room reserved for the important occasions of life.

"What is that?" The first words out of Moira's mouth, when she saw Hy in the sole blouse and salmon skirt.

"Your wedding outfit, I hope."

"But it's…it's…" Moira touched the fabric. "What is it?"

"Fish skin."

Moira pulled her hand back, and held it away from her body as if it had been contaminated. She looked around for something to wipe it on. Nothing. Everything in here was "good."

"It's your heritage, Moira." That argument had worked before. It might again. Hy had nothing to prove that Mi'kmaq had worn fish skin. But they might have.

Hy saw hesitation in Moira's eyes. The fact was, the blouse and skirt were beautiful and unusual, neither of which Moira was. She could see it though. The rarity. The quality.

But the hesitation dragged on. Moira opened her mouth without saying anything. Hy heard the door open.

"We're in here," she called out. Ian, in the hall, cocked an eyebrow. The front room. Must be important.

When he opened the door and saw Hy standing there, Hy who never wore dresses or skirts, in this fabulous outfit, the breath was knocked out of him. When he recovered it, one word came from the depths of him.

"Stunning."

Hy smiled, a big generous smile, with no undercurrent of cheekiness.

"Yes, isn't it?"

He touched the fabric of the skirt.

"Salmon," she said.

He stroked the blouse.

"And this?'

"Sole."

"Of course I've read about native North Americans using birds and fish to make shoes and clothing, but I've never seen it before. Is this something for the 200th?"

"Not exactly. This is what Moira's considering wearing at her wedding." Hy hoped that by saying it – in front of Ian – she would force Moira's hand.

Ian was confused. If it was Moira's wedding outfit, why was Hy wearing it? He put it down to a woman thing.

"Well, it's stunning. Beautiful."

Moira's mind was racing. Ian was looking at Hy the way she'd like him to look at her, even though she was marrying Frank. Frank had asked, the only man who ever had. Ian had not, but he was the one she still loved.

"Clever link to our heritage celebrations. Very clever, Moira.

You'll look great in it, even better than Hy with your dark hair." Ian knew exactly what he was saying and why. He'd caught Hy's look, and knew he was supposed to conspire to convince Moira to wear the outfit.

He pulled it off. What he'd said sealed it. Almost. What he said next most definitely did.

"You wear that, and I'll give you away."

Moira nearly swooned.

It was the next best thing to marrying him.

Right now, she was anxious for him to go so she could try the outfit on. And show Hy up. When Ian did finally leave, with a wink to Hy on the way out, Moira abandoned her usual modesty, and slipped out of her housedress to reveal sensible cotton underclothes. Frank liked them. It was as far as he'd ever got.

"Matched only by the couture houses in Paris. Actually only one of them…" said Hy, pinning the top, where it hung on Moira. She had no breasts.

"But *Cosmo* says nothing – "

There was renewed doubt in Moira's eyes, creeping back after Ian's exhilarating pronouncement: "Stunning." She could still hear it, and now she had herself almost convinced that she, not Hy, had been wearing the clothing when he'd said it.

"*Cosmo*, forget *Cosmo*." Hy broke a thread with her teeth.

"You are on the leading edge of fashion, Moira…what do they call it now? Oh, yes – fashion forward."

"Fashion forward?"

"Yup."

Moira, who wasn't in the habit of glowing, glowed.

She always felt that she presented herself well, far better than the rest of the ladies of the Institute, keeping up-to-date on fashion through the Sears catalogue. But she had secretly known that, if anything, she was fashion backward, not forward. She had a niggling thought that this might be fashion backward, too. After all, hadn't fish skin been worn in the past? Had her Mi'kmaq ancestors worn it? She winced at the thought of her ancestry, still not fully at ease with the idea.

She was on the point – reluctantly – of allowing her family history to be included in the book.

"Else what would you say about the Toombs?" Gus had pointed out to Hy. "You can't leave them out, and them living there right next to the hall all these generations. But they never done anything. Not until this." Gus was taking a greater interest in "the book" since she'd washed her hands of it.

Moira had Marie's letter still, but she finally gave it to Hy at a fitting one day. She set her qualms aside when she saw what Hy had found for her. The outfit was on and off the hanger every day as Moira tried it on over and over again, admiring herself in the mirror.

It – she – was utterly unique.

"Perfect for your physique," Hy had said. Moira was, at best, stick thin, scrawny. She didn't look it in the sole top, though.

The salmon skirt rippled to the floor in a sheen of fabric. When Moira tried it on with the top, the two complemented one another perfectly and looked just right on her.

"Born to it," said Hy. "All we need now is a finishing touch."

"A finishing touch? What?"

"I don't know now. Yet. But I will. I'll know it when I see it."

Frank gave Marlene a cheeky grin and a wink, behind Moira's back. Marlene flushed red. Small and mousy, Marlene was not without her charms. Her mother would say – and did –

that she had "a good bust." Her facial features were largely unremarkable, except for her lips. They, like her bust, were generous and well-formed. Kissable, so Frank thought. Her usual expression of dissatisfaction formed her lips in a pout, which made them more kissable.

It didn't take much to satisfy Frank. A nice kiss could set him up for the day. A bit of fooling around while waiting for the main prize – Moira.

Frank was the only man who could possibly consider Moira a prize. He thought of her as a dark chocolate cream – bitter and crisp on the outside, but with a delicious interior to be savoured. And now that they had discovered her Mi'kmaq heritage, Frank thought of her as his Indian princess.

Moira had not come around to it herself. She'd always made much of the fact that her father was a waste management supervisor. A garbage man. Elitist and racist, she'd not been happy to find out that a grandmother, several times great, had been a Mi'kmaw, no matter the circumstances.

"But it's so romantic," Marlene gushed when she heard the story. "You must do a presentation for us on the 200th."

It was a romantic story, with a rough start, that was told in the letter that Moira had inherited.

The native woman had taken in a shipwrecked Toombs. Shipwrecked, sick with scurvy and rude. She ignored his cursing, cleaned him, made him a comfortable bed and fed him tree bark tea against scurvy.

She was graceful, quiet in her movements, silent except for her eyes that implored him not to curse, not to spit out the concoction she had made him to cure him. As he got better, the cursing diminished and then ceased altogether. Interest grew in him, and one day, his strength returned, he grabbed her and threw her to the ground. She whimpered, but lay still, speaking only with her eyes, as he fumbled with her clothes.

And then he stopped. The look in her eyes spoke to him, and with a curse that he could not do what he would, he threw himself off her. He grunted, and made motions with his hands for her to fetch him food.

It wasn't a great start to love and marriage.

But the two became used to one another, began to understand one another, and when he recovered, he took on the duties of the man of the house. She taught him to hunt and to trap, to smoke meats and fish, to make his own clothes.

They exchanged words and learned a bit of each other's language, and they began to convey meaning in their glances.

Meaning that could mean only one thing.

The inevitable happened. They became man and wife – or that is how Marie referred to it in the few pages found among Gus's collection.

Whether they were actually ever married is doubtful.

That was another thing that bothered Moira. Conceived in sin. All the way down the line. But surely all those legitimate marriages should have wiped that out?

It made Moira even more determined to save herself for marriage, to continue the cleansing that all those legitimate marriages had accomplished. She'd also begun to have a suspicion that she wasn't going to like "it," that she wouldn't want to do "it" as often as Frank did. So that had made her stall on the wedding date. Frank seemed to think their engagement was a license for lovemaking. Once they were married, it would be harder to turn him away.

Like now. Why couldn't he be satisfied with a little peck on the cheek when he headed off in the morning? Here he was, yanking at her skirt, trying to pull it up, feeling her bottom, and she wriggling, which only seemed to make him more excited.

Finally, he gave up. With a peck on the cheek, he smacked her bottom and left the kitchen. Then she remembered – the list of errands she wanted him to do in town.

She chased after him to be stopped in her tracks by what she saw in the hallway. Frank had grabbed that Marlene, and was giving her a full kiss on the lips, hauling her up off the floor into his arms.

Moira was too shocked to say anything.

Frank dropped Marlene. She looked flushed and pretty.

Moira said nothing. Retreated quietly back through the door into the kitchen.

Perhaps she was going to have to be more giving.

She'd start with Frank's favourite meal tonight.

Wieners.

And seal the wedding date. A.S.A.P.

Hy found what she was looking for in an unexpected place. She'd gone back to Big Bay to "stage" the wedding – figure out where the flowers would go, where the pair would take their vows, where guests could watch from.

She found another boutique open in one of Ben and Annabelle Mack's shacks. Their son Nathan's girlfriend Lili had opened an outlet for her fresh flowers.

Hy placed an order with her immediately for Moira's wedding. Moira might be miffed that she hadn't been consulted, but when Hy told her she'd picked up the bill, she knew Moira would be happy with whatever she'd chosen. For one thing, it wouldn't be mean and small.

That business done, Hy noticed a display case of jewellery.

"This stuff is gorgeous," she said. Lili opened the case and let her have a better look.

"Just beautiful."

"I'm making it myself. A modern take on traditional North American jewellery. Not just Mik'maq, which I am, in part, but Inuit, and Navaho as well." Hy picked up an elaborate bead-embroidered cobalt necklace and earrings, the beads matching beautifully in colour and roped in a chain of ascending sizes. When she saw it, she knew it.

"Some people have actually commissioned pieces."

"Is this for anybody?" Hy fingered the tightly knit beads.

"No."

"Can I buy it for Moira?"

"Moira?"

"For her wedding."

Lili frowned. "No, you can't."

Hy frowned, disappointed.

Lili smiled, picked it up and gave it to Hy.

"It's a gift."

"You'll never make a living that way."

Lili smiled, even deeper.

"I know."

Chapter Sixteen

"She's comin'."

The words were out of Gus's mouth before Hy was even through the door.

"Who?"

"Who else would it be?"

"Uh…" Hy stood still at the doorway, as if that would give her the answer. "You got me."

Gus held up the tiny garment she was knitting.

Hy beamed.

"Not…"

"The same." A look of smug satisfaction crossed Gus's face.

"Dot?"

A nod.

"Dot one and Dot two?"

Gus looked puzzled. Hy had forgotten the child's name. "Little Dot." That's what Gus always called her.

Hy came into the room and slumped in a chair.

"A homecoming. A heritage homecoming. A real cause for celebration." She tried to keep her eyes averted from the fat, messy pile of papers and photographs on the dresser beside the chair. The book was not likely to happen now with Dot and the baby coming.

As if she had read Hy's thoughts, Gus nodded at the file folder. "Mebbe Dot will help me with that."

"I thought Dot's thing was science, not English."

"She's very organized," said Gus. "She could make sense of a crazy quilt."

Hy left, anxious to finally meet the marvel that was Gus's long-awaited and only daughter, and hopeful that Dot might bring the bicentennial book back on track. Would she be able to exorcise the ghost of Gus's mother?

He's coming.

Dot's homecoming was swept right out of Hy's mind when she reached her own home and fired up the computer.

When she read the message on the screen, she did sit down.

Finn's coming.

If this was online dating, it was getting serious.

Hy's face was warm, flushed. Her eyes turned toward Shipwreck Hill. The lights had just come on at Ian's house.

What will Ian think? Tell him now? Wait?

Tell Finn not to come?

She began to write.

"That's great, Finn. I can't wait to meet you…"

She looked up again at Shipwreck Hill. The flickering light coming from the living room told her that Ian was on his computer, too. But he wouldn't be navigating on Facebook, though to her surprise, Hy had found his page on the social network. His only friend was Moira Toombs. Hy figured Moira must have set it up.

The knowledge that Ian was a Facebook innocent added

to Hy's guilt about Finn, but didn't change her intention to welcome him to The Shores.

www.theshores200.com
The newspapers of the day say the fire that killed one of the Sullivan brothers was "an accident." The villagers say it was murder. They say one started the fire to deliberately kill the other, because he wanted the house. It had happened before in that family, brothers squabbling over ownership, ending in fratricide. They say the Sullivan house is built on blood.

On the morning of Moira's wedding, in the front room of the Toombs residence, Hy transformed her into an exotic creature, in the silky sole blouse, shimmering salmon skirt and beautiful blue beaded necklace. Hy had enjoyed the makeover, but the big reward came when Moira opened the china cabinet and the banged-up cigarette case and gave the ancestral letter to Hy.

"For the book," she said.

Moira stood, for fear of damaging her outfit, the whole time while Hy slipped into her bridesmaid's dress.

The bride's outfit had changed, but Hy was wearing the same dress as the year before, when the marriage ceremony on the beach had been interrupted. She'd had time to make it more flattering, but it's hard for a redhead to work with purple. She was wearing the dress with gumboots. That was even less flattering. She would put on the requisite heels for the wedding, but the wharf was slippery with fish oil and water and she didn't want to fall and ruin her dress.

It was a typical Big Bay morning, with a Scotch mist seeping across the wharf, that fine mist Red Island reserved for special outdoor occasions.

The setting wasn't anywhere near what Moira had imagined from the pages of *Cosmo*. Thanks to Marlene, a half-dozen of the fish shacks were freshly painted, although the colours chosen looked more garish than picturesque. The Scotch mist had moistened the wooden decking, which was slick with seagull scat as well. At the head of the pier, the fishermen had erected a canopy for the ceremony, a green army tarp that was flapping in the wind and refusing to allow flowers to be attached to it. They lay where the wind had thrown them, in sad-looking bunches on the dock.

The dock was lined on either side with window boxes, whose flowers had suffered an overnight beating from the wind and rain. They drooped miserably – purple and pink petunias ragged and splotched with fading colour; lobelia dragging across the wood planks, beaten into the boards and unable to rise to the day. Only the marigolds stood up bravely, splotches of chirpy orange soldiering on through the weather.

The guests – the entire village had been invited – hadn't ventured onto the wharf. They stood gathered around in the gravel parking lot, some with arms aloft, holding onto umbrellas that kept flipping inside out. Others were sitting on their tailgates. The villagers knew they wouldn't be able to hear much, but they could see, and that was just fine. They'd all been to so many weddings they could have officiated as well as the Reverend Rose. The reverend and Frank were already standing, shivering, at the end of the pier, where the ceremony was to take place in a few moments.

Hy was glad of her boots, because she was barely onto the wharf when she stepped onto a pile of gull poo.

"Yech, gross." She hopped about on one foot, grabbing at the soiled boot and looking at the bottom. "Gross." She put the

Bodies and Sole

foot down and walked gingerly to Cat's, to clean it off. She left gumboot prints all the way along the dock.

Moira arrived, driven by Ian in his truck. She was smirking, delighted at the opportunity to spend time with Ian, to be escorted by him, even though she was getting married within minutes to Frank.

She was also fully convinced of herself as an Indian princess, and alighted from the truck with an unusual air of confidence. There were the requisite *oohs* and *ahs* upon sight of the bride. But some of the oohs – from the direction of the Women's Institute group – sounded more like *"ew."*

If Moira heard it, she chose to ignore it. She lifted her skirt so as not to get Red Island clay on it, and, head high, Moira, the Mi'kmaw bride, took a few steps forward and slid on the same pile of poo as Hy. But she went down and landed right in it.

Hy came tearing down the wharf, slipping and sliding, to help her up.

"My dress. My God."

"We'll clean it up. It'll be fine." For the second time in a week, Hy felt truly sorry for Moira. She wasn't crying – yet – but her eyes were swimming with tears and mascara was running down her cheeks. Bad to worse.

Hy scurried back to Cat's, leaving Moira to the inept commiserations of Ian. Cat, standing outside his door, had seen the whole thing.

"A cloth…some water…soap…" Hy panted.

He just stood there, shaking his head.

"Nope." It sounded like.

"Nope?"

He shook his head again, and spoke more distinctly.

"No hope."

"No hope."

"No hope?"

"No hope." He gestured in Moira's direction. She was now clinging onto Ian and sobbing into his shoulder. He was looking exceptionally uncomfortable, patting her back.

"Ohmigod." Hy pointed at the back of Moira's skirt.

It was happening in front of their eyes.

"It's disintegrating."

"Yup. Told you. Enzymes and stuff. Not good. Not good."

"No. Not good at all."

When Hy got back to Moira, slumped in Ian's arms, the entire backside of the skirt had disintegrated. Frank had run down from the end of the pier and relieved Ian, trying to console her, with no success. Cat produced an oilskin jacket, and Frank, Hy and Ian helped Moira back into Ian's truck. He had spread a copy of *The Guardian* newspaper on the passenger seat.

Moira wept all the way home, and wouldn't let Frank in when he showed up shortly after.

Another unsuccessful wedding.

Would there be a third?

Would it be third time lucky?

And whatever was the bride going to wear?

The fish skin outfit had already found its way into the compost bin.

Hy didn't dare phone Moira or drop by. And she quickly copied Marie's letter, certain that Moira would demand it back.

Chapter Seventeen

www.theshores200.com

The Macks are, and have been for 200 years, the most prominent family in The Shores. They truly can lay claim to having had an ancestor who swam ashore from the sinking Annabella. *A 15-year-old boy from Ireland, he no sooner landed than he began procreating with local Irish, Scots, English, Welsh, Mi'kmaw and French lasses. But his legitimate line became the first white settlers in The Shores and he quickly established himself as fisherman, farmer, general-store owner and informal banker.*

She was home.

The tongues would be wagging shortly, with something worth wagging about. Maybe that was why she was taking her time on this last leg of the journey.

She'd been surprised herself that the Campbell Causeway that joined The

Shores to the rest of Red Island was still under construction. It almost always was.

Of course, she'd heard about the catastrophe several years before that had ripped the causeway in two, destroyed five houses, pushed cars into the water, tossed boats up onto the road, and killed nine people, all within thirteen-and-a-half minutes.

The province had fixed the causeway, but never well, and provided a small open car ferry, bought from a neighbouring province, to provide regular seasonal service in place of the causeway.

She found it pleasant taking the old river ferry the short distance across the inlet. She felt like taking her time to return home. Reluctant to get the gossiping tongues going? Maybe, a bit. But she felt more as if she were savouring it, this return after so many years.

She hadn't told the family her exact arrival time. She wanted it to be a surprise.

What if Ma and Pa weren't home?

They were always home. And where would they go when the whole village was about to celebrate its 200th anniversary? She was arriving in time to be part of the celebration. It would be a heritage homecoming.

She was out of the car for the brief crossing, leaning on the metal gates at the front of the flat-bottomed boat. The wind was brisk, carrying moisture that misted her lips, and she brushed her tongue across them.

Salt.

The taste of home.

She breathed in deeply. The cold air stung her nostrils.

Salt, sand and the sea.

The smell of home.

It was then that she saw him. She hadn't known there was another passenger on the ferry. Hers was the only car. He had been on the back of the boat and now strode past her just as the ferry made its bumpy connection to land. She returned to her car. The baby was still asleep in the back seat, eyes closed to this first sight of home. Because it was home for her, too, though she hadn't been born here, had never lived here. All her history was here.

As the ferry slid into place and the gates clanked open, he put down his backpack and stretched. All dressed in black, his limbs so long and thin, he made her think of a spider, minus a few legs. He was up the ramp before she'd engaged the ignition, but she quickly caught up and slowed down, lowering the window on the passenger side and calling out to him:

"Do you need a lift?"

He smiled, an engaging smile, not the least like an arachnid, and shook his head.

"Thank you, but I'm fine. I don't have far to go."

"The Shores?"

"Yes."

"Well, that's all there is."

"I know. So they say." He winked, waved a long arm and strode off.

The Shores. All there is.

The thought stayed with her, up and down hills and hollows, familiar as no other part of the world was – and she'd been in many of them. This land and seascape was imprinted on her brain, traced in her heart, engraved on her spirit.

All there is. She'd had to get away from it to know it. It had seemed so suffocating. Now, it seemed like a whole world to her. As big as the world she'd seen. All of it.

All there is.

When she came to the high hill above the village, her heart filled with the sight. Her history, her heritage. There, smack in the centre, was the hall. Close by, a lot, "For Sale," where the Old General Store had been. The other empty lot across the road belonged to her, where the one-room schoolhouse had once been, and where she had gone to school. It was kept tidy, clear of invading brush and bandit spruce, grass clipped.

She had been gone too long.

Suddenly, she couldn't wait – stall? – a moment longer. She released the brake and went speeding down toward home.

He would be here soon.

She'd hesitated about telling Ian, but finally decided she'd better before he found out the worst way – bumping into him in the village.

About his coming, Hy wasn't sure how she felt, but she was pretty sure how Ian would feel about it. Not happy. With reluctant footsteps, she dragged her bicycle up Shipwreck Hill.

"On Facebook? Give me a break." Ian's face was etched with disgust. How would he feel, Hy wondered, if he found out he was on Facebook, too, with Moira as his only friend?

"Yes. I met him on Facebook."

Ian's forehead wrinkled.

"Are you…?"

"No. Nothing like that." Not true, she thought. Not true. It was like that. She was interested. Definitely interested. And he? "So who is he? What's his name?"

"Finn. Finnegan."

"That's it? One name?" Ian's lip curled.

"No, two. Finn Finnegan."

"Finn. And Finn again? Does that make him Finn Finn?"

He was being deliberately annoying.

"I hope you'll behave when he comes."

"So I'm to meet this marvel? I'm honoured."

Not honoured. Jealous. Of someone he hadn't met. Of someone who might mean something to Hy.

Or might not.

Ian's only consolation was that Hy didn't seem able to make a commitment to anyone. Certainly not to him.

Ian had no idea of the baggage he dragged around with him.

"What's going on here?"

A disembodied voice woke her from a light nap.

Her eyes popped open.

She rubbed them.

Rubbed them again.

Was the Skype on?

No. Here they were. The two of them.

Gus jumped up out of the chair faster than she'd moved since her eightieth birthday, and that was quite a few years past.

She grabbed the bundle Dot held out to her.

Little Dot. Her granddaughter.

And Dot, her daughter. She wanted to hug her, but couldn't, not with the babe in her arms. And she wasn't letting go.

Little Dot. Born in the Antarctic. And here she'd managed to get out alive.

It had been a perfectly normal birth, in a somewhat abnormal place, to an older mother. Dot was past forty when she had Little Dot – as Gus had been herself. But, she always said, she'd had seven under her belt first, whereas for Dot this was the first – and only? – one.

The bundle was squirming. This baby was no baby anymore. A year old. She wanted onto the floor and the inviting mess that beckoned her.

Gus let her down. Little Dot trampled with glee all over the quilt patches, then began sliding on the photographs and clippings.

"August, no." Dot scooped up the child.

"No name for a child." Gus shook her head. Better than Augusta, her own, but still, she thought Little Dot suited.

"I know you call her Little Dot, but it's a mouthful."

"Dottie then." That settled, Gus reached out her arms to the child. "Let's see what we have in the kitchen for you."

Dot sighed. She surveyed the mess on the floor again. She began to shift the photos and clippings around, like pieces of a puzzle, fascinated by the lore that lay on the kitchen floor.

Gus returned with Dottie grabbing onto one of her fingers. With the other hand she was attempting to stuff a blueberry muffin into her mouth. Walking and eating at the same time was a new skill, leaving a trail of muffin on the floor.

Dot bent down to pick up the crumbs.

"Oh, don't bother." Gus sat down in her chair and pulled her granddaughter onto her knee, ignoring the crumbs and blueberries staining her apron. That's what aprons were for, wasn't it? Gus shook her head as Dot began grabbing at papers and photographs, picking up pieces of the past like so many crumbs.

"Maybe you'll make sense of that. I haven't, not since I started it. Now I'm supposed to finish it for this here celebration and it's driving me crazy. As crazy as that quilt." She pointed down at the patches, crushed beneath her feet.

"I don't know. I see a certain order here. You can take it chronologically, or by theme. Or both. Separate parts."

"Mebbe you're right. Why don't you do it, now that you're here? P'raps we might make something of it after all."

And then she got to the real point:

"Why didn't you tell us when you was comin'? We might not have been here."

Dot smiled.

"Oh sure, when was the last time you were not here?"

Gus said nothing.

"Where's Pa?"

"Abel?"

"Who else?"

Gus smirked. "Well now…"

Not here.

The man dressed in black with the spidery arms and legs walked along The Island Way, drawing stares from villagers going back and forth from Winterside and Charlottetown.

Ian got a real eyeful when he passed by, just as Finn Finnegan was marching up to Hy's door. A quick survey of the house gave Ian the information he wanted. Hy wasn't there. Her bicycle was gone. Her truck, he knew, would be in the garage, because the door was closed. It would have been propped open if she was out in the truck.

Should he confront the man? Prevent him from going in when Hy wasn't there? Inviting Facebook strangers to visit. It might be dangerous.

Ian slowed his truck, its wheels keeping pace with his thoughts. Well, it wouldn't be dangerous if she wasn't there. He picked up speed again, turned up Shipwreck Hill.

He'd drop by later to see everything was okay. Right now he had a date himself, he thought, smiling. With the online forensic course. And Jamieson. Good-looking woman. Great hair. And a sensible mind, more like a man. She thought in black and white, a language Ian could understand. Hy, with her flashing red curls, communicated in technicolour.

At the moment, Hy was trying to cheer up a weeping Moira. Frank had asked her to come over and see if she could make her feel better.

"I've told her we should just hook up with a Justice of the Peace and have a quiet ceremony, but she won't hear of it," he explained to Hy when she arrived.

"She's got her heart set on a proper ceremony, but she doesn't want to make a fool of herself in public again." He shrugged his shoulders. "Rock and a hard place."

He led Hy to the kitchen where Moira was spilling her tears into a batch of blueberry muffin mix.

Hy didn't know what to say, how to help. For a while, she allowed Moira to weep, her back heaving.

"Morti… I'm so mortified."

"C'mon, Moira, it could happen to anyone."

They both knew that was a lie. For one thing, it hadn't happened to anyone. It had happened to Moira. Twice.

"You still want to marry Frank?"

Moira hiccupped two big breaths of air, by way of a "yes."

"Then do it simply, as Frank suggests. Justice of the Peace."

Two more hiccups of air, accompanied by a sharp shake of the head.

No.

"At the hall, then. Nothing fancy. A traditional hall wedding."

Moira had an envelope crushed in her hand. She held it out for Hy to take, and with a flick of her hand indicated that Hy should open it.

It was from Moira's aunts Bessie and Jessie, Moira's only

relatives besides her sister Madeline. They were planning to visit.

Moira had managed to control her sobbing.

"They think I'm already married."

"Well, won't they be happy to be able to come to the ceremony. In the hall."

Moira gave a slow nod. "In the hall."

"Soon."

"Soon."

Slowly, Hy coaxed Moira into the hint of a smile, and soon had her planning for a Justice of the Peace on home turf – the hall.

"We could write our own vows," said Moira, remembering a recent article from *Cosmo*.

Finn, not knowing the local ways, knocked on Hy's door. There was no answer. He knocked again. Waited a while. He tried the doorknob. It gave. Slowly he pushed open the door, peeking inside as he did.

He smiled. It told the whole story. An assortment of mostly antique furniture, bright tapestries, up-to-date electronics, and – looking in the fridge – he found nothing to eat. Or rather, nothing edible. Shrunken dried-out food, a pasta dish or two that had seen better days, lumps of cheese of various varieties and eras and a couple of bottles of white wine.

He pulled off his backpack, rummaged inside it for some treasured spices and went right to work.

Chapter Eighteen

The rental car parked in the driveway at Macks' could mean only one thing. Dot had arrived. Hy sped her bicycle the short distance from Moira's, jumping off it before the wheels had stopped spinning, and bounded up the front steps.

Hy had never met Dot. She had lived in The Shores for over twenty years, but had arrived just after Dot left. Only once in all that time had Dot returned home, and Hy had been away.

Once in twenty years, thought Hy. What did that long absence mean? There didn't seem to be any bad blood between Gus and Dot – Hy had witnessed their easy relationship on Skype. But there must be something. Twenty years away. It said complex, not simple, relationship.

Whacky charged past Hy when she opened the door, streaked straight for where she wasn't wanted, as cats do. Straight up to Dot and pawing at Dottie, who perched on her mother's hip.

Dot in person wasn't much different than Dot on Skype. They'd conversed a bit when Dot was pregnant with Dottie in Antarctica, so Hy was used to her open smile and breezy self-confidence.

Now, in person, Hy liked Dot for herself and she was glad, but she knew she would have liked her anyway, if only for

Gus's sake. How could she not? The lovely smile lighting up her old friend's face, eyes sparkling with joy, settling on her own most loved child, and grandchild. Bustling across the room to hug them both and relieve her daughter of the baby. Simple pleasure. Nothing complex about that.

Until she sat down in her rocker.

"And where's himself?"

Dot frowned.

"Well…?"

"Well, there's been a parting of ways."

"Never." Gus shoved the baby back at Dot. "Let me get you a cup of tea."

Gus scurried off to busy herself in the pantry – her reaction to all stripes of emotional shock.

"It's cold down there," Dot whispered to Hy. "Someone to warm your bed can cloud your judgment." She grinned. Hy smiled back. Gus fussed and fussed in the pantry, unable, at first, to find the tea, then the milk. She opened and closed the fridge several times before she located it – in the fridge.

She emerged – but without the squares, returned to the pantry, still holding the tea tray, came back with the squares but without the tea.

Hy jumped up and helped sort it out, while Dot nursed the baby, who had begun to fuss.

Gus wasn't sure she approved of the display in public, but she was wrangling with a bigger issue from the calming rock of her chair. It was getting less simple all the time.

"And so you'll be staying here. Home." It was the only comfort Gus could find in the situation.

Dot darted a glance at Hy, adopted as a co-conspirator.

"Ma, I don't know…"

"Don't know? How could you not know? With the babe, where would you go?"

"Where I usually go."

"Traipsing all over the world?"

"That's what I usually do."

Gus sighed. A heavy sigh. She pointed to the dresser where Dot had stuffed the papers and photos of the heritage project back into the cardboard file. They were about to come out again.

"Bring me that folder, Hy."

Ian had been useless during the weekly online forensics session with Jamieson, constantly jumping up to look out the window, and confirm, from the sight of Hy's bicycle, that she was still with Gus.

"Settle down," Jamieson barked, annoyed when he jumped up for the fourth or fifth time.

"Did you digest this? Can I go to the next page?"

Ian returned from the window. The light beaming in flashed a sheen over Jamieson's black hair. He hardly noticed. He hardly noticed the screen either. He skimmed over the information.

"Yes. Uh-huh." He sounded distracted, but Jamieson took him at his word and clicked "Next."

Ian stood for a moment or two, watching the simulation of the case study crime, of a woman, sitting in a car, shot through the head on a lonely stretch of road.

When the video ended, Ian drifted back to the window. Hy's bike was still there.

Jamieson stuck in her USB, downloaded a few items and clicked off the screen.

"There are still two more sections and a quiz." She ejected

the USB and picked up her notebook and pen. "We'll catch up tomorrow. I see you're in no mood today."

She walked over to the window.

McAllister's bike outside Gus Mack's? Why should that disturb him?

It didn't. Not as long as it was there.

When it moved, so did Ian. He jumped into his truck and headed down to Hy's.

He was dressed in the shirt and pants that had arrived that day from L.L.Bean. The tidiest they would ever look. After which they would land on a chair, become crushed under more clothes, be dragged out and stuffed in the washer and dryer, and then left in the dryer for days to allow the wrinkles to set. Ian never looked crisp. At best, rumpled.

Finn was crisp and had the look of someone who was always that way, even when he was living out of a backpack. His clothes were L.L.Bean, like Ian's. Unlike Ian, Finn didn't look as if he'd borrowed the skin he was in. The clothes looked made for him. A good-looking outdoors guy.

A spidery-thin, good-looking outdoors guy, tasting the tomato sauce that was bubbling up on Hy's stove. She arrived home to a house filled with the aroma of a fine Italian meal.

"I take it you're Finn. If you're not…"

"The very same. I hope you don't mind my making myself at home like this…"

"Not at all. Anyone who cooks for me is always welcome."

"You don't make it easy."

"I know, I know. The cupboards are usually bare or rotting."

"However, I have devised a delectable shrimp in tomato sauce. With the house wine. Have a seat."

Just as he spoke, Ian charged though the door.

"Pardon me for interrupting," he glanced first at Hy, then rested his gaze on Finn. A full head of hair, Ian noted with distaste. He wasn't the least bit sorry about having interrupted them, she could see that. She was annoyed. She knew she liked Finn, she could tell that right off, and here was Ian barging in. She felt she had no choice but to invite him to what otherwise might have turned into a romantic dinner.

"We're just sitting down. Please join us. There's plenty."

Ian never said no to a meal. And he saw all the signs of a romantic dinner hatching, so he was quite happy to accept the invitation. Very foolish of Hy, he thought. She didn't know this man and here he was cooking in her house, eating in her house…sleeping in her house?

He sat down and picked up a fork.

For a few moments, eating and comments about how delicious the food was filled what otherwise might have been an uncomfortable silence. But it came, as it was bound to. Dinner had reached the point where conversation was required.

"So you're a scientific man?" Finn started it up.

"How do you know?"

"Hy and I have communicated quite a bit. I understand you have a keen interest in science. Then we have something in common."

Hy felt a spark of hope that this meeting might go okay. Finn was making overtures.

Ian raised an eyebrow.

"You think?" His voice was thick with doubt.

"I would think – although you have not gone as far with it as I did."

"Did?"

"Oh, I don't bother with the stuff I used to anymore."
So much for overtures.

"But when you *did* bother with the stuff…?" Hy sensed he was going in for the kill, looking for a slim connection to science, if at all.

"Not science exactly."

Ian looked triumphant.

"Medicine. Medical doctor. My specialty was forensics."

"Was?"

"I'm an environmentalist now. Got into the medical thing because it was what my mother wanted. Forensics… I don't know. It seemed to be on the cutting edge, so to speak."

"Forensics?" A spark of interest from Ian. "Dabbling in that myself at the moment."

"I had no real interest. My mother felt I should have a trade, a back-up. I chose forensics because I thought it would appall her and I'd be off the hook. It did appall her, but she waited it out, thinking I would cave in. I waited, too. We were both so stubborn that I finally found myself with the rubber gloves and scalpel carving into a cadaver."

Ian's face whitened at the image.

Definitely a dabbler, not a carver, thought Hy.

The talk had put them all a bit off their meal, but Ian soon rallied and managed to have a second helping.

The folder became something that Gus and Dot began to shape their renewed relationship around.

Dot had all the contents of the folder spread on the kitchen floor again. Dottie was crawling all over them, shuffling them around.

Gus sighed.

Dot dove for a yellow piece of paper with a scribble on it.

"Here's a partial list of contents."

"Well, now, and if it isn't. I been looking all over for that. In and outside my head. Couldn't remember for the life of me."

"And here's your first settler."

"Ebenezer Mack. Yes, that's right."

"Might as well go chronologically with the people, the families, and then do some of the interest pieces. Like first barn, first car, all the firsts together with any photos that you have."

Gus was nodding and rocking.

"Old Ebenezer. The stories they told about him." She smiled. Her eyes closed in reminiscence.

Dot picked up papers and photographs and was sorting them in sequence. Gus was a bit like Tom Sawyer whitewashing the fence. She'd started it up and now Dot was doing the work.

"Old Ebenezer. Did you know him?"

Gus laughed and her eyes came open.

"No, but his name was spoke in my house as if he were still alive. Lived to be one hundred and twelve. Or so they say. No record of it."

There was about to be. Dot pulled out her iPhone and hit *Record*.

A few hours later, the floor was clean of clippings, scraps of paper and photographs. Dottie was tucked upstairs in bed, and Dot's iPhone was full of stories.

Dot had been asking questions.

Gus had done what she did best – told her stories.

Gus Mack's tales of the past – a documentary account unrivalled anywhere.

Chapter Nineteen

Ian now had over two thousand Facebook friends, many of them called Finn Finnegan, or some variation. On his quest to find out who Finn was, he'd stumbled onto his own Facebook page. He wondered, briefly, how it had been created, and then used it for his own quest to find out about Finn. The Finn he wanted to find out about had not yet confirmed his friend request.

That Finn was friends with Hy, on and off Facebook, had become painfully clear to Ian following the awkward dinner.

Quite apart from his jealousy, he was genuinely concerned that Hy had a man she didn't know staying in her house. So concerned that he'd offered him a bed at his.

Both Finn and Hy had laughed it off.

This evening, he'd seen them strolling down The Shore Lane. Hand in hand. Down to the shore, as the sun set. Very romantic. Their heads close together. Talking. Laughing.

Ian thought the man looked like a spider.

This growing closeness between Hy and Finn made Ian more determined than ever to find him out. He'd confirmed

Finn's status as a doctor and forensic anthropologist. He'd also found some references to his environmental activism, but he was looking for something more.

Everybody had a secret they'd rather other people didn't know. This Finnegan character would be no different.

The skull was killing time. The gulls were, too. A pair of them picked him up, beaks stuck through the holes where his eyes had once been. They carried him over the water, a flock of gulls pursuing them, deluded into thinking he was edible.

They pecked at and removed the seaweed stuck to his head, and, finding nothing more of interest, let go.

The skull dropped to the water with a splash, very near the hole in the ocean floor where it had been stuck for fifty years.

But the tide caught it up. It wasn't destined to be hidden anymore.

It was headed, once again, for the shore.

Hy's FB Status: The skin can stretch to ten times its size, so it's no wonder we get wrinkles. But if you use one of those anti-wrinkle creams, a substance in it may come from a cadaver.
Likes: 1
Comments: Eeeew.

Vera creamed her face, looking with displeasure into the mirror. All the lines. All the wrinkles, set by the sour expression she'd maintained ever since she was six years old and a boy had smacked her on the head in the school playground. She went dashing after him, arms raised, and, just as she was catching up with him and beginning to scream, red-faced and mouth stretched wide, the button on her skirt popped and it fell to the ground. Vera's anger melted into a pool of shame, gathered, with the skirt, around her ankles. She grabbed it, hung onto it tight around her waist with one hand; the other she clutched over one ear, to muffle the sounds of laughter following her as she dashed from the playground and into the school.

It was then that Vera had decided that life was not fair. The boy had misbehaved and she was the one who was punished. The boy had actually smacked her on the head because he liked her, but she would never see it that way. And she would never forgive the rest of the children for laughing at her.

Vera's expression had turned sour somewhere between her skirt dropping and the echoing laughter. By the time she left school that day, the expression was set, as if the wind had changed and made it stay that way.

She'd grown into it, so that now what had not been suitable on a six-year-old child was perfectly suited to a bitter sixty-year-old woman. She saved her best approximations of a smile for the men she wooed, but actually counted on her other qualities to attract them.

Chief among them, she was able to appear caring. Competent and caring. She didn't have to be good-looking. The men in the age group Vera favoured weren't interested in sex anymore, although some thought they might be. That was soon taken care of. No, what they wanted was someone to play nurse. For real.

Wipe their bums and noses, Vera thought, not for the first time, as she applied a thin line of lipstick to her pale, receding lips.

They didn't know they were doing it for a price, but of course they were.

A high price.

"Do you mind talking about your family?"

Finn and Hy were sitting over a glass of wine as dusk fell on another rainy day at The Shores. The ride-ons were idle, and Hy was thinking how peaceful it was. And how nice it was to have an amiable companion, a man, in the house.

Especially one as neat and tidy as Finn. But he'd made no overtures. Time enough, she smiled, thinking of the phrase that came quickly and often to Gus's lips.

The smile wasn't an answer to Finn's question. She hadn't really heard what he'd said.

"Mind?" She was buying time. Time for whatever it was he'd asked to come to her.

"I guess you do."

"Mind?" It wasn't coming to her.

"Talking about your family."

Oh.

"Not really. I, well – it's complicated." With a bit of wine in her, Hy wasn't in the mood to talk about the past.

"I don't mean to be nosy."

"Not much to be nosy about. There is no family. Hasn't been for as long as I can remember. All dead, including my bitter old grandmother, the only one I ever knew. Never knew my father, my mother."

"Well, of course, I know about your mother. I'm sorry." His two thick black eyebrows, like a pair of caterpillars knitted in a frown. Ian would have been grateful to have that much hair on his head.

"Nothing to be sorry about. I have no feelings for any of them, especially not the bitter old granny." She gave a weak smile. She sipped the last of her wine and stood up.

"I'm going to bed." She walked over to a library desk and pulled out a magazine. She opened it, and handed it to him.

"This'll tell you everything."

She left him there, reading everything she thought he didn't know. But he did know, quite a bit. That's why he was here. He hadn't been asking, he'd been probing.

He had read into her reaction a warning not to mention her family again.

Better back off for a bit. What he knew would keep. He didn't want to shock her.

Finn Finnegan.

Finding out this guy's secret was not turning out to be easy. Ian scrolled through social media. He checked births and deaths over fifty years, until, finally, he found what he was looking for.

The accident. The mother. The child.

He hoped it hadn't gone too far. Hy would be appalled.

It was his duty to bring it up, even if that scumbag hadn't. How could he keep something like this from her? Why?

He was a pervert. He must be.

But really the only question now was who and how to confront.

Both, he decided. Together. Let Finn squirm in the web of his lie. Let Hy be embarrassed. She deserved it.

Hy was in for a surprise, but quite a different one, the next time she went to Macks'. Dot handed her a USB drive and a neat folder of printed pages, mixed with photographs, graphics and original documents.

"Dot," Hy beamed. "You're a treasure."

"It's Ma that did it," she said, nodding at Gus, who held up her hands to deny it.

"Every word of it, Ma. I captured her on this little thing." She held up her iPhone. "Word for word. Didn't change a thing."

"It's a miracle." Hy hugged the manuscript.

"Reckon you're right about that," said Gus. "Got almost the entire top of my crazy quilt pieced at the same time. That's a miracle, too."

Dottie was on the floor, grabbing up scraps of material and stuffing them in her mouth. No one stopped her. You could eat off Gus's floor.

Gus looked down, eyes and mouth both smiling.

"She helped me. Chose the pieces. Whatever she'd pick, I'd fit it in, so I didn't have to think at all. Came out beautiful." She held up squares one by one, and Dottie smiled, squealed and clapped her hands.

Her squeals almost masked the sound of the screen door squeaking open. Finn popped his head around the corner.

"You," said Dot.

He straightened and smiled, delighted. "You," he said.

"You?" Hy.

"You. You. You." Dottie, smacked her hands on the floor, pleased that the grown-ups were speaking her language.

Gus said nothing. She thought they were all as crazy as her quilt.

"Dot. Finn." Hy looked from one to the other, with a puzzled expression. "You know each other?"

Dot smiled. "Met on the ferry."

Hy wasn't sure she liked the way they were looking at each other. Eating each other up. Finn hadn't looked at her that way. He'd made no overtures of any kind. They'd been just like brother and sister. They'd held hands, but it was purely companionable. She'd been considering that maybe he was gay.

Hy wasn't sure exactly how it happened, but, after a brief conversation, Finn and Dot were off to the shore, Gus was babysitting Dottie, and she was headed home, manuscript in the basket of her bike.

Was Finn using her as a cheap hotel?

It was on the way home, some of Gus's familiar phrases ringing in her head, that Hy had an idea for the title and for publication. Time Enough. There wasn't time enough. Hy hoped Gus would last forever, but of course she wouldn't. And the village wouldn't last forever, not now that there were more tourists than villagers. It would be a slow death.

Time was. Another of the local expressions, and the more she thought about it, the more she liked it. *Time Was.* Yes. *Time Was.*

She'd had a look through the folder Dot had given her and Gus's stories, her way of speaking, her old-fashioned phrases and point of view shone through it. She knew what she was going to do with it. This didn't have to be a vanity publication. It could stand on its own with a real publisher. The publisher of her mother's book. If she had to, she'd apply a little pressure.

She didn't have to.

When she got home, she copied a sample and pitched the manuscript to the publisher. After giving them a couple of hours, she made a direct phone call.

Brad Perkins took the call. She knew then that she was in. Brad was the co-publisher at Real Words Press. He was also a bit sweet on Hy. And he loved what he'd seen of *Time Was.*

"I'll front it. I'll back it." She rambled before he could even say a word. "I'll pay the losses if there are any. But I don't think there will be. I think you'll have a steady little income earner."

Hy smiled a sly smile when she got off the phone. Done. She screwed up her forehead. Nearly done.

Brad had jumped on it, especially given Hy's agreement to take an editing role. Toss her mother's name in the mix and one book could feed off the acclaim of the other.

Now Hy had to pass the idea by Gus and Dot. Tell them that the original plan for a vanity publication had been scrapped, and now *Time Was* would be produced by a real publisher, who saw in it similarities to *A Life on the Land,* but replicating the popular bestseller in its own Gus-like way.

Hy returned to Gus with the news.

Gus blushed red. She was too self-effacing to believe that it had anything to do with her.

"Have to thank Dot," she said. "She did it all."

Finn's arm was around Dot's shoulder when they returned from their stroll on the beach. Dottie quickly clamped onto his long skinny black leg.

Bonding, thought Hy.

"Not me, Ma. You."

"Maybe it was your mother, Gus, looking over your shoulder." Hy was trying not to look at Finn and Dot.

Gus smiled softly.

"Happen it was."

Chapter Twenty

Hy and Finn were at the table, just about to sit down for supper, when Ian burst through the door.

"Your brother." He pointed at Finn.

"My what?" Hy stared at both men blankly.

"Your brother. He's your brother."

"Ian, that's biologically impossible. Don't be ridiculous."

"He's not being ridiculous." Finn had stayed standing. So did Hy and Ian. Mute. All three without a word.

And then they all spoke at the same time.

"I…" Hy.

"I…" Ian.

"I…" Finn.

And they all sat down. At the same time.

"Finn, is this true?" Hy felt foolish. Embarrassed. She'd had thoughts – about her brother? Ian jumped in before Finn could answer.

"Yes. Yes, it's true."

A big grin spread across Ian's face. He knew it was true. His research had told him, but it was satisfying to see Finn acknowledge it. It was also satisfying to see Hy with the air blown out of her, her would-be lover turned into a brother.

"Half-brother," Finn added.

Ian gave Finn a hard look, his eyes darting at Hy. "You haven't...?" He was hoping Finn was just a would-be lover, not a *fait accompli*.

"Of course not." Finn did not like Ian's suggestion.

Hy flushed to think of how close she had hugged Finn before bed some nights. She had felt the resistance in his body, the stiffening. No wonder.

"That would mean my father...your father..."

"Yup. My father, then your father."

"But you were never in touch before. Why not? And why the secrecy now?"

Finn pulled out his wallet. From the wallet he slipped out a piece of paper, folded many times. He unfolded it carefully, but it came apart at the well-worn seams.

It was a magazine article. An interview with Hy in her twenties, on the release of the coffee table version of her mother's seminal back-to-the-woods book. It was an American magazine interested in her connection through her deserter father. The father who'd died when out trapping in northern Canada. Who'd left her mother and the infant Hy to rough it in the woods. Who'd been responsible for her grandfather's death when the bush plane he flew in to rescue them had crashed. Killed him. Killed her mother.

"I hate my father," Finn read from the article. "He killed my mother and he nearly killed me. I never went looking for any relatives and they never came looking. I have no family and that's fine with me."

He passed the piece of paper over to her. It was the same article she'd given him. She hadn't looked at it in years. Her first thought was that in the photograph taken to accompany the article she looked impossibly young. Her second thought was that she looked strikingly like Finn. Not the hair. His, a shock of black, sticking out straight from his skull. Hers those red curls that so enchanted Ian.

No, not the hair. It was something in the jaw, the mouth, the eyes.

She passed it back to him.

"It hardly suggests you would welcome me, your long-lost brother."

"Well, no…"

"I tried to open it up last night, but you shut it down."

"True."

"My mother never told me who my father was," he said. "I had no one but her. That's the way she wanted it. My grandparents were dead, and she had been an only child. You're my closest living relative. She told me, finally, when she was dying of cancer. She felt guilty, I guess. She felt I should have someone. And you were innocent. Innocent of your father's crimes."

"Crimes?"

"He ran off with your mother. He had two women pregnant at the same time. We're only a few months apart."

"I said I hated him, and that's before I knew that." Hy got up and grabbed a bottle of organic Merlot from the hutch beside the table. She pulled out three glasses and poured.

"So that's why you were reluctant to say who you were in our Facebook messages. But how does coming here make it any better?"

"Human contact. Human contact, always better than the machine." He jabbed a finger at Hy's laptop, propped open on the table. Hy's message postings were open, including the one she had sent to Finn before he came to the village.

"I'm so excited you're coming. Can't wait until you get here."

Oh brother, thought Ian. He stood up.

"Guess you two have a lot to talk about. I'll be going."

Finn turned to Hy as the screen door squeaked and slammed behind Ian.

"Boyfriend?" Finn jutted his chin in the direction of the door.

"No…yes…sort of."

"Maybe that's the problem."

The sound of a gentle summer rain closed the evening around them.

They sat in silence. Brother and sister. It was a lot for Hy to absorb. But like the summer rain, it was comforting.

She was no longer alone in the world.

The next morning found Hy at Ian's, after Finn took off with Dot to walk the shore. There was another fine mist, but the village men were out on their mowers despite it. It had rained, mostly overnight, ever since Marlene tried to issue her no-mow edict. The village men were determined not to appear as if they were co-operating. The grass was wet and hardly needed mowing, but got it anyway.

Marlene had picked herself up and dusted herself off after the unsuccessful meeting at the hall. And she'd learned a few things.

She had devised a new scheme and another flyer. In this one, she spelled The Shores correctly.

"No mention of a public meeting." Hy grazed the paper she'd brought in from Ian's mailbox.

"So she can't err there."

"Beware." Hy held up a finger and waited.

"Err. There. Beware." Jasmine loved rhymes.

Ian groaned. "Now she'll be all over that for weeks." He stood up and stretched, his back sore from hunching over the computer. "So what's it about?"

"It's a survey. Looks like Marlene's cutting her losses. It says: 'Tick the box that best describes how long you'd be willing to leave your grass uncut. One week, six days…'" It goes all the way down to one day."

"But nowhere that says 'not at all'?"

Hy shook her head.

"That's where she's made her mistake." Ian smiled a sly smile. "Plenty of people would answer her survey if they had that option."

Ian was right. No one answered the survey. Marlene considered taking the spark plugs out of the local mowing machines, except she wouldn't know how to do it. Instead, she hatched another plan.

A few phone calls to the Tourism Department and John Deere soon had her grinning as she created her next flyer.

She popped it in boxes. Villagers patiently pulled it out. Those who crumpled it up and threw it away before reading it soon dove back into their recycling bags, straightened it, and filled it out.

Finn and Dot strolled on the shore, and Dot fell in love all over again with her birthplace, through Finn's eyes. Finn was from Boston and knew as much about the shore as she did, about the water and its ways, the gulls and theirs, and the shellfish that were tossed up on the shore and abandoned by the tide.

They were easy in each other's company, as if they had known each other for years. They were both also in a temporary, transitional time in their lives and open to where it would lead them.

At the moment, it was leading them away from the sea rock to the far cape, away from the skull that had surfaced again. It had been hiding for some time in a pile of cape rock. No one had discovered it yet. But it had been in the water for fifty years. It could bide its time on the beach a little longer.

And then the skull could, perhaps, rest in peace.

But it wasn't going to be found today.

The water had tickled it up from the rocks and deposited it on a clump of sand.

Quite visible now.

But not to Finn and Dot, who only had eyes for each other.

www.theshores200.com
Occasionally a pre-Columbian artifact will be found on the shore. Or a shard of a Ming dynasty treasure. They're the last remains of a millionaire art collector who lived in a fabulous A-frame on a very precarious overhang of the cape. It came crashing down in a savage storm several years ago, a storm that threw hundreds of lobster traps up on the shore and ended the season early.

Hy left Ian's, happy that the distance between them was easing now that Finn was no longer a reason for tensions. She smiled at how foolish she'd been to fall for her brother. Well, half-brother. Still. She was getting used to the idea of having family, after having been alone in the world for so long. She was connected to Finn now. And through Finn to Dot. And, through Dot, linked even more closely to Gus.

Family. It felt good.

Her pleasant thoughts were interrupted by the mewling coming from the roof of the Sullivan house. It was pitiful.

Whacky?

Hy jumped on her bike and pumped so hard she lost her footing on the pedals. She bumped over the clamshell driveway, and threw the bike down before she had fully dismounted, scraping and bruising her leg.

There was Whacky on the highest peak, apparently terrified to come down. Hy had heard that cats can always get down from the places they climb up, but she wasn't so sure about that.

The pitiful creature was staring right at her, desperate appeal in its eyes.

She'd better do something.

She went around to the back door. When she disappeared from sight, Whacky's crying became even more pitiful, signaling to Hy that it really was in distress.

She knocked on the door. No response. Rang the Victorian doorbell. Nothing. Then looked at the driveway. No vehicle. Of course, why hadn't she noticed?

She would need a ladder.

The shed. There it was, hooked along the side of the building. Extension ladder. Would it be long enough?

It would have to be.

She hauled it off its hooks and half-carried, half-dragged it around the house.

Whacky was alert, waiting for her to return, big eyes glued to her every movement.

She set up the ladder. It wasn't going to be long enough. Behind her, there was a wooden picnic table. She shoved it forward, and wrestled the ladder into position on top of it. Better. She looked up the length of it, still coming several feet shy of the cat. Terrifying height. She tested the ladder's stability, a hand on the bottom rung. It shook. Vibrated.

Was she crazy?

She began to mount the rungs, taking it slowly, testing each new step before she put her full weight on it. The cat's mewling had turned to whimpering. She inched up, rung by rung.

And then she stopped.

She stopped because of what she saw through the second floor window. The sight made her dizzy.

A creature? A man? What?

And another, or something like it, just barely visible through the window of the next room.

Vera Gloom's art? Giant balsawood insects?

Hy was frozen in place, her eyes trying to make sense of what she was seeing, something so bizarre she couldn't comprehend it.

She closed her eyes.

Opened them again.

He – it – appeared to be waving at her.

She shook her head. That made the ladder tremble. She was trembling, too. Trembling at what she was seeing. *Human?*

The cat began a new racket of mewling and meowing. Hy barely noticed it, she was so mesmerized by what she was seeing through the window.

Human?

A gust of wind came up.

Alive?

The ladder shifted.

"Are you nuts?"

The voice cut through the mist of confusion.

Hy looked down. Almost lost her balance. The ladder pulled

away from the house, and then slammed back, hard.

Jamieson.

Jamieson had crawled up onto the picnic table and was gripping the ladder.

She had seen Hy from the road. She'd braked, backed up without checking her rearview mirror and pulled into the driveway, spitting clamshells as she sped over the grass to the picnic table, leaving ruts in the lawn.

"Get down!"

"Easy for you to say. I've got your cat up here."

"That's not my cat, that's – "

At the sound of Jamieson's voice, the tiny creature peeked from behind the dormer where she was hiding.

"Get her, and get down."

Right, thought Hy. Now we know where her priorities are.

Whacky was perhaps just close enough now to grab. Hy stretched forward. The cat pulled back.

She was now well out of reach. Hy stretched out both arms towards the cat, but it didn't budge. She called "kitty, kitty, kitty," but still it didn't move. Then she remembered she had shells in her pocket. They would rattle and they would smell of salt. She pulled them out and shook them in her hand.

The wind came up. Wafted the salt scent at the cat.

Whacky caught the scent and inched forward.

Still out of reach.

"I can't. I can't reach her," Hy yelled down at Jamieson. The ladder shifted. Jamieson tightened her grip on it.

"Climb up on the roof then."

"Now it's you who's nuts."

Whacky meowed plaintively. Looked directly with her big cat eyes into Jamieson's.

If Jamieson could ever be said to melt, she did then.

And then she did the most unusual thing.

She began to purr. Human volume. But a cat's purr. The little creature's ears twitched.

It responded to Jamieson, purr for purr, stealing slowly forward toward Hy.

When Whacky was close enough, Hy grabbed her, and the cat dug her claws right into her shoulder. Hy tried to ignore the pain shooting through her, and felt with one foot to the rung below. And then the next. And the next, glad of Jamieson's sure hands on the ladder.

Jamieson's knuckles were white, her teeth clenched as she mentally helped propel Hy and Whacky down to safety. As soon as Hy's feet hit the picnic table, Jamieson let go of the ladder and it came shuddering down, clattering to the ground, scraping the shingles as it collapsed on the lawn.

Jamieson grabbed Whacky from Hy's shoulder, her claws still anchored there, and hugged her close, murmuring and purring into her tiny ear.

"Glad you showed up." Hy was inspecting the pool of blood seeping through her t-shirt.

"You never should have gone up there."

"It was to save your cat."

Jamieson was still holding the creature close. It was licking her face. Grooming her.

"It's not my cat. It's…"

"Never mind that. I just saw the craziest thing inside that house. You've got to get a search warrant."

Whacky had clawed its way down Jamieson's body, leaving a trail of long white hair down the front of her black uniform. It was circling her feet and weaving through her legs, leaving fur all around the bottom of her trousers.

"And just why should I get a search warrant?"

A car pulled into the driveway. Vera. She got out of the vehicle and marched straight at Hy and Jamieson. She pointed to the ruts in the lawn.

"What's the reason for this?"

She looked over at the ladder. She pointed at it.

"And that?"

Hy didn't say a word.

Nor did Jamieson. She scooped up Whacky as if she needed to protect her from Vera.

She might, thought Hy.

"Animal rescue," Hy choked out. Jamieson nodded, mute.

"Well, see that you clean it up. If it's not done satisfactorily, or causes me any expense, you will be hearing from my lawyers."

She turned, marched back to the car, yanked out some grocery bags, and went into the house.

"Bodies," Hy's voice was a whisper in Jamieson's ear, just rising above the cat's purr.

"That's what I saw in there. Bodies."

Chapter Twenty-One

The flyers came flying back to Marlene. Every villager had filled one in. There were photocopies, too, filled out on behalf of children, infants and one boy still in the womb. His parents figured since he had a name already – Brian – he should be eligible.

The villagers were clamouring for a chance to win a John Deere riding mower. The chariot of the lawn-mowing gods. The Rolls of green arables. The Mercedes of mulch.

Billy Pride filled out an entry, with difficulty. Writing had never been his strong suit. But what he lacked in calligraphic ability, he made up for in heart. His tongue stuck out to help him form the letters as he answered the question: "Why do you want to win the EZTrak John Deere mower?"

He wrote that he wanted it so he could marry tiny Madeline Toombs, Moira's sister. His own machine was breaking down, and it was the source of his spring, summer and fall income, maintaining the grounds of the summer cottages. He used his mower as a car, too. Without it, he'd be stuck home, jobless, and penniless, with his constantly complaining mother.

Marlene was reconciled to having only one day mow-free. She realized the cut lawns would be tidier, prettier for the tourists.

You could have too much authenticity.

It was on the day of her triumph, the lawn-cutting agreement with the village, that it began to rain.

Every day.

All summer.

Some tried, but no one was able to keep a lawn mowed anywhere in The Shores.

Until the sun shone, finally, on celebration day, straining the promise of a day without mowers.

Hy kept harassing Jamieson about the bodies she claimed she'd seen in the Sullivan house. Jamieson thought the whole thing was ridiculous and continued to resist her.

"You have an overactive imagination."

"Oh, sure. So I was imagining things when I tripped over Lance Lord on the beach?"

"No. Although it was a bit far-fetched."

"Far-fetched, maybe, but true."

"I'll grant you that."

"And Fitz, knocking me into the creek."

Jamieson said nothing.

"And Miss pudgy paws, flattened under a rock?"

Jamieson knew that if there were a body to be found, Hy would be the one to find it. She had stumbled over or onto a number of murder victims in The Shores in the past few years.

But what Hy had described was surely not possible. Was surely a product of her vivid imagination. Or a product of Vera Gloom's artistry. It was all over the village that she was an artist. Could this not be artistry? These bodies?

"They were so real, and unreal, at the same time." Hy's expression lit up. "I know. Taxidermy. It might be taxidermy. She's had them stuffed."

"That would be illegal."

"Would it?"

"I believe so. If not, it should be."

"A lot of things should be, but aren't."

"That I can find out."

"And then you can get a search warrant and go in and see."

Jamieson bristled at Hy telling her what to do, but she was curious to see what Hy had seen. She just couldn't figure out any way to justify a search warrant.

"But grounds. I need grounds." Why was she even arguing this? There was precedent. Here at The Shores, Jamieson had loosened up on what exactly was correct law enforcement and what was not. She'd bent the rules before, and no doubt would again. Hy had helped in every single investigation, but this wasn't an investigation, was it?

"What bodies could they be? No one here is missing."

"Bodies from away, of course," Hy said, with a grin. "Could Vera Gloom be a murderess who's imported her victims?"

Hy wouldn't let up. She swore she'd seen bodies – two of them. Jamieson couldn't say she was mistaken. Jamieson hadn't seen anything.

"They were real. Not art, I swear. There was a quality about them that said really dead."

"What quality is that – really dead – and how do you sense it through a window? Have to do better than that, McAllister."

"You know what I mean. You've seen really dead from a distance. You can just tell."

Hy was right, but Jamieson wasn't going to admit it and weaken her very reasonable point of view. Hy had been overexcited. She was seeing things. Or reading into the things she'd seen.

Real, thought Hy. But in an unusual, inhuman way. Were there just two? How many more might there be in that big house?

Chapter Twenty-Two

The Teepee B&B

Heritage Home of The Shores' Oldest Family
A Fine Blend of the Three Cultures that made Red Island
Come experience it for yourself during this heritage year –

"200 Years and Counting"

"I told her it was wigwam, not teepee. Guess she likes the rhyme. And this – a fine blend of three cultures?"

Hy had pulled up Moira's website on Ian's Mac. "She makes it sound like coffee."

Ian smirked.

"You have, as they say, created a monster."

Hy groaned. "I know. But at least she's embraced her origins."

The new website had not brought Moira any new business, so she was still slaving away cleaning the beachside rental cottages and the Sullivan house.

It was a house a family could rattle around in, and yet there were only two people there, thought Moira. One old lady who couldn't make much of a mess. And the other, a man half-dead.

Moira didn't know about the ex-husbands upstairs, but she was about to find out. Moira was a snoop, and could hardly keep to a few rooms on the bottom floor as she'd been instructed. She was determined to get a look at the whole place, including the upstairs, as soon as she got the chance.

But Vera was always in the house and in and out of the rooms Moira was cleaning.

Finally, she got lucky. The landscaping company that was taking care of "the grounds," as Vera liked to refer to them, arrived with some shrubs and trees, and Vera went out to supervise.

Moira hurried up with her work, darting looks out the window, to see Vera now clothed in outdoor gardening regalia, complete with a pair of Lee Valley boots.

She'd be a while.

Moira dashed up the stairs, and threw open the first door.

She could see only the back of his head.

Pale. Very pale.

He appeared quite absorbed in his book. Moira tiptoed a little closer.

"What are you doing here?" Moira jumped back.

But the voice had come from behind her, and it was a woman's. Vera.

"You are not meant to be upstairs." Her voice was flat, but it contained a tone of warning, of menace.

Vera grabbed Moira by the elbow and marched her down the stairs and into the kitchen. She pushed her down on a chair, but kept standing herself, towering above Moira.

"What did you see?"

Moira wondered what she was meant to have seen or not seen.

"Nothing. I saw nothing."

"Come. You saw something."

"I did?" At the moment, Moira was staring up at Vera's jiggling jowls, hoping she'd never be that old and ugly. Vera leaned over and Moira could smell her stale breath, the decay under her dentures.

"I saw the back of the head of an elderly gentleman."

"That's all?" Vera loomed over her.

"I thought he looked sickly pale."

Vera straightened.

"Did he speak to you?"

Moira shook her head.

"Did you speak to him?"

Moira shook her head again. There hadn't been time, even if she wanted to.

"Let's discuss the terms of your continuing employment."

Moira felt her throat closing. She was unable to speak.

"You will never go upstairs again."

Moira nodded her head several times.

"You will never utter a word to anyone about this."

Moira didn't shake her head or speak. She just stared wide-eyed at Vera.

Vera grabbed hold of Moira's arm and twisted the skin. Moira shook her head vigorously. She felt that if she tried to speak, she would choke.

"Not a word. Or what happened to them may happen to you."

What had happened to them? Who were "they"?

"Happens to us all. We get old." Vera let go of Moira's arm.

Old? That one had looked more than old. His skin. It was... She couldn't describe it.

Vera smiled her version of a smile, laced with a threat.

"The boys don't like to be disturbed. It upsets them. It upsets me. And you wouldn't want that."

Moira was quite sure she didn't want that.

"I don't want people talking about the boys. Make sure you don't."

The boys, wondered Moira. Who were they? Had she seen one of them?

She was quite sure she didn't want to see him again. Not after this. She found it creepy, an antidote to her natural snoopiness. She would stay well away from upstairs. She wished she could stay away from the house altogether, but she needed money coming in.

Moira couldn't leave fast enough.

She kept darting glances behind her as if she were being pursued. She wasn't, but she was being watched.

Vera stood at the large windows of the front room, eyes burning into Moira's back. Once, looking back, Moira caught her eyes, and flinched as if they really were burning. She picked up her pace until she reached the road. Out of Vera's sight, she shot one more look back.

Hy had just come out of the police house, and caught the curious expression on Moira's face. She watched as Moira propelled down Shipwreck Hill, stumbling in her haste and nearly falling several times.

Hy stepped out into the road, and Moira screamed, tripped, and fell forward.

Hy grabbed her.

"Steady. What's up?"

Moira regained her balance and stared at Hy. Said nothing. Just stared. Mute. Fear, yes definitely fear, in her eyes.

"What's going on, Moira?" Had she seen something in the

house? Something that would explain what Hy had seen?

Moira remained mute. She tried to push Hy back, but Hy restrained her.

"Did you see something in there?"

Moira shook her head.

"No?"

Moira shook her head again.

"Are you sure?"

Moira nodded her head.

Hy grabbed her by the shoulders. "Speak to me, Moira."

Moira gulped. Nothing came out.

"Did you see bodies in there?"

Pause. Nothing.

"Did you see art?"

A shake of the head.

"No giant insects?"

Moira's eyes opened wide and she shook her head.

"Well, something's scared you, and I mean to find out what it is."

Finally, Moira choked out a word.

"Nothing."

"Nothing?"

"Nothing."

Hy let go her grip on Moira.

Nothing, my foot, she thought as she watched Moira stumble down the hill.

Chapter Twenty-Three

Everyone in the village was soon talking about Vera's "boys," not knowing really what they were talking about. Moira couldn't keep the secret. Who could? She'd told Frank. Frank had told the UPS guy in Winterside, whose wife was April Dewey's cousin. The cousin told April who told her partner, Murdo. He told Jamieson, his one contribution to police work that summer. Jamieson discussed it with Ian, who told Hy, who wondered why Moira hadn't just told her directly in the first place.

"The boys," the villagers concluded, were Vera Gloom's ex-husbands. Strange they'd all be living there together. And strange that they were never seen. Old and infirm probably. More dead than alive.

With the village buzzing with "the boys," Hy hoped Jamieson might now be forced to make inquiries. Buzzing with rumours, thought Jamieson. Gossip. This was not a police investigation, unless, as Hy was now maintaining, the woman had had her former husbands stuffed.

Hy's FB Status: In the 1800s British sportsmen used to hunt and shoot pygmies in the Congo. Then they'd have them stuffed. A pawn shop in New York recently had one for sale.

Likes: 0

Comments: Double eeeeeew.

Cat.

He'd know.

Hy wasn't sure why, but she had a feeling about it. She headed for Big Bay.

She almost turned back on the way there. The incessant rain had started out as a spit, not enough to stop her from pedaling in comfort.

By the time she got to Big Bay, it was a downpour. She was drenched. The rain had soaked into her clothes, they were clinging to her skin and water was running off her clothing in rivulets and dripping off her face.

Big Bay was closed up. The boats were in for the day and construction workers on the new stores had gone home.

Cat lived above the store and she was certain he'd be home. She banged on the door – a few times, leaning up against it to get some shelter from the slim overhang of roof.

It felt like the door flew open, and she tumbled in. Cat reached out to steady her and then helped her across the stoop.

"Slippery as a salmon's back. Here…" He unhooked a throw from beside the door and wrapped it around her.

"I keep it here for just this reason." He beckoned her to the back stairs. "Coffee or tea?"

She nodded, shivered and followed him up the stairs.

They were settled down with their coffees when Hy told him why she'd come.

"Do you know anything about taxidermy?"

"Well, yes. I was a taxidermist, time was."

"Do you know any taxidermists who would stuff a human?"

His eyes opened wide.

"Not just at the moment. Odd question."

"I have reasons. Don't really want to talk about them now."

Cat raised his eyebrows.

"Anyone I know?"

Hy smiled, taking his meaning.

"No. I don't want anyone stuffed. I just want to know if it happens."

"It does."

"Have you?"

"No, no, not me. I've been asked. And I've known people who've done it."

"Legally?"

"Yes and no. Meaning it's not legal, but if you want to fight it out in court you can. There's a company advertises on the Internet to preserve your loved ones. 'Where legal,' it says. Where that is, I don't know. Funny thing is, the law is clear on stuffing animals, but not people. You can't sell stuffed wildlife in Canada under the Wildlife Protection Act."

"What about humans?"

"For humans it's not so clear. The protection bodies have is only that they have the right to rest in peace. Otherwise, once the person leaves it, presuming that's what they do, they lose ownership – and their next of kin, usually the spouse, has control."

"What kind of control?"

"Over disposal of the body, burial, preparation, possession, autopsy, damages for mutilation of the body. All within accepted social norms."

"Taxidermy not being one of them."

"I would say not."

"How do you know all this?"

"Well, when I was asked to do it, I looked it up. I wanted to know what ground I stood on."

"And that was not stuffing humans."

"No. Nor animals either. I just use the skin. Fish skin only." He smiled. "And the odd reptile."

Hy's FB Status: Roy Rogers had his faithful mount...mounted. When he died, he's rumoured to have said he'd like to be skinned out and mounted on Trigger.

Likes: 15

Comments: You're getting deep.

Six feet deep! LOL.

Hy's visit with Cat had convinced her that people did stuff their loved ones, but she wanted proof, real proof, before she went badgering Jamieson anymore to inspect Vera's house.

A phone call to the taxidermy place Cat had mentioned would do it. She'd have to get her best friend Annabelle in on it. Annabelle would never forgive her if she didn't.

The rain had tapered off. Still wet, Hy cycled over to Annabelle's.

She pushed her way in as soon as Annabelle opened the door.

"Is Ben in?"

"No, do you need him for something?"

"Not at all. Will he be out for a while?"

"I expect so. He's mucking about with the *Annaben*. Engine trouble." The *Annaben*, also known as the *Loveboat*, was the boat Ben and Annabelle used to fish lobster.

"I was just going to have a glass of wine. Chase this glum day away. Join me?"

"Sure. But only one. We need to be clearheaded for what I have in mind."

"And just what do you have in mind?"

Hy explained her plan, and Annabelle, grinning a big grin, fell in with it, only insisting that she be the one to make the phone call.

The two women sat down to plot tactics – what they should say, what they should ask. They agreed they'd say it was to stuff the husband. They finished a glass of wine. Started another.

"So, go on. Phone." Hy was thinking they should not have had that wine for courage. Annabelle had an attack of the giggles.

"I'll do it then." Hy grabbed the phone.

"No. It's okay. I want to do it."

Annabelle dialed the number on the piece of paper in front of her. They waited while it rang. Three times.

"I hope it's not voicemail."

Another two rings.

"Real People Taxidermy."

Not voicemail.

Annabelle cleared her throat.

"Yes, I was wondering…yes…how did you…oh, yes, of course." Annabelle gave Hy the thumbs up.

"Well it wasn't myself…oh really…two for one? Oh well…could I give that…really?" Annabelle's eyes opened wide. "Really? And how much would that be?" Eyes wider. Big grin.

"I'll get back to you…soon as I speak to…yes…that's correct."

She slammed down the phone and burst out laughing.

Hy grinned. "She did all the talking."

Annabelle stifled her laughter.

"She knew right away that I was phoning for a husband. 'Happens all the time,' she said."

"And the two for one?"

"Both of us – me and Ben. And…" She drew out the word and paused dramatically, "they could stuff my boobs, as if they need it…"

"As if…"

"And…" Annabelle clapped a hand over her mouth to stifle a laugh. "Ben could be stuffed with an erection."

"With what?" Ben had just come in the back door. Hy hadn't seen him in time to warn Annabelle, who seemed not the least fazed.

"An erection, dear. You could get it stuffed, just like Tutankhamen."

"You think it needs stuffing?"

"Certainly not."

Ben sat down for a glass of wine and the two women explained what they'd been up to. He shook his head when they finished their story.

"Time was, this was just a quiet little fishing village. If I had my druthers it still would be."

"Be careful what you wish for, Ben," Hy warned, as she got up to leave. She slipped into her soaking rain jacket. "That Marlene woman's trying to turn it into just that."

Time was, she thought as she left. She'd chosen a good name for the book.

Chapter Twenty-Four

"I wonder if you could throw together a little something for Cyril."

Moira had been about to refuse. She was a cleaner, not a cook. But then Vera spoke the magic words.

"Lime Jello."

Vera opened a cupboard door, and stacked inside it were dozens of boxes of lime Jello.

"He loves lime Jello."

So did Moira.

She hardly ever ate it as a child, not because it was pricey or unhealthy. It was loaded with sugar, but no one worried about sugar then.

No, Moira's mother was mean, and very mean about anything that gave her husband and children pleasure. Disappointed in life, she wanted to be sure that they were disappointed, too.

Lime Jello.

Moira gazed up at the boxes of her favourite childhood treat. She lifted an arm and touched them delicately with her fingertips.

Vera nearly slammed Moira's fingers in the cupboard door when she closed it.

"Yes, well, I'd like you to make it for him. Keep a constant supply going. I can't keep up with it."

It was as if she'd given Moira a gift. She made the first batch immediately, using a clear glass bowl, the better to see the beautiful colour of the jelly. The powder was white with a green tinge, bursting into emerald when she poured the boiling water onto it, and stirred it around.

There was hardly any room in the fridge for the Jello. It was bursting with bottled water. Vera was constantly "hydrating." Moira was always having to pick up the plastic bottles around the house and recycle them. She cleared a space for the bowl of Jello and popped it in.

She came to check on it several times while she was cleaning. As it began to gel, it had a sloppy texture. After an hour or so, it had fully hardened, and she spooned some into a bowl, smiling as it jiggled into place.

And then she ate it. Took another bowlful. Wolfed that down. And another. And another. Until, finally, she was spooning it straight out of the big bowl into her mouth.

She ate it all.

When she saw what she had done, she was horrified. She looked around her as if someone might have been watching. But no, Vera was napping. She was a sound sleeper, Moira knew, and exact. Moira checked the clock. Still another hour. Time to make another batch of Jello. This one would never be missed.

Neither were the rest of them in the next days and weeks. Moira got in the habit of making up two boxes at a time, "hers" in a nice crystal bowl she'd found. The cut glass created prisms of green. The colour appealed to Moira as much as the taste and the amusing jiggle.

The jiggle. Perhaps that's what her mother had disliked. Food that jiggled. Food that was fun. Her mother's food was never fun. Tough meat. Grey gravy. Lumpy mashed potatoes. Moira's talent for baking light-as-air blueberry muffins had remained hidden until her mother passed away. In an uncharacteristic gesture of rebellion, Moira made and served the muffins at her mother's wake, a grim expression of satisfaction on her face.

There was a smile on her face now, as she held up the cut crystal bowl, enchanted by the green glimmerings created by the light cutting through the glass. Then she lowered it, and began to eat. Straight out of the bowl, another pleasure her mother had denied her. She never intended to eat it all, every time. She'd have just a bit. Stop. Just a bit more. Pause. A tiny bit more. In no time, it was all gone.

On this day, she'd miscalculated. Not the amount of Jello in the bowl. The amount of time Vera would be having her nap. As Moira was holding the bowl up to her face and licking the last bits of gel sticking to the glass, Vera walked in.

Moira looked up. Shock. Fear. Embarrassment.

Vera looked…well, Vera looked shocked, too. For a moment. Then her eyes performed a quick calculation. The result was apparently satisfactory, because she smiled.

"You like lime Jello, too."

Moira brought the bowl down from her face. She stared into it and nodded, not wanting to meet Vera's eyes. She wasn't scared of Vera anymore. She'd become more relaxed. Nothing awful had happened, had it? She tried not to think of "the boys" upstairs. Let the village think they were elderly ex-husbands. She thought they were…well, she preferred not to think about what they were.

"You must have as much of it as you want. There's certainly

plenty." Vera looked sober. "I fear it will outlast him."

"Oh, no, surely – "

"Does he look like a well man to you?"

"Well, no, but – "

"In fact, would you say he's looking very ill, more ill…?"

"Perhaps." Moira drew the word out, as if in doubt.

But there was no doubt.

Cyril was very ill.

And getting worse all the time.

Cyril was so bad that he could hardly swallow Jello. It seemed to Moira that he didn't want to eat it. When she failed to get him to eat, she'd call on Vera and Vera would force it down him. Sometimes he choked on it, and sometimes, when Vera left, he spat it out of his mouth.

Yet Vera said he loved lime Jello.

Moira couldn't imagine a person not loving it.

Hy was getting a macabre enjoyment out of her postings. She was nowhere nearer finding out just what Vera Gloom had stashed away in her upstairs bedrooms, but she was getting a twisted kick out of researching cadavers.

Hy's FB Status: For hundreds of years in the Far East, medicines were made out of mummies. Today, in the modern west, doctors are plumping up wealthy clients' cheeks with collagen-busting confections made from cadavers.

Likes: 3

Comments: Drop dead good looks?

Hy leaned back, smiling. Obviously Vera Gloom had not taken part in deathly cosmetic surgery. Her face was like a prune.

Or as if she were sucking on vinegar. Probably, thought Hy, from her continual expressions of disapproval and distaste.

All through July, it rained. No one was out on a ride-on.

All through July, Hy thought about what she'd seen, or thought she'd seen, at the Sullivan house.

There was no way she could convince Jamieson to make an official visit. She'd tried over and over again.

They were going through the same old argument one day at Ian's.

"The remains belong to the family," Jamieson insisted. "It's their decision as to what to do with them."

Anything but cremation, she thought privately. That's how her own parents had died. Cremation. Before the fact. They'd burned to death. In a fire Jamieson had accidentally started.

"What if I decided to engage in some home-made cryonics and had grandma in the freezer downstairs?"

Jamieson looked at her sharply.

"Do you?"

Hy grinned. Sometimes Jamieson had simply no sense of humour at all.

"Yes. And grandpa. Abel, too, in case you've been looking for him."

"I doubt that would be legal."

"Probably not." Ian was in his usual position, on a stool in front of his computer, a beautiful brand new iMac.

"However…" He turned to look at the two women. "There was a case in France, more than a decade ago, in which a court ruled a couple had to come out of the fridge in the basement and be buried or cremated. The old fella had just died, but the wife had been down there almost twenty years. The son was fighting their right to stay where they were."

"And?" Hy walked over and stroked Jasmine's head. The parrot was where she usually was when Ian was on the computer. On his shoulder.

"He lost. The government lawyer said they could hardly rest in peace if anyone could go and have a peek anytime."

"Maybe that's what they wanted." Hy grinned and chucked Jasmine under the beak. Jasmine nibbled her fingers. Hy let her, briefly. Finger nibbling was a crapshoot with Jasmine. Even with someone she liked, it could turn ugly.

"Our religions demand and have rituals for, respect for the dead, but what is done to a body is a tangle of legalities. For instance – " Ian scrolled down and clicked a couple of times.

"In the US, for example, sex with a dead body…"

"Ian!" Hy moved back, away from him, away from the screen. Jamieson just stood there, waiting.

"…sex with a dead body isn't rape. In most states. Unless…" He held up a finger, "…you thought the body was alive while you were doing it."

"That's just gross and disgusting, Ian." Hy coaxed Jasmine onto her arm and slumped down on the couch, stroking the bird on the head.

"Maybe, but it's the truth. Doing it with a former person is actually only illegal in sixteen states."

"Well, I don't think we're talking about doing it with the dead." Hy scrunched up her face. "Are we?"

"So it seems that what's done with human remains may not be a matter of law, or laws, laid down." Jamieson had begun to pace, hands locked behind her. "It's precedent – dealing with each case as it comes up."

"Precisely."

Hy jumped in. "If there are stuffed humans in Vera's house, do we have a case?"

Ian shrugged. "You tell me."

"I don't even know that there are bodies." Jamieson's tone was dismissive.

"I told you there were."

"Seen through a window, under stress."

"I told you what I saw. Human bodies. Not moving. Dead. Definitely dead."

Jamieson sighed. "You seem more certain of that now than you did then."

"I've given it a lot of thought."

"I'd call it selective memory. And, anyway, what do you expect me to do? Go knock on the door and say, 'Excuse me, Mrs. Gloom, I'd like to search the house. Someone says she saw two dead bodies upstairs. She was peeking into your house from your ladder'?"

"Yes. Something like that."

Jamieson shrugged.

"Sorry. Have to have more to go on."

"Well, figure out something." Hy grinned. "I'm deadly curious."

Hy's FB Status: You don't want to hide grandma in the freezer. When you take her out, she might crack. She's three-quarters water.
Likes: 5
Comments: Does that make grandma a stiff drink?

Finn and Dot strolled the beach for several hours a day in spite of the rainy summer weather. On the rare nice day, they would walk out to the end of the rocks spilling from the cape at Macks' shore and do Tai Chi, facing the water and the sunrise or sunset.

They made a handsome sight – he with his long spider appendages, and she with her willowy form, meeting him motion for motion and stretch for stretch. They performed the moves like a slow ballet, tall black figure beside tall black figure, black from the roots to the tips of their hair.

They were in tune with the universe, but not entirely with the shore, though they thought they were.

Day after day, they did not find the skull. It was eluding them, so clever were its secret places, its playing on the tide. It was a game of hide and seek they didn't know they were part of. One day the skull lay, eyes up to the sky, exposed on the bare stretch of sand between the incoming tide and the high water mark. Granted, it looked like a grubby soccer ball, a bit deflated, but that's not why they didn't see it. They raced right past it, Dot accidentally kicking it, as she tore along trying to keep up with Finn. She stumbled, and he came back to help her, and in the kiss that followed, their thoughts were far from finding a treasure on the beach, even such a treasure as this.

The blow from Dot's foot sent the skull skittering into a cluster of sandstone, where it lodged beside a decaying piece of white-and-grey buoy, becoming just another piece of broken-up fishermen's junk on the beach.

It had been hidden for half a century. Why would it give itself up now? Why seek notoriety, long after it had been cleaned of every scrap of flesh, drained of every feeling, every emotion, every engagement with the physical world?

The skull had long ago given up everything – its entire body and organs, clothes, boat, house, all its possessions.

Well, not quite all, and maybe that's why it was nursing these last private moments, guarding the last thing belonging to the cranium.

The last possession and the manner of his death.

Not by drowning.

No, not by drowning.

As the hole in his head, even after all this time, made clear.

Shot. Swallowed by the sea. In that order.

Chapter Twenty-Five

"I think I've found what you may have seen at Gloom's."

"Serious?"

"Yup."

Hy raced up to Ian's right after he called. She was in such a rush, she didn't bother to put on a rain jacket. She was halfway there when the skies opened. She burst into Ian's kitchen, dripping all over the floor.

He went upstairs and grabbed a sweatshirt and sweatpants for her. She ducked into the bathroom and changed, struggling to drag the dry clothes over her wet skin, cursing with impatience.

Ian had stumbled on a site while researching what happens to dead bodies. As soon as he opened it, he knew that this was what Hy had been describing. He was rewarded by the look on her face when she saw what was on the screen.

"Oh my God." She very nearly crossed herself.

She had to sit down.

"This is too bizarre," she said.

"Pretty strange." Ian reached over and clicked on a series of images.

"That's it," she said.

"What you saw?"

"I'm sure it's what I saw. These are what I saw."

"I've heard of this, but I've never seen it. Never been tempted to look, until now."

"I'm tempted." Hy looked up, an appeal in her eyes.

"No. Hy. No."

"Oh c'mon, Ian. I have to see. To be sure. If I'm sure, I won't let up on Jamieson. I'll make her do something about it… them. And if this is what they are, she should."

"I dunno, Hy, they may be perfectly legal. All of these are. For medical purposes, the literature says, although these appear to be an exhibit, a show. But legal, Hy, I should think, to be out in the public like that."

"I don't care. There's something that's not right there. I'm going to find out. Are you with me?"

Ian sighed.

"I am. You know I am. How can I resist?"

"A mystery?"

"Yeah." He was silent for a moment. "A mystery."

What he really couldn't resist was her request for him to help. It had been a while since she'd done that. And he couldn't resist his need to protect her from herself.

Moira wasn't feeling well. She mentioned it at the Women's Institute meeting and there were a few snickers.

But she couldn't be pregnant. She and Frank hadn't gone that far.

She also had what Frank called "the runs." She wished he wouldn't call it that. She didn't like to think of herself as someone who had those.

But she did.

She also had headaches. She was dizzy.

Was it something she'd eaten?

Moira wasn't going to let nausea get in the way of her third attempt to marry Frank. She refused this time to have church vows. She was superstitious. The first time, they almost landed her married to the wrong man.

She went online to find out how they could write their own vows. She didn't find anything she liked. It was all too flowery, too unlike her. What Frank was like never entered her mind. Moira shared that with other brides: the wedding wasn't about him.

People looked all misty-eyed when she said she and Frank were writing their own vows. Everyone except Hy. She sneered. She couldn't help it. She couldn't imagine what Moira could possibly write. Moira didn't see the sneer. Hy had turned away from her to hide it. The two were in the hall, setting it up for the wedding the following weekend.

Third time lucky, Hy thought as she shifted a chair into place.

A swell of nausea gripped Moira. It started as a cramp, surged through her stomach and gripped her intestines. She doubled up.

Hy put a hand on her shoulder.

"Moira, what's wrong?"

Moira said nothing. Her face was distorted. *Was it going to go up? Or down?*

Hy could hear Moira's intestines grumbling. Gently, she tried to guide her to the bathroom. Moira could only shuffle along, nursing her pain with arms wrapped around her belly.

Hy left her at the bathroom door, and returned to the chairs. She hoped their vows weren't lengthy. People never wanted to sit in these hard wooden school chairs for long.

A groan came from the bathroom.

If there were any vows.

Surely Moira's wedding was not going to be sabotaged a third time?

The groan, it turned out, was one of relief. But Moira knew it wouldn't be for long. The sick feeling would start welling up again in her intestines and come out one end or the other. What was wrong with her?

Lime Jello?

The idea had been in the back of her mind. It was the only thing new in her diet, and the only thing not made in her own clean kitchen. But she had made it herself. Straight out of the sealed box. She kept coming back to that.

So what could possibly be wrong with it? Wrong with her?

www.theshores200.com
The last time the Sullivan house was inhabited it was uninhabitable. The Fitzpatricks pitched a tent in winter in the kitchen and lived with rats and mice in desperate poverty. There were two deaths, but the story did have a happy ending – the discovery of a family treasure. The family left quickly after that.

At one time, it would have been more difficult to convince Ian to break into a house, but he was happy Hy had asked him. His compliance had closed the distance between them, put them back on easy terms with one another.

And his scientific curiosity was aroused. To see one of those things in the flesh. Did it count as flesh?

They waited until Vera went to town. Tuesday was her town day, when she visited the fellow who parked his truck in the centre of Winterside and sold fresh fish out of the back. She'd be a few hours. The causeway was still under construction, and the old river ferry only took eight cars at a time. Tuesday was a popular day, because of the fish guy, so it created what passed for a traffic jam.

Vera would certainly be gone long enough for Hy and Ian to have a good look around the house's twenty-four rooms.

But both outside doors were locked.

"She's got something to hide." Hy took one more try at turning the doorknob.

"She's from away."

"So are we." Hy and Ian had soon adopted the Red Island habit of leaving their doors unlocked, but Vera obviously had not.

"There – the kitchen windows. Sliders. Just like mine. I can get in there."

"But that would be break and enter."

"So would going through the door."

"Not if it was unlocked."

Hy had grabbed onto the window ledge.

"Help me up."

Ian knit his two hands together and she stepped into them. He hoisted her up, face turning red with the effort.

"Hurry up." His voice was breathless.

"Going as fast as I can."

She managed to slide an opening large enough to squeeze through. Jumped down on the other side. Ran to the door to let Ian in.

Even though they now had good reason to believe no one was in the house besides them, they tiptoed. In silence, as if someone might hear them.

Hy hadn't seen the place since the Fitzpatricks had lived there when it was practically a condemned building.

The old wood floors shone with paste wax. The windows beamed light onto the beautiful wood wainscoting, milled work on the doors and around the windows and up the staircase.

"Wow." Hy gazed up at the ceiling, painted cream like the walls. "Perfectly restored."

"Cost a bucket of money to do this."

"Sssh." Hy went suddenly quiet. "What's that?" Ian listened, and after a moment, heard it, too. Laboured breathing coming from the front room.

Hy eased open the door. There was no response from the bed, just the rattly breathing and demi-snores.

Hy closed the door carefully.

"So we're not alone, but he's right out of it. Maybe she drugs him when she leaves him alone."

"Better be quiet, anyway."

They crept up the stairs. There were a series of doors down either side of the long, broad hallway. Some open. Some closed.

A ball of fur streaked past them, nearly tripping Hy.

"Damn Whacky! Must've got in the kitchen window. Stupid me. Left it open." She chased after the feline, but it outwitted her – scurrying into one of the rooms and sliding under the bed. Hy knelt to the floor, swept her arms under the bed. Got clawed. She whipped out her arms and put the bleeding hand to her mouth.

She came up from the floor by the side of the bed and saw the body.

Not stuffed.

Much creepier than that.

She went white.

Human.

Dead.

Preserved in plastic.

"There." Triumph in her voice, aimed at Ian, who had slipped in behind her. There on the bed was an old man, propped up on pillows. He was wearing silk pyjamas and a wine velvet robe.

Perfectly normal.

Except he was dead.

And you could see right though him in places.

"Plasticized," said Ian, in a whisper.

He strode forward to inspect more closely.

"Fixed in formaldehyde, dehydrated, bathed in acetone, filled with plastic – polymer, epoxy – cured with heat or ultraviolet light…and, voilà, a perfectly preserved cadaver."

He shook his head, admiration in his eyes. "I've heard of this, but never seen it."

"I wish I hadn't." Hy backed away. "It's creepy. You can see his leg muscles…"

"What there is of them. These are used for medical display. There are a couple of shows – one in New York – that exist under the guise of being educational. Well, you saw the website at my house."

"Creepier now." Hy shuddered.

"This one, with his leg muscles showing, must be an example of a couch potato." Hy pulled out her cellphone, held it up and took several photographs.

"For the record." Maybe this would help convince Jamieson, if she dared to show them to her.

"An odd sort of immortality. Perfect for our plastic times." Admiration continued to shine in Ian's eyes.

As they left the room, Hy couldn't find Whacky anywhere. She looked under the bed again, behind the curtains, but there was no feline to be found.

In the next room was one of the bodies Hy had seen from the ladder – another old guy, with a pipe in his mouth, sitting by the fireplace, reading a book. His brain was exposed on one side. On the other, his hair was gingery and tousled. She took more photographs.

In the final room, a man was standing at an easel, arm aloft and hand holding a paint brush. The water colour on the easel was half-done. His hands revealed spidery webs of blood vessels.

"The guy who waved at me."

"Don't you have to work quickly on a water colour?" Ian peered over the corpse's shoulder at the painting.

Hy grinned in spite of herself. She took a photograph.

"Jamieson could see him without coming in the house." Hy looked out the window to see where the best viewpoint would be from below.

"Why bring Jamieson into it?"

"Surely this isn't legal. You can't do this to people, can you?"

"I believe it's perfectly legal. Done for the right reasons. In the right circumstances. You saw on the site. All above board."

"Then how about how these men died? Three in a row. She's a serial widow."

"Well…"

They looked in every one of the rooms on that floor and the next. Nothing in any of them.

"Guess it's just the three," said Ian, with a grin.

On the way down the hall, they were silent, not knowing what to think, what to say. Until Hy remembered the cat.

"We've got to find her. We can't leave her in here."

They opened and closed doors, called "kitty, kitty, kitty,"

but Whacky didn't show.

"Where's Jamieson when we need her?" Hy was thinking about her purring talents.

"Jamieson? How could she help? I thought she didn't like cats."

"Long story."

"She may have got out the same way she got in. By the open window."

Hy nodded. You're probably right."

"There you go." Ian pointed and leaned down to pick a piece of gingery fluff off the floor. He handed it to Hy. It was rough, a bit like soft steel wool.

She screwed up her face.

"What is it?"

"Hair."

"That's not cat hair."

"No, it's not."

The man reading the book. Ginger hair. Tousled – by the cat?

"Yech!" Hy made a motion to drop it, but Ian closed his hand around hers.

"Hang on to it. If you think there's been foul play, a forensic analysis of that might prove it for you." He let go of her hand. Reluctantly. It had been pleasant to hold it, no matter what it contained.

She looked down at her hand. Opened it. Stuffed the hair in her pocket. Maybe she would do something with it. Or convince Jamieson to do something with it.

On their way out, Hy set down her cellphone and closed the kitchen window. Just as she did, Whacky bounded up and streaked through the opening.

"Two birds with one stone," she murmured.

Chapter Twenty-Six

Moira had never sought Hy's advice, but she was desperate. So desperate that she called out to Hy on her way down Shipwreck Lane. *Moira.* Hy didn't want to be bothered with Moira. She wanted to think about what she would now say to Jamieson, to get her to take seriously what Vera had in her house. Except that it had been a break and enter. She didn't know how she was going to get around that.

With no immediate answer, Hy strolled over to Moira. The marching marigolds on either side of her stoop were drenched from the unending summer rains.

"Do you think…"

Hy looked up sharply. Moira, asking her opinion?

"It's just that this nausea, it won't let up. It's not like anything I've experienced. I'm wondering if…if…it might be…poison."

"Poison?"

Moira nodded.

"From where? From what?"

"Lime Jello."

"Lime Jello?" It seemed an unusual food for Moira.

"Yes. At the house." Moira jerked her head in the direction of

Shipwreck Hill. "I make it for him. And I've been making it for myself, too."

"Him?"

"Her husband."

"And is it the only new food in your diet?"

Moira nodded.

"And how's he...?"

"Not good. But he's old and dying."

"Dying anyway, or because of the Jello?"

Moira slumped down on a chair. Her voice, when it came, was thin and weak.

"I don't know."

"Well there's one way to find out."

Moira looked up, hope in her eyes. "There is?"

"Get a sample of that Jello."

"That won't be easy." Moira was imagining herself shoving some jiggling jelly into a pocket.

"Look. You're not well enough to work. If she's poisoning you, then it won't surprise her. I'll go in your place. Give me a letter confirming I work for you, and I'll get some Jello out."

Moira hesitated. It went against her principles. She was a snoop, but she wasn't a liar. A wave of nausea gripped her stomach and stabbed like small knives cutting through her bowels.

"Okay." It would be a chance to use her new letterhead. *Nice As You Please*. It looked so pretty with the sloping periwinkle blue cursive at the top of the pale blue sheets.

"This is to introduce Hyacinth McAllister, a trusted and bonded member of the *Nice As You Please* staff. Arrangements as usual."

"Bonded? I'm not bonded. It's not like you to lie, Moira."

"If the way I feel right now has anything to do with her, then it's the least I'm entitled to."

Moira, showing a bit of mettle against authority. Nice for a change.

"And what does 'arrangements as usual' mean?"

"That's a mannerly way of saying she pays me as usual. But I'll give you what you're owed."

Hy laughed. "As for that…paid for snooping? I should be paying you." Hy folded the paper. "Now I'll have to figure out how to get a sample of that lime Jello."

"What will you do with it?"

"Something," said Hy. "Something." She was suddenly thinking of that hair sample. Still in her jacket pocket? Would Finn be able to do something? Analyze them? Get someone to do it for him?

She patted her pocket and realized she did not have her cellphone. She had left it on the counter at the Sullivan house.

"You'll do the usual."

Hy lifted an eyebrow, questioning.

"Make the Jello." Vera's tone was irritable. Hadn't Moira told this woman anything?

"It's here." Vera opened the cupboard stuffed with boxes of lime Jello. "Then do the chores. When you're finished, the Jello should be ready and Cyril can have some. So can you, if you wish. Never touch it myself."

I bet you don't, thought Hy.

"I'm going to have my nap now. Upstairs. You've no need of going there, so you won't disturb me."

No need.

There was no need. Hy had seen it all, and it had repelled

her. She was here for the Jello. Just the Jello.

She grabbed a box. Inspected it closely. Factory sealed. No doubt. Both the exterior cardboard and the wax paper lining inside that held the powder Jello were secure. Hy took the water straight from the tap, boiled it in the kettle, mixed the Jello in the bowl, covered it and put it in the fridge to set.

She began a cursory cleaning of the kitchen. She moved out into the dining room, so clean it didn't even need a dusting.

Then she heard the rasping, the laboured breathing from the front room. *Cyril.* She eased open the dividing doors. If it weren't for the pained sounds he was making, there was little evidence that a human was lying in the hospital bed. The blankets simply appeared messy, his body under them sunken, shapeless.

"Cyril?" Hy whispered. There was no response from the bed.

She crept closer. She could see his eyes now, just above the sheet. Closed.

She came right up to the bed and his eyes popped open. She jumped back, startled.

His eyes were fixed on her. Whatever was in them held her. What was it? An appeal? Yes, an appeal.

He eased the rest of his face out from under the sheet. Drool slid down from the right side of his mouth, carrying a small, strangled sound.

"V…v…"

"Vera?" Hy guessed.

He closed and opened his eyes.

"Yes?" She nodded her head. He repeated the motion, and began to try to speak again.

"K…k…kl…kl…klng."

"Killing you?"

He shut and opened his eyes.

"With lime Jello?"

Before Cyril could answer, Vera stormed into the room.

"What are you doing here? Is he asking for his lime Jello?"

Fear struck through Cyril's eyes.

"No. But he sounded restless, so I came in."

"You have no need to be here. There's plenty for you to do elsewhere. Leave him be. You'll only upset him. I haven't been able to sleep. I've come down for a pill."

She grabbed one of the several bottles cluttering Cyril's bedside table, shook out a couple of peach-coloured pills, tossed them in her mouth and swallowed them dry.

"There. That should do the trick." She banged the bottle back down on the table, turned and marched out. The room was vibrating with Vera's anger, turned dark with her presence. It lightened when she left.

"See I am not disturbed," she called back as the door slammed behind her.

Hy picked up the bottle of pills. The prescription was for Cyril, not Vera. She shrugged and put it down. She turned to Cyril. His eyes were closed. *Asleep? Dead?* Hy listened for his rattled breathing, and, satisfied that he was still alive, left the room.

As she busied herself with cleaning that didn't really need to be done, Hy rummaged in drawers and cabinets in the dim hope of finding her cell phone, with its images of the creatures upstairs. Preserved out of love? Surely not. Vera Gloom didn't seem capable of love. Preserved in spite of having been murdered? Poisoned? By lime Jello? Could traces of the poison still be found? In their hair, for instance?

Hy allowed a half-hour to pass, by which time she assumed

Vera would be asleep and not yet ready to wake, not with those two pills in her system.

She slipped quietly up the stairs. In spite of her horror at what she had seen when she was last here, she couldn't stop herself, compelled by a desire for more clues. Hy had one hair sample but she wanted them from the other two.

She was vibrating with fear, shaking with the prospect of being found out by a woman she thought was a murderess. Hy liked the word. It made Vera seem so thoroughly wicked. Murderess. Husband killer.

Hy wished she'd brought scissors. What was she going to do – tug the hair out of a dead scalp and send a plastic cadaver pitching over onto the floor, breaking off a body part? The thought made her shudder.

But there, on his night table, was a pair of nail scissors. Hy grabbed them, and turned to Charlie, his hand uplifted as always.

How much hair would she need? How much would these tiny scissors cut? Hy selected a lock, smaller than she would have liked, but small enough for the scissors to handle. Barely. They were blunt, and Hy had to saw through the hair, tingling with disgust as bits of it gave way while others clung, until she finally had what she hoped was enough. She shoved the clump into her pocket and sped from the room.

She didn't get far.

"I thought I said you were not to come upstairs."

Hy turned around to face the voice and the dark presence of Vera Gloom shadowing the hallway.

Chapter Twenty-Seven

Finally, they saw it.

Maybe it was willing to be seen for the first time, to give up its final secrets, to make his archenemy, his killer, answer to his death. His secrets weren't his alone to tell. That thought may have put the smile in the skull's jaw. The smile that all skulls have, but this one was there for a reason. He had managed to cling to the prized possession his enemy would have taken from him.

And now everyone would know that he had not been drowned at sea, though he couldn't swim. Would perhaps look for the rest of him, most of which was there in that hole in the ocean floor. He might be reassembled, a curiosity in the hall. Who knew?

So he gave up his secret to them, the lovers strolling hand in hand down the shore, laughing and pushing at each other, playing tag, so that they would have missed him yet again if Dot had not seen a beautiful rock, stopped to pick it up, and then the two of them were stalking down the beach, eyes riveted to the sand, looking for treasures, not knowing they were about to come upon the greatest treasure of the summer.

Him.

They saw it at the same time, pointed, and ran. Then came to a complete stop and just stared down. Dot had no immediate desire to touch it, although she was curious. It was Finn, the forensic anthropologist, who picked it up, held it up, and grinned straight into the skeletal grin.

"Modern day," he said, turning it around in his hands. "But old."

"How old?"

"Been in that water a while. Before you were born, I bet."

He winked and passed the skull to her. Finn was still living at Hy's and they had bonded seamlessly as brother and sister, but his heart was lodged down The Shore Lane with Dot.

Vera Gloom gave as close to a smile as she could give – a bitter, twisted sort of thing, almost a grimace.

"Well, you've seen them now, haven't you?" She paused, her distorted expression twisting a notch more. Hy swallowed, preparing to say something. *Yes? More than once?*

"But you've seen them before, haven't you?" Vera slipped Hy's cellphone from the pocket of her dress, faced it towards Hy and clicked through the camera roll, displaying the photographs Hy had taken of the plastic corpses, and continuing to some selfies that made it clear whose camera it was.

"You might as well see them again. My boys. Let me explain."

Explain? What explanation could there possibly be?

"We live, all three and I, in the greatest harmony." Vera swept forward and extended an arm in a gesture for Hy to follow her.

The door to Blair's room was closed.

It creaked open. Already the old house was reclaiming itself after the renovation, finding its former posture, its familiar creaks, structural habits and flaws, settling into its remembered self. Shiny sanded floors and patched-up plaster couldn't hide its essential soul. A dark soul. It had been no surprise, really, for Hy to find these bodies here. A shock, yes, but no surprise that darkness and madness were revisiting the Sullivan house. Darkness and madness had always resided here. Why would that change because the wainscoting had been freshened, the plaster shored up, the rats sequestered to the attic, where they belonged in a respectable home?

This was not a respectable home. Never had been, though it was beautiful. The sad history of family strife and murder was built into the bones of the house. But what had been the seed that had created it, continued to create it to this day?

Did Gus even know? It was nowhere spelled out in her history of The Shores. Or was it – a clue hidden to even Gus? Hy determined to have another look at the manuscript.

For now, she followed Vera through the door. This was the third time Hy had seen Blair, but she was not inured to the sight. Revulsion shivered up her spine, the backs of her legs and arms tingled with distaste.

Vera marched over to the chair, and yanked the book from his hands.

"You must be finished this by now, Blair. It offends me that you take such interest in it."

The book was called *The Nude Through the Ages*.

"You should give it back to Charlie." She straightened his collar. "It is his, after all, a Christmas present from me last year."

Hy watched with fascination, as Vera brushed off Blair's sweater, skimming over the hole where his heart was. Where his heart was displayed. Displayed. That was the word. Meant to be seen.

But, for Vera, it was as if that display box of Blair's heart wasn't there. For Vera, it appeared as if Blair were alive, as she fussed over him and chatted with him.

"Messy boy." Vera continued to brush his sweater. "Crumbs all over you."

Hy couldn't see any crumbs. The woman was mad. And she herself was mad to be standing here with her. Even so, she dared to open a door to reality.

"I see nothing. No crumbs."

Vera took one more long, slow swipe at Blair's sweater, catching her rings in the hem. She held her hand there momentarily. She caressed it, lost in the sparkle of the blue diamonds. Hy was transfixed, too, on the blue diamonds. Blue diamonds. Hadn't she come across something about them recently, something she'd meant to read?

Vera caught Hy looking at her hands, at the rings. She looked up at Hy, her expression, if possible, even more twisted. Madness, surely, gleaming in her eyes. She frowned. Her eyes shifted. Only her features moved. The rest of her body was rigid, hand still caught in place.

Then she smiled. No smile at all.

"You're right," she said. "No crumbs. Of course not. He's dead. They're all dead."

Vera's features distorted. She unhooked her rings from the sweater. A tear trickled down her cheek, taking a long route crisscross from wrinkle to wrinkle.

"Dead." The word came on a sob. "All dead?" She looked at Hy in appeal. It was as if she were realizing it for the first time. And, in this moment, she was. *Blair dead. Charlie dead. Hank dead. Oh my God. And the blue boys. The blue boys, too.*

Hy said nothing, eyes glued to Vera, her emotions visual,

changing from instant to instant, now returning to reality. Vera caressed Blair's plastic heart.

"Did you see this?" The expression in her eyes became tender.

Hy shuddered. Touching his heart. Sure, plastic. But didn't that make it worse, not better?

"We showcased his heart."

"We?"

"The creators and I."

"Creators?"

"The people who performed the plastination. My decision, really, because Blair was all heart. Generous to a fault. With myself…" The twist came back into her smile. "…and with others. Especially with others."

She turned to look at Blair again.

"Others, Blair. That's what stood between us. Others."

Hy saw malevolence in Vera's eyes. So much for the love she professed.

"But…how could you do this? Is it…legal?"

"Perfectly legal. Ask your Mountie there…the one who's been snooping around."

"Jamieson? Has she…?"

"Seen the boys? No. But I've seen her looking in this direction. She's passed by."

Hy smiled. So she had managed to get through to Jamieson – at least to the point where she was showing curiosity.

"Come." Vera's tone and gestures were abrupt, summoning Hy from the room to the one next door.

Charlie was standing, as always, back to the light, in front of his easel, arm poised, paint brush in hand, the collection of unfinished paintings propped against the easel legs at his feet.

The painting was of Sullivan house.

How had he painted it if he was dead when he got here?

"Do you paint?" she asked Vera.

"Me? No. Of course not. It's Charlie's. Such talent."

This was the mad Vera, not the sane one. Believing that Charlie was alive and still her husband.

"Good. Oh very good." Vera peered over his shoulder. "Come see." She beckoned Hy, who moved closer to look at the painting.

"Not that," Vera snapped. "This."

She grabbed Hy and pulled her around so that she could see the side of Charlie's skull. Like Blair's heart, Charlie's brain had been plasticized and exposed.

"An attempt to understand what makes up the creative brain," Vera explained. And then Hy knew. At any moment, Vera might be mad or sane, but even when she was sane, she was utterly mad.

And dangerous?

Hy felt as if she could throw up, but she knew she'd have to follow Vera into the next room.

The couch potato, that's how Hy thought of him. Reclining on the bed, remote control in hand, watching TV, a home and garden show.

Vera grabbed the remote and clicked the set off. She pulled the blanket from across Hank's knees. It hadn't been there yesterday. Hy didn't need reminding that each leg was slit – one along the thigh muscle, the other showing the calf.

"A study of what happens to muscles rarely used. I had to carry him over the threshold." Again that cold Vera smile.

"But enough. Our treat is waiting for us downstairs."

Lime Jello.

Chapter Twenty-Eight

"Look what we found."

Gus smiled at the familiar words. Eight kids living by the shore were always finding something and bringing it home. The boys would leave their finds out in the yard, on the picnic table, around the well house, and forget about them. Dot would bring them in. Shells, rocks, wounded birds. Once the boys had dragged the corpse of a sea cow up to the house.

But the catch of today was not a sea cow.

It was Roger Murray.

"Plain as day," as Gus said the moment she saw him. Some of him.

Finn kicked off his shoes and came into the room, holding the skull high.

"Well, I'll be." Gus put down her knitting and leaned forward. "If it isn't Roger Murray."

"You know him?"

Gus nodded her head.

"Been waitin' for him to show up."

Vera watched in silence as Hy reluctantly spooned Jello into her mouth. Hy loved lime. As a child, like Moira, she had loved lime Jello best, but all she could think of now was that somehow she was eating poison. She could hardly swallow. She could hardly stop herself from spitting it up.

When she had finished, Vera instructed Hy to feed Cyril his Jello. She didn't want to. It might make her an accessory to murder. But more unsettling than that was the pathetic, pleading look in Cyril's eyes.

Hy had no choice, because Vera stood at her elbow, supervising.

Her hand trembled as she guided the spoon to Cyril's mouth. He was trembling, too. So was the Jello. A lump of it jiggled with thin green drool down the side of his mouth onto the pillowcase. Then the lump flopped off the bed and onto the floor.

"Clumsy woman. Clean that up."

Hy grabbed a paper towel from the roll on the bedside table and ducked under the bed. She scooped some of the Jello into her apron pocket, and brought the rest up in the paper towel. She threw it into the garbage can.

Vera watched with disapproval, and Hy hurried to leave before the Jello could soak through her pocket.

"What's that?"

It had.

"Oh, it fell on my apron before I got it in the garbage. Just a stain."

A feeling of nausea was overwhelming Hy. She began to back out of the room, hand over her mouth. She couldn't speak, couldn't make her apologies, she just kept the hand clamped over her mouth and raced down the hallway.

The oriental runner flew up from underneath her, and she

pitched forward, hand no longer on her mouth, but shoved forward to break her fall.

Thump!

She came down with a thud, and, for a moment, thought she had broken her wrist, the pain was so severe.

The soft sound of fabric hitting the floor broke through the pain. She turned her head. Vera Gloom was standing at the end of the runner, with that twisted smile on her face.

"Just straightening it." She didn't even try to look sincere.

Hy glared at her. She pushed herself to her feet, wincing at the pressure on her wrist. Not broken. Cracked maybe? She stepped onto the wood floor.

She was dizzy. And still nauseous. The fall was the final trigger.

She leaned forward and puked.

Lime Jello.

Little clumps of it, the rest a liquid green. Nothing else in her stomach, but she retched and retched, dry heaves.

Vera didn't move. She stood at the other end of the hallway, smirking, a tight unpleasant smirk.

Normally Hy, embarrassed, would have cleaned up after herself, but she didn't even offer. She glared again at Vera, and left by the front door. After she closed it, she wiped a hand across her mouth, to get rid of the taste of Jello and of Vera.

Lime Jello. Did it mean anything? Was there anything to it? In it?

She plunged a hand into her pocket. Kleenex. She spat out whatever remained in her mouth into it. She would ask Finn if he could analyze it.

She stuffed the Kleenex into her pocket and hurried up the path and out onto the road. Behind her, Vera fished the lime

Jello out of the garbage, grabbed the bowl containing the rest, and poured it into a hole in the garden. She threw in Hy's cell phone and stuffed a shrub into it.

The shrub wilted almost immediately and was dead the next morning.

Hy was worried about Cyril. What the gelatin might be doing to him. Might have done to the other husbands. Jello as a murder weapon? Jamieson would never swallow it. Hy needed evidence.

She went straight down to see Finn, where she knew he'd be – at Gus's. She felt as if she'd been given a macabre preview of Bachelor Number One, Bachelor Number Two and Bachelor Number Three. Except they were husbands. Ex-husbands. Late husbands.

Or the Lion, the Tin Man and the Scarecrow? Not quite, but nearly – with the exposed heart, brain and muscles for courage.

"You know him?" Dot repeated her question to Gus and extended her hands. Finn popped the skull into them. His eyes lit up in amusement.

"Yes and I do. I'd know him anywhere. Been waiting for him to show up."

"Waiting?" Dot set the skull down on the table in front of the picture window.

"He disappeared fifty year ago. I remember the day. Him and Orwell Crane, went out on a boat together in a storm. Only Orwell came back. Said Roger had gone over the side in a big swell. He couldn't swim. Neither could Orwell. So Roger drownded, so he said. No one could say different."

"There's a hole in the skull," said Dot. "A bullet hole?"

Finn shrugged. "Hard to say."

"Ain't you studied all that? And you can't say?"

Finn picked up the skull and sat down with it, examining it closely.

"It's small, but it's male."

Gus nodded. "Roger was a small man."

Just then Hy burst into the house.

"You look a fright," said Dot. Where have you been?"

Hy caught sight of the skull in Finn's hands.

"I might ask you the same."

"I asked first," said Dot, noticing the apron – Hy in an apron? – and the green stain on the pocket. Hy pulled out the hair from the other pocket, and told them what she'd seen and done at Sullivan house. Then she asked if Finn could do any forensic work on the hair and the Jello.

"I don't know about the Jello – or even the hair. I don't have a lab, any way of telling…"

He was feeling the texture of the hair. Watching him made Hy shiver.

"I could… I could send it to a friend of mine. Went through the forensics course with him. He's working in the field. Might do me a favour and have a look at this."

"Good."

"It might take weeks, though. Those labs get more work than they can handle, and he'd be doing it on the side."

"Understood. Now what about this skull?"

"Found it on the shore."

Hy was glad that for once it wasn't she who'd stumbled across human remains.

"And, as I was saying, it's male."

"How do you know it's male?"

"The male brow ridge is more rounded and bonier between

the eyebrows and the nose." As he spoke, Finn traced the parts of the skull he was describing. "Here, the mastoid area behind the ear is larger. The jaw is more squared, and see how the forehead slants backward. The nasal cavity's longer and narrower. No doubt it's a male."

Hy sat down beside Finn and peered at the skull with Dot.

"Any way to tell if it's an adult male?" Dot asked. "You said the skull is small."

"Oh, it's an adult all right."

"And you know that because?"

"We're born with skulls made up of smaller bits of bone, but as we grow older, the bones fuse together. By about the age of thirty, the process is complete. It is in this skull, so it's a male older than thirty."

"Roger Murray was thirty-three." Gus's tone said Finn had proved her point.

"You can set age by teeth, too, can't you?" Hy peered closely at the skull's grinning mouth.

"Yes, by the wear on them. Normal wear. These are well-worn."

"Crackin' open shellfish." Gus broke a thread in her teeth. "He were a great one for that."

Hy had often been tempted to crack open a lobster claw with her teeth. An instinctive move, but not a wise one. She winced at the thought.

"Is that how he lost that one?"

"Which one?"

Hy pointed to the prominent gap where a front tooth was missing.

"The missing tooth. What about that?"

"Gold," said Gus. "It were gold."

"We better call Jamieson." Hy, a bit lost without her cellphone, went to the landline in the dining room.

Jamieson wasn't there, or wasn't answering. Hy left a message on her voicemail.

"Got a body part here. You might be interested."

She returned, grinning, to the kitchen.

"Well, it's been fifty year, hasn't it now…"

Gus was talking to the skull.

Chapter Twenty-Nine

Hy's FB Status: There's a diamond made from a strand of Ludwig Van Beethoven's hair. It's valued at a million dollars.
Likes: 7
Comments: Music to my ears.
                I'm deaf to the idea.

Hy's dreams – often active – were peppered that night with skulls, bodies like large preying insects, body parts exposed and plasticized, and diamonds.

Diamonds. Blue diamonds flashed through her consciousness – until she was actually conscious, sitting up in bed.

Blue diamonds. Of course.

Her laptop was lying on the bed beside her. She snatched it up and Googled corpses turned into diamonds. She'd come across the site before and found it fascinating, but thought it was irrelevant to her interest in Vera Gloom. Until she got a good look at those rings, glittering on Vera's hands.

Blue diamonds. Made so by boron traces in the human body. It took six to nine months to make a diamond from a person. Similar to the time it took to make a baby.

Blue diamonds. Vera had at least two.

So there were maybe two other husbands – on ice.

Jamieson had never seen a lace doily used for this purpose before. Not even a plastic one. Finn had set the skull down on the table under the picture window. Resting atop the doily, it grinned into the room. It looked quite out of place beside the porcelain teacup with the pretty forget-me-not pattern.

"There's the problem of identification," said Jamieson.

"No problem," said Gus. "I'd know him anywhere."

Jamieson turned around sharply from her study of the skull. "How?"

"That front tooth there. That tooth."

Jamieson turned back to the skull, puzzled. There was nothing remarkable about the front tooth. Just a tooth. No particular marks of decay.

"What is it about the tooth?"

"It's missin'."

"Oh, the one that isn't there." *Gus could be exasperating. What could she possibly mean?* "If it isn't there, how could you know it?"

"It was gold. I bet that's why it's missin'."

What Gus was saying still didn't make a lot of sense to Jamieson, but her police instincts alerted to the word gold. *A gold tooth. Something of value. Taken? Or lost?*

Jamieson moved closer to the table. Scanned the skull, without touching it, though Lord knows it had certainly been bashed about a lot since the man had died.

Died – how?

"Roger Murray. He'll have been kilt. Shot dead by Orwell Crane as I allus expected. For the tooth."

Killed – for a tooth? Even a gold one?

It was as if Gus could read Jamieson's mind. She kept answering her mental questions.

"I should say it wasn't all the tooth. Bad blood between those families for generations. Fights about land, about women, about fishing territory. And about the tooth. The tooth did belong to Orwell in the first place."

"What?" Jamieson turned from the skull to stare at Gus in disbelief.

Gus rocked and nodded. It was as if she were saying: "I know."

"That tooth was in Orwell's mouth first. Then he lost it in a bet to Roger. Dentist took it out of Orwell, re-shaped it, then stuck it in Roger's mouth. Any time those two was together Orwell couldn't take his eye off that tooth. Sometimes you thought he was going to rip it right out of Roger's mouth." Gus had been concentrating on knitting the heel of the sock. Now she looked up.

"Reckon he did, in the end. That day they went out together in the storm. Never could figure why they did that – if one didn't force the other." She shook her head and looked at the skull.

"Orwell came back. Roger didn't. Don't think Orwell ended up with the tooth. We never saw it on him after."

"Is this Orwell still alive?" Jamieson's policing instincts were on alert.

Gus let out a big guffaw and slapped her thigh, sending the knitting that was resting there onto the floor.

"Oh, no," she said when she finally straightened up. "Gone within the month after Roger. Abscessed tooth. Went rotten on him. Got an infection. Died. What do they call that?"

Jamieson raised an eyebrow.

"Irony?"

"Yeah, that'll be it. Fittin' anyroad."

Gus rocked her chair a couple of times, contemplating.

"You want to take a look through his things, see if you can find that tooth, Wally Fraser's got all Orwell's stuff in his shed. They were cousins. I 'spec Frasers had a good look through it for anything valuable, but I think they thought like we all did, that Roger had gone down with his tooth."

"There's no telling what happened with the tooth," Finn finally spoke up.

"And you are?" There was a note of disdain in Jamieson's tone and look.

"Finn Finnegan. Hy's half-brother. I'm a forensic anthropologist."

The disdainful look was replaced by one approaching respect. Confusion, too. McAllister had a brother?

"Can you date this skull?"

"Not to a year. And not to a ballpark without the proper equipment, but I can tell you it's modern rather than ancient."

"How?"

"Fillings, for one thing. Silver amalgam."

"Anything else?"

"Well, he didn't die yesterday. There's wear and tear on the skull."

"Could it be Roger Murray as Gus claims?"

"Don't see why not. Fifty years old is not inconceivable for this artifact."

"Any way of knowing for sure?"

"No."

"None?"

"Short of DNA profiling, and I doubt you'd convince the brass to go for it in a case this old, none. We forensic people tend to specialize in casting doubt rather than affirming absolutely, I'm sorry to say."

"If we found the gold tooth?"

"Well, if the tooth fit..." Finn grinned. Jamieson did not smile back.

"And the hole in the head?"

Finn stuck his finger right into it. Jamieson opened her mouth, ready to object, then thought better of it when she saw he was examining it. He was a professional, after all, as near to one as they'd get at The Shores.

"Happened too long ago to really tell anything. This could be a bullet hole." His finger circled the inside of the hole. "But it's too smooth to say, possibly worn and made larger by the water, the waves, the sand, all the stuff it's come in contact with." He pulled his finger out of the hole.

"If it is a bullet hole, there are signs that this is where it entered. The skull has two tables. When a bullet enters the skull it creates a 'punched-out' hole in the outer table, with sharp edges. You can see a suggestion of that here. Hard to see the inner table, but close examination might find the beveled look of the exit wound."

"Might?"

Finn nodded. "There's not much to go on. No soft tissue to tell us anything. No suspect. No crime scene. No fingermarks."

"No DNA?"

"Problematical with bone, and for what? What police department or forensic lab would touch this? It's not just a cold case, it's freezing, if this is the guy you think it is. And I can tell you that skull's been floating around the shore for decades. This happened long ago, to people who would be dead now if they weren't already." He grinned at the idiocy of what he'd just said. "You've got yourself a heritage murder. Motives and modus operandi buried in the past. So what's the point?"

"Justice is the point," said Jamieson stiffly. "Justice should be served."

"Don't see how it can be. But if you want to pursue it, I say you've got to I.D. the fellow first."

"I already told her who it is." There was an edge of irritation, annoyance in Gus's tone. She leaned forward and pointed at the skull. "Roger Murray. Know him anywhere. Even sitting on my doily without his gold tooth."

Jamieson sighed. It was hard enough keeping track of modern murders at The Shores. She certainly didn't need a heritage murder.

But it appears that's what she had got.

In the form of a skull on Gus Mack's table.

Grinning at her from the past.

"Just been checking out Vera's contribution to our heritage celebrations."

Hy had not bothered to knock on Jamieson's door. She'd waltzed right in and plunked herself down in a hard chair beside Jamieson's desk. Jamieson was writing her weekly report for headquarters. She had to produce hard copy because the Internet connection was iffy and insecure. At one time, suspecting no one ever read her reports, Jamieson had been sending in blank papers, until she got found out. Now, dutifully, she submitted the boring details of everyday crime in the village. Boys caught peeing on the hall steps. Ninety-eight-year-old Willard Cole caught driving without a license – he wasn't allowed one anymore. Olive MacLean reporting the theft of ice cream from her freezer.

Sometimes Jamieson longed for a good murder.

"What?"

"Vera's contribution to the 200th."

"Yes?"

"Two hundred years of husband."

Jamieson wrinkled her brow.

"I've seen them."

"You've told me that before."

"No, I mean really seen them. Up close and plastic."

"Plastic?"

"Yes, human bodies plasticized. Her husbands."

Jamieson put down her pen and pushed her chair out from the desk. Hy had her attention.

"Her husbands?"

"Well, three of them anyway. The plasticized ones." Hy's tone became more serious. "And then there's the live one. Cyril. At least I think he's still alive. " She leaned forward, urgent. "I think she's killing him."

Jamieson let out a heavy sigh.

"I think he's dying."

"I understand he's an old man. Not well."

"Well, yes, but…" Hy didn't want to say anything about the lime Jello. Or the diamonds. Keep these in her back pocket until proven. Jamieson would never believe her if she brought them up now.

"And how did you manage to see them? Did Mrs. Gloom show them to you?"

"Yes…actually."

Jamieson raised an eyebrow. There was something in Hy's tone. Something lacking the ring of truth.

"She did?"

"Yes. The second time. I've seen them twice," Hy said stubbornly. "So I know what I've seen."

"The second time? When was the first?"

Hy said nothing.

"You were in her house?"

Hy nodded.

"Without her knowledge?"

Hy nodded again. Then opened her mouth to speak.

Jamieson held up a hand.

"Don't say anything. I really would have to charge you if I knew about this." Jamieson was constantly threatening to charge Hy, but never had yet.

"What were you doing there, anyway?" It was really a rhetorical question, laced with disbelief and exasperation. "No, don't answer," she said quickly. "I don't want to know."

"I had to see them. Had to. And I was right…"

"The means justify the end?"

"Yes. I had to know."

"Good. Excellent. There's a firm foundation for an investigation."

Jamieson picked up her pen.

"She's not an artist, you know. I've Googled her. There's nothing."

Hy wrinkled her brow. What could she say to convince Jamieson to do something, anything?

"You could ask to see her artwork."

"Why would I do that?"

"Because it's not art. It's bodies. Don't you think you should be on top of any bodies floating around the neighbourhood?"

"I hope not on top of them."

"Jamieson, please. Do this for me. I'm not steering you wrong.

Have I ever?"
 "A bit askew at times."
 "Just speak to the woman, that's all I ask."
 Silence. Then it came to Hy.
 "Speak to Moira. Ask her what she's seen."

Chapter Thirty

Moira wouldn't speak. She was struck dumb by being questioned by Jamieson in an official capacity. She didn't know what she should say – about Vera, about Hy, about the lime Jello.

"So nothing unusual?" Jamieson closed her notebook.

Moira shook her head.

"I haven't seen any of them."

"Them?"

"She calls them her boys." Moira wanted to offer up something to Jamieson. She was also hoping that, given a little tidbit, Jamieson would leave. Her stomach was giving her trouble again, and she didn't want to bring that up with the police.

Next, Jamieson dropped in on Vera Gloom. She lunged right in when Vera came to the door.

"There's some wild talk going around the neighbourhood." Jamieson's tone was apologetic.

"Yes?" Vera's eyebrows darted upward. She frowned.

"I'd just like to be able to set the record straight."

"What record?"

"People are talking of…of…bodies in your upstairs rooms."

Vera smiled her Vera smile, nasty and dismissive.

"Yes, I have three lifelike bodily representations here. Works of art. My former husbands."

"Works of art and former husbands? Both?"

"Yes. Preserved in plastic. Perfectly legal, I assure you. The bodies were used in medical programs for study of the heart, the brain and musculature. When they were finished with them, what was I to do? None will fit in a standard coffin, they can't be cremated, so I have kept them at home. They want for nothing."

They want for nothing. Odd.

Vera did not offer to show Jamieson the bodies, and Jamieson didn't ask. It was unusual, weird, creepy, but not, so far as she could tell, illegal.

And that's what she told Hy who'd been spying on her from Ian's, and came out just as Jamieson returned to the police house.

"So I've been over and it appears to be all above board."

"Did you see Cyril?"

"He was sleeping."

"Did you see them?"

"No. She didn't offer and I didn't ask."

"Did she say they were preserved for medical purposes?"

"Yes."

"At the time. But here they are, not serving any medical purpose."

"I don't think there are any laws against what she's doing. I think it's perfectly legal. For one thing, they crossed the border."

"How do you know?"

"Frank. He helped unload them when they arrived."

"So you did go to see Moira? What did she say?"

"Very little. I didn't like to press. She looked quite ill."

If you only knew, thought Hy.

"Okay, it may be legal, but it's weird. What makes it weirder is the husbands. Three of them dead, in mighty quick succession I would say. All in their eighties and she just scraping sixty."

Jamieson shrugged.

That wasn't a crime either.

Was it?

Hy's FB Status: The best bodies from which to make a "mummy elixir," a highly desirable health potion in the Orient, are young, virile men, especially gingers.

Likes: 9

Comments: Red Island could be a major supplier. We're full of gingers.

"Poison?" Moira had felt the effects, but she still didn't get it. "But I made it myself, out of sealed boxes."

"And the water?"

"The water? Out of the well, of course. There was bottled water in the fridge, but that was for her. For drinking."

"We need a sample of that well water."

"Easy enough," said Hy. "Moira, when you go there tomorrow, bring some water back."

It sounded easy enough, but it didn't turn out that way.

Vera chose that day not to take a nap, and to busy herself around the kitchen, so that she was always there when Moira came in, hoping to get a water sample. She had no idea how much was needed, but assumed the more the better. She had a jam jar in her apron pocket, but it was hard to conceal – especially when she dropped a spoon, leaned down to pick it up, and the jar fell out. Vera whipped around when she heard it clatter to the floor.

She said nothing. Just raised an eyebrow. High.

Moira stared at the jar. Paralyzed.

"Yours?" Vera's eyebrow was stuck on high.

Moira nodded, mute. Still paralyzed.

"Well, pick it up." Vera said nothing more for several moments. Moira hoped the incident was ended.

"You were looking, perhaps, for a sample of my water?"

Moira flushed bright red.

"No. Of course not."

"Of course not." The eyebrow was down, the mouth had settled into a grim line. "Then what?"

"Some Jello. I just wanted to take home some Jello."

Vera marched over to the cupboard, and swung the doors open.

"Help yourself." She tossed out a few boxes in Moira's direction. Moira fumbled to catch them and dropped the jar again.

Contempt sketched across Vera's face.

Moira left that day with some boxes of lime Jello, but no water.

She saw Hy's bicycle outside Ian's, so she stopped in. Finn was there, too.

"Give me that anyway." Finn inspected the box Moira handed him, flipping it over on all sides and fingering the seams. It appeared to be factory sealed. Still –

"You never know." He slipped the box into his knapsack. Moira left.

"We'll have to get some water from the well." Hy looked at Finn and Ian.

"Tonight."

"Are you nuts?" Ian thought he'd done his bit with the search of the house.

"Well, that lets you out on the clandestine bit. Finn, are

you in?"

"Wouldn't miss it."

"What about Dot?"

"She won't want to be left out. She could be our eyes and ears."

"The lookout."

"I'll go ask her."

Finn always grabbed any chance to see Dot, thought Hy. He'd have moved in with her by now if Gus had allowed it.

When the door closed behind him, Hy turned to Ian.

"You have to divert Jamieson."

"Why?"

"Because she has a clear view of the house. She could see us."

"No, I mean, why me? Why not Finn?"

Even though Ian now knew Finn was Hy's brother, a fine thread of jealousy still ran through him. Jealousy of anyone who could divert her attention. Even of Dot.

"Because he's already going to the well. And because, if you invite Jamieson over, she'll come."

"Invite her over? Couldn't I just drop in on her?"

"That wouldn't stop her looking out her window."

"Invite her over – why? What for?"

Exasperating. The word might have been coined for him.

"I don't know…your forensics course…"

"It's over." He looked glum.

"She aced it," Hy guessed, correctly.

His frown deepened.

"You didn't."

"Not quite." He ran a hand through the rapidly disappearing hair on the top of his head. Perplexed. How had Jamieson scored better than he had? They had done everything together.

"Invite her for dinner then."

He looked appalled. Because the idea excited him more than he liked to admit. Because he didn't know what he'd cook. Because he didn't know what he'd say. Do.

Dinner with Jamieson. What would it be like? Business – or pleasure? He flushed to the roots of his fast disappearing hair.

Hy noticed. How could she not? She knew Ian was sweet on Jamieson. It didn't bother her. She couldn't see it going anywhere. It was the hair. Raven black. And the porcelain skin, of course. Who wouldn't be attracted? But Jamieson… and Ian…in a clinch? Hy smiled at the image.

"But what would I…? I can't…"

"Finn will cook the meal. Here. In advance. All you'll have to do is warm it up." Hy gave him a mischievous look. "And her. If you can."

"But I have to invite her in the first place. What if she doesn't come?"

"Oh, she'll come."

Ian might not know what the forensic course and Jamieson's regular morning visits were all about. Jamieson might not even know herself. But Hy did.

"She'll come," she repeated, with added conviction. "Piece of cake."

"Can I email?" Ian had been stewing over how he would invite Jamieson, and had just brightened at the thought that he could do it online.

"No. Phone. For one thing, you know her Internet sucks. Isn't that why she's here all the time? She might not get your message, and then where will we be?"

"Okay. Okay." He still looked glum. Then he brightened.

"What's for supper?"

"No idea. Probably something Italian. That's Finn's specialty."

Hy was so caught up in the plan to get a sample of Vera's well water, all thoughts of the mystery skull were swept from her mind and she didn't tell Ian about it as she normally would have.

When Hy left, Ian's brow furrowed at the prospect of the task ahead – phoning Jamieson. He looked over at Jasmine, sleeping, her parrot beak tucked into her wing. Too bad she couldn't carry on the conversation for him.

It was a conversation that didn't turn out to be the "piece of cake" Hy had predicted. In spite of Hy's certainty that Jamieson would jump at an invitation from Ian, it took some persuasion.

When he phoned, Jamieson was thinking about the skull. She had left it at Gus's. She didn't really know what to do with it. Take it back to the police house? And when it was at the police house? What then?

Finn had clinched it by offering to have a more professional look at it, though he warned his resources were limited.

In a way, Jamieson had brought the skull home with her. It might be sitting on that doily at Macks', but it was very much on Jamieson's mind. Another murder at her door. Granted, an old murder, probably dating back to before she was born, certainly before she became a police constable. Still, a murder that might be solved.

So, when Ian phoned, and made his request, her thoughts were far away. *How long had it been rolling around on the shore? Was that a gunshot wound? Had there been a murder at sea?*

"What?" she said in answer to his invitation. She hadn't heard a word. She couldn't have processed it if she had. He asked again. This time she heard the words, but she didn't understand what he was saying. *Had he said, "Come to dinner"?*

Surely not.

But he had. And, in an agony of self-doubt, he repeated it one more time.

"Dinner?" she responded finally.

Roger Murray. Could it be Roger Murray? Could an old skull, knocking about the shore for half a century, be identified as easily as that? By the untrained eye of Gus Mack?

"Yes. Dinner." He almost stuttered, this had become so difficult.

And what of the tooth?

"Oh…well…uh…when?"

The missing gold tooth. A motive for murder?

"Tonight." He tried to keep the exasperation out of his tone, but it was as if she wasn't listening to him, was somewhere else, thinking about something else.

That was true, but Jamieson dragged herself enough into the moment to find Ian's invitation didn't have the ring of truth to it, to her practiced ear.

Why was Ian now inviting her to dinner? Could there be a reason behind it, an ulterior motive?

"That's a nice invitation, but I had planned to review the forensics course." She'd actually been planning to see if she could get into Wally Fraser's shed, but that wasn't any of Ian's business.

"Review the forensics course? We could do that together. Over dinner."

"Some things are best done alone," she said. "Without sauce on the course material."

"Then do that another night, but come here tonight." Was there a desperate edge to his voice? There was, and she picked up on it.

"Couldn't dinner hold until another night?"

Bodies and Sole

"But it's all made – "

All made? Before the invitation was issued. Made by Ian? Not known for his cooking? It had now become interesting to Jamieson because it was so suspicious.

Roger Murray. She wrote it down on her desk calendar. *Oliver Crane. Wally Fraser.* She made a note of them, too. As if she would forget.

"So, tonight?" She jumped up, drawn suddenly into Ian's world, and walked with the phone to the bathroom. Looked in the mirror. She'd need a shower to lift her straight black hair and give it some fullness. She'd need drying time. People ate at four in The Shores.

"When tonight?" Already she had pulled off a sock with one hand, clasping the phone with the other.

"I thought eight o'clock." Ian had heard interest spark in Jamieson's voice. He felt on surer ground now.

Plenty of time. She stopped hopping around as she yanked off the second sock.

"Alright," she said.

A real dinnertime. Not The Shores standard of four. Interesting. What would they eat? What would they talk about?

What would they do?

"See you then, then." Ian was positively cheery, although, once off the phone, he began to immediately worry where supper was.

Jamieson was preparing for a shower and what she had already begun to think of as her date with Ian, but her thoughts had turned back to Roger Murray. Roger Murray and Orwell Crane, and her mind had begun exploring Wally Fraser's shed.

Chapter Thirty-One

When Hy got back to Macks', Dot announced that the mission she and Finn had dubbed "waterfall" couldn't take place until midnight.

"Why midnight?" Hy asked.

"Isn't that the official time for clandestine events?" Finn grinned, as he sped out the door, Ian's dinner in hand. He'd made a big vegetarian lasagna.

"Moonset," said Dot, who had a mind for these things. "Darkest. Best take no chances."

"True," Hy nodded. "The well is fairly close to the house and we won't have any cover there."

She and Dot sat down to eat the lasagna Finn had left them. When they finished, she looked at her watch. Eight o'clock. Maybe Jamieson wouldn't be there yet. She should phone Ian and warn him he was going to have to play host for a while.

Jamieson arrived promptly, her porcelain skin flushed a flattering pink by the cool night air – and something else?

Anticipation? That was certainly in her eyes. The aroma of a fine Italian meal filled her nostrils. Ian? Cooking this? For her?

Jamieson was just about to say something.

Ian's cell phone rang, playing "She Blinded Me With Science."

He snatched it up, grateful for the distraction. He had been at a loss for words and had no idea Jamieson had been prepared to fill the gap.

He looked at the screen.

Hy. Rescue? Complication?

"Yup," he said.

"Is she there?"

He crushed the phone against his ear, turned his back on Jamieson and walked a few steps out of the kitchen so she wouldn't overhear.

"Yes."

"You're going to have to keep her there for a few hours."

"A few…how many?"

"Four."

"Four?" Ian forgot to keep his voice down, and Jamieson could hear him clearly.

Four what? she wondered.

"At least."

"That's a long time."

Four. Four hours. What's this about?

"Well, the moon's still lighting the sky. We have to wait until it sets. It'll be midnight or later before we can do it."

Ian groaned.

"What will we do?"

"I don't care. Kiss her if you have to."

He turned back toward Jamieson. She had slipped out of her jacket. She usually wore no-wrinkle shirts or sweaters. She was wearing a silk blouse. Static made it cling to her.

"Okay. Bye." He put the phone down and watched Jamieson pulling the clinging blouse away from her skin.

This might not be too bad, after all.

Hy's FB Status: A burning corpse produces more electricity than a 120 volt battery. Three Swedish cities get ten percent of their power from crematoria.

Likes: 14

Comments: Gives new meaning to body heat.

Dead clever.

They were dressed all in black. Hy. Finn. And Dot. Moving as quietly as they could in the night. Trying not to brush against the rose bushes that were everywhere.

There was one light on – in a room on the second floor. Otherwise the house was in darkness. The one light, though, was disturbing. It made Dot hang back.

Hy grabbed her arm and pulled her forward.

"We'll see her before she'll ever see us," she whispered.

Hy led the way. She knew exactly where the well was. So did everybody at The Shores. Everyone in the village knew where everyone's well was, and a lot more besides.

Even though Hy knew where it was, the well pipe was hard to locate in the dark, and she tripped over it, landing in an ungainly position, with arms and legs in all the wrong places.

The light in the house went out. It was then they realized it had been providing the only illumination they had to see and remove the well pipe cover.

Hy found the first nut by feel, and, by trial and error, selected the right fit in her wrench set. She tried to budge the nut. Not a chance. She was glad Finn was there to do it. But they didn't come easy. One down. Three to go.

The light went back on in the house.

The meal, dripping with cheese and fresh tomato sauce, was delicious.

"Absolutely delicious," Jamieson said, not for the first time.

"Mmmm…" Ian grunted, his mouth still full.

"And you made it yourself?"

"Mmmm…," He grunted, the full extent of his conversation at the moment. She didn't believe him. For one thing, the dish was from Hy's set. Not that Hy could have cooked it either. Maybe could have, but highly unlikely that she would have. Hy hated to cook. She'd have to have an ulterior motive to do so.

Ulterior. Motive. Just why am I here?

"Who called you earlier? Was it Hy?"

Ian pointed to his full mouth as an excuse for not responding. Jamieson persisted, like a dentist trying to make a patient speak with a mouth wide open and full of instruments.

"What was that about four hours? What's going on? What's she up to?"

Ian turned bright red. He felt the heat in his cheeks. Jamieson didn't miss it. She'd taken courses in body language.

"Four hours. I've been here over two. Are you supposed to keep me here another two hours? For what? What is going on?"

"No, no, no, nothing like that. We'd been arguing about moonrises and sets, that's all. She thought she'd found the answer. I'm not sure."

Jamieson wasn't sure either, but she went along with it, for now. She was certain that Ian was supposed to keep her there, for some reason, for four hours. She was just as sure that Hy was involved, quite likely masterminding the operation, whatever it was. Nothing to do with the skull, she assumed. Maybe more of that nonsense about Mrs. Gloom and her dead husbands.

Relax and enjoy the evening.

A nasty streak in Jamieson spoke: *McAllister shouldn't mind if I borrow her boyfriend for the evening.*

She knew that Ian was interested – slightly – in her, at least he liked her hair, her skin. Both were better than good. She sometimes felt Ian wanted to reach out and smooth down her hair, or stroke her cheek.

When they had finished the meal, and Ian had chucked the dishes in a sink already brimming with dirty dishes, such a moment came.

They were sitting on the couch, quite close, and he reached over and touched her hair.

"So lovely," he said, then dropped his hand and took a sip of the wine that had flowed into their cups all evening.

And he's in his, she thought. *His cups. Don't take it seriously.* He was clearly attracted to her, but she knew his obsession was Hy. *This could get messy.*

She was completely unprepared for his next move. He undid the clasp that held her hair back in a long black ponytail. It fell forward in a curtain obscuring her face. With one finger, he slipped it back over her shoulder.

Jasmine screeched. She didn't like any woman, except Hy, getting close to Ian.

Ian appeared ready to ignore the bird, and leaned forward, about to plant a kiss on Jamieson's smooth white cheek.

She held up a hand and pushed him back.

"Don't do that." *So much for borrowing the boyfriend.*

Jasmine's screeches, which had spiraled upward and filled

the air with a sound as piercing as a smoke alarm, ebbed off.

"Kiss you? I thought you would like it."

"Not like that, I don't." *He wasn't trying to kiss her. He was stalling for time.*

"What do you mean?"

"I mean. Not like that. Not unless you mean it." Four hours, she was thinking. It was a set-up.

"I did mean it."

"I don't think so, and when you think about it, you won't think so either. So, don't do it unless you mean it…"

Ian was confused. Truth was, he didn't know whether he had meant it or not. It was a nice thought, but Jamieson wasn't Hy.

Hy was the elephant in the room, thought Jamieson. And there was another animal species keeping her and Ian apart. The parrot.

Jamieson bet that Hy had counted on Jasmine to guard her ground.

A figure came to the window.

The three shrank down, trying to be invisible behind the rose bushes. They hardly dared breathe. Hy was getting pins and needles in her left foot and right hand, where she put the pressure to hold her steady.

The figure – Vera it must be – closed the curtain and the light went out again.

The three relaxed.

The light went on.

Tense.

Off.

Relax.

"Jesus." Hy slumped onto the ground. "Will she make up

her mind?"

It took a long time to get the nuts and bolts undone and the cap off the well pipe. They had a long coil of rope with a jar attached to it to lower into the water.

Finn eased it down silently.

Down.

Down.

Down.

The rope uncoiled quickly. There were only a few loops left, and still the jar was going down, with no sound of water.

Down.

Down.

Down.

Down to the last loop. They tensed.

Splash. It hit water, with just a few inches left.

Finn hauled it up carefully, so as not to spill the contents. He handed the jar to Hy, and began to screw the nuts back in place.

"Damn," he said, his hand searching in the grass.

"I've lost the last one. I should have put them in my pocket. They were right here on the ground." He continued feeling around. Hy and Dot joined him, but had no luck.

"Leave it," said Hy, finally. "No one will notice. Or if they do, they won't suspect."

They were so anxious to get away, it was hard not to run. But they took it slowly, quietly, Finn holding the precious jar of water. Hy didn't trust herself with it. Nor would Finn and Dot have, had they known how clumsy she was.

"Nearly four hours now." Jamieson looked at her watch. "Can you tell me yet what this is all about? Why you're meant to keep me here?"

Ian was flustered. It was clear Jamieson knew it was a ploy, just not what it was about. He couldn't tell her and betray Hy, but he felt bad about concealing the truth from Jamieson.

"Well…," he said, and that's the only clue he would give. He'd said the word. He'd been honest. If she didn't pick up on it…

She didn't, but she decided to toss him a bone. A skull. See if he knew. Maybe create trouble of her own.

"Is it something to do with the skull?"

He looked genuinely shocked.

"The skull? What skull?"

He clearly didn't know about it. McAllister hadn't told him. Strange. It must mean she was too occupied with something else, whatever it was she was up to tonight, to keep him in the loop. She had a sudden, panicked thought.

Was McAllister raiding Wally Fraser's shed?

Jamieson was tempted to leave and go check, then thought better of it. The shed was close to the Frasers' house and Wally spent most of his evenings out there, smoking. McAllister wouldn't have been able to sneak in. Jamieson relaxed.

Or did it have something to do with her obsession with the Sullivan house?

She told Ian about the skull. They spent the rest of the evening talking about it, tying the limited amount they knew about forensics to what Finn had said, anxious to find out what more he might have discovered.

Jamieson had allowed herself a few hours of private life, a few hours with a borrowed man, but the conversation had made her itchy to be back on duty. Besides, any involvement with Ian was bound to be unsatisfactory. McAllister would always stand between them.

Jamieson looked at the digital clock on the coffee table.

"Looks like our four hours are up."

Ian was surprised. The past hour had flown by like ten minutes.

He smiled and helped her up off the couch, gripping her hand in his, their eyes meeting in a companionable warmth. It had turned out to be a good evening.

Her hair was still loose, shining in the lamplight, swaying in a curtain across her back. She pulled it back and clasped it, her breasts outlined by the silk blouse.

Ian had to turn away, because he liked what he saw way too much.

He walked Jamieson to the door and began to open it, when he spied three people coming down Shipwreck Hill.

Finn. Hy. Dot.

Jamieson had turned to say good night. Ian shut the door quickly and he lied.

"I do mean it this time," he said. He grabbed Jamieson by the shoulders, pulled her close and kissed her – just as the trio was going by.

Long and deep, he kissed Jamieson. He had to give them time. Time to get past the door. Time to get down the hill. Time to turn the corner and be out of sight. He didn't know how much time that actually was. His brain was trying to follow their footsteps, to estimate, but he got lost in the kiss.

Sank deep in it.

He enjoyed it.

So did she.

Hy did not, when she saw it through the window.

Backfire. Big backfire.

Because when Hy was out of sight and Ian no longer had to kiss Jamieson to distract her, he kissed her again.

And again.

The skies opened. Thunder rolled up the shore. Rain drilled down on the three dressed in black as they ran for shelter, Finn hugging a jar of liquid death to his chest; Hy nourishing a small hurt in hers.
Every contact leaves a trace.

Chapter Thirty-Two

Moira did not look the picture of a happy bride on her wedding day. She'd tried to avoid the lime Jello at Vera's the previous day, but Vera had been suspicious, and so she'd been forced to eat some. And forced to feed some to Cyril as well.

Pathetic, that was. Every time it was the same. His eyes moistening up in what she assumed were tears of frustration. Gripping his mouth closed as she tried to slip the spoon in. Vera's eyes on them both the whole time.

Lime green drool running from the corners of his mouth.

The Jello dropping in blobs onto his chin, sliding into the creases of his jowls and onto the napkin tucked under his chin.

She didn't like feeding him. She felt it made her a poisoner, a murderer, and that made the adrenalin course through her at the thought of her elderly neighbour, the late Elmer Whitehead. She had often given him her leftovers. Last year she'd unloaded red kidney beans that hadn't been boiled long enough, and he'd died. She couldn't be guilty of that again.

But Vera watched her like a hawk.

When Moira brought in Cyril's lunch tray, sans Jello, Vera barked out a command that she bring it.

She fetched it, and when he showed no interest in it, Vera barked again:

"Feed him."

"Feed him?"

"The Jello."

Reluctantly, Moira picked up the spoon. She held it to his closed lips. He refused to open them. His eyes stared into hers. They were saying something.

"Stupid woman." Vera grabbed the spoon from Moira, and forced the Jello into him. He let it spill out of the corners of his mouth and down his chin. Vera forced another spoonful in. And on it went, the lime Jello landing on his chest as often as in his mouth.

Moira retreated to the kitchen, and Vera followed her there.

"Aren't you going to have some?"

"Well, I thought, no…"

Vera whipped open the fridge, hauled out the bowl of Jello and spooned some into a dish for Moira. She shoved it at her.

"Here. Take some."

Reluctantly, Moira did, but refused to finish the bowl.

And now here it was, her wedding day – her third wedding day – and she felt so sick she'd be lucky if she could make it down the aisle, from the back of the hall up onto the stage.

But she was determined, determined that nothing would stop her from exchanging her self-written vows with Frank and becoming his wife, a respectable married woman, someone who was wanted by a man.

It was those thoughts that propelled her down the aisle on the arm of Billy Pride, her sister Madeline's boyfriend. She'd given up on Ian as being bad luck. She'd decided her impure thoughts about him had jinxed her.

Moira was wearing black, an outfit she kept for funerals. The latest *Cosmo* had said black was the chic colour for weddings. It hadn't meant for the bride, but Moira misunderstood. Besides, black was safe. If she threw up, it wouldn't ruin the garment. And she was very close to doing that, every inch of the way.

It was not a very long distance, but it took time. Moira had to stop frequently as waves of nausea gripped her.

Frank, up on the stage, looking down on his bride, wondered if she was going to bolt on him. That's what it looked like every time she stopped, her eyes darting desperately in the direction of the bathroom that was also the direction of the door.

But she made it with Hy and Madeline, her bridesmaids, leading the way.

The Justice of the Peace said a few words and then it was the turn of the bride and groom to pledge their troth. There was a hush. The whole village had been waiting to see what Frank and Moira had written.

"I take you to be my husband till death us do part."

"I take you to be my wife till death us do part."

That was it? That's what the glances around the room said. There was some grumbling before the justice pronounced the two married, and then half-hearted applause.

Moira made a beeline for the toilet.

She didn't come out until the guests were gone.

They'd consumed their tea and cake, and, despairing of the bride appearing, or of someone popping open a bottle of bubbly, they all left, more disappointed than any of them had ever been in a wedding.

The groom, who had waited so long to taste Moira's charms, was going to be the most disappointed of all.

By the time Moira got over feeling nauseous, they would be

almost an old married couple. And Frank would be considering taking up again with his lady customers.

But the marriage had been a good trade-off. The muffins were great, and he was now master of a sweet little property at The Shores, fast becoming the most popular tourist destination on Red Island. The sweetest property. And the sourest wife.

There was no traditional wedding night.

Hy's FB Status: A woman in England sent her husband winging off into the next world. She had his ashes packed in gun cartridges. Then she and friends went on a shooting party at an estate in Scotland. Her late mate bagged over 100 birds before he was well and truly done.
Likes: 0
Comments: She should be shot.

Jamieson headed to Frasers' for an informal investigation.

She told Wally she needed to look through Orwell Crane's things. She didn't say why – just that it was part of a police investigation. If she had to, she'd get a warrant. She didn't have to. Wally didn't mind letting Jamieson into his shed. He was proud of it. A place for everything and everything in its place. His John Deere mower had pride of place – smack in the centre of the shed. It was polished to a showroom shine, looking as if it had never come near a blade of grass. Sadly – and it made Wally frown to think of it – it had been used very little this rainy summer.

Taking her cue from Wally, Jamieson hugged the wall around the tractor, careful not to brush it with the fabric of her uniform.

The back of the shed was lined with shelves. Deepest in, as one would expect of artifacts a good fifty years old, were

Orwell Crane's things. A large antique trunk and a shelf of boxes. Precious little to show for a whole life.

Precious? Was there something precious in there?

"Don't know why I kep' 'em really. Not just Orwell's. Quite a few relations in here. Aunts and uncles, spinsters and bachelors. Seemed a shame to throw anything out. They do take up a bit of space. But being kin 'n all, I thought I better. Someone might pop up who was closer kin, and what could I say – I'd recycled it all?"

Jamieson murmured agreement. They stood, looking at Orwell's things, Jamieson hesitant to dive in.

"Go ahead," said Wally. "I'll leave you to it. Just be careful of Johnny on your way out."

Johnny?

Wally grinned, patted the ride-on and winked at Jamieson.

Fonder of the tractor than his wife, I bet. It was certainly better-looking. But not as tough. Gladys was a bulldog of a woman.

Jamieson started with the trunk. She didn't really know what she was looking for. A gold tooth? Not likely. Besides, they hadn't even identified the skull as Roger Murray, although Jamieson wouldn't be surprised if Gus were right.

The trunk was full of clothing, mostly in need of a good wash. There were boots, shoes, outerwear, but nothing of any interest. At least not to her.

Whitey had come up from Macks', and was now sniffing and rolling about in the clothing on the floor.

Jamieson looked in the boxes next. In the first one, she found a series of threatening, misspelled notes from Roger Murray to Orwell. They weren't dated, but, by the nature of the threats, appeared to be in chronological order, with the last a taunt

Bodies and Sole

to go out on a boat in a storm together, and find out who was "the better man."

If Gus was right about the identity of the skull, they had done just that.

She set the notes aside. They could be evidence if this case were ever opened.

Another box revealed a set of mismatched dishes. There was one full of papers that Jamieson rustled through carelessly. Bills. Unpaid or disputed. A high school diploma. A few ragged, creased photographs of men and their boats. *The family album?* There was a box of ancient tools and fishing tackle, and not much else.

Firearms?

"No, Orwell never had a gun, not a hunting rifle, nothing." Wally had come back to see how she was doing and was closing up the shed on his beloved "Johnny."

"Not a man for killing, in spite of what they said."

"And they said?"

"Well, that he had killed Roger Murray out there." Wally looked toward the shore. "Never believed it myself. Orwell said Roger fell over the side. Drunk, probably. Orwell sure was when he got back. Actin' awful funny. Course, you couldn't blame him. He was near drowned."

"And Roger?"

"Roger?"

"Did he have a gun?"

"Did he? Whole collection of guns. Left to his nephew."

"Who's his nephew?"

"Jared MacPherson. Thought everyone knew that. Course, he wasn't his nephew then. Wasn't born yet. But he got the guns."

Jamieson groaned inwardly. Jared MacPherson. The local

scumbag. Jared MacPherson, who seemed always to be involved in some way with whatever dirty business was going on in The Shores. And now this. On the sidelines of a heritage killing.

Jamieson thanked Wally and got his permission to take the threatening notes. Whitey had jumped into a box and was clawing the contents, shredding the paper bills of a half-century ago. Jamieson pried her out and headed down The Island Way to Jared's house. He'd recently scored some cedar shingles in some shifty deal, and had just finished shingling half of the house. The bottom half. Then he'd run out – of supplies and energy. The plan had been to open the house as the only square house with a mansard roof in all of The Shores. Charge admission. Rake it in.

Killer, Jamieson thought when Jared opened the door to her knock. She thought he was responsible or implicated in a couple of deaths in the village, only she couldn't prove it.

There was a cigarette hanging out of his frown at seeing her. He held the door open just a crack and grunted for his "hello."

"I understand you inherited Roger Murray's gun collection."

His eyes narrowed, wondering what she was after. He took a haul on the cigarette, removed it from his mouth, and threw it at her feet.

She stepped on it and ground it out. It was meant as an aggressive gesture. A warning.

"And if I did?" A challenge.

"One of his guns may be a murder weapon."

"Nothing to do with me." Jared was always fast on the defensive.

"I know. You weren't even alive then."

"Left them to his sister's first-born son." He straightened up a bit. Pride at being first at something. "First born. Me. But I never got them. Parents sold them before I was old enough to 'herit them. Said it was for my education. But it was for booze."

The apple doesn't fall far from the tree.

"How many guns were there?"

"Twelve."

"That's it?" Jamieson got the feeling that Jared was lying about something. He was fidgeting, his hands gripping at the sides of his trousers.

"That's it." He pulled a pouch of tobacco out of his shirt pocket and began rolling another cigarette.

Jamieson stood for a moment, watching his hands shake. Then she thanked him and left. The sweet smell of marijuana followed her down the front walk.

I should bust him, she thought. But she wasn't going to. She could spend all her time – valuable police time – busting Jared. As far as she knew – and she did keep an eye on it – Jared had only personal stash right now. He wasn't dealing. Besides, she had a hunch Jared knew something she wanted to know, so she wasn't going to get too fussy about a joint.

Chapter Thirty-Three

Moira was just glad to be married.

It hadn't been a dream wedding out of *Cosmo,* but at least there had been a wedding this time.

She and Frank were well and truly married. Almost. The marriage had not been consummated. The first night, it was nausea. The second night, lingering nausea. The third night to the eighth night she had her "monthly visitor." And then he stopped asking. They rolled onto their own sides of the bed, backs to each other.

Everyone knew. Moira would have been mortified to know that everyone knew that she and Frank had not consummated their marriage. Frank had made no secret of it. He'd complained to anyone who'd listen.

"Perhaps someone should tell her it could render the marriage invalid." Ian suggested to Hy one morning when she dropped by, minutes after Jamieson left. That had been happening a lot lately. Had it been the kiss? Kisses? Hy hadn't said anything. It was as if she didn't care.

She did, but she didn't care to show her feelings.

"Would you be the one to tell her?"

Ian's eyes opened wide with horror.

"No. Never. Not me."

"Well, don't think I'm going to."

"How about April?"

Hy had just taken a sip of coffee. It came spitting back out of her mouth.

April Dewey had been married to a philandering husband. Though they had six kids, he'd managed to get their marriage annulled. April had broken faith with the church as a result.

Wiping the coffee off her sweater, Hy grinned at Ian.

"No. Not April, either."

"Jamieson?"

For a moment, Hy considered it. "Well, it is a legal matter." She shook her head.

"No. Jamieson could never do it. She certainly wouldn't consider it police business."

"Let it go, then."

"Let it go."

There was a line-up into Gus's kitchen. Word about the skull had spread around the village.

Gladys Fraser had seen Finn take it into the house. When Wally told her Jamieson had been into the shed to look at Orwell Crane's things, she put two and two together. She made a quick call to Olive MacLean to tell her to meet her on the way to Macks'. They bumped into Gus's neighbour, Estelle Joudry, who was heading over, too. She was always on the alert for anything interesting going on at her neighbours' and had also seen the skull go in.

A hired hand on Ben Mack's farm and friend of Jared MacPherson had overheard Annabelle on the phone talking with Hy about the skull. When he went down to Jared's after work for a joint, he told him about the skull and that it was Roger Murray. If there were a gold tooth in it, that rightly belonged to him, Jared figured, and he, too, made his way up to Gus's.

Finn let them in, but he wouldn't let anyone touch the skull.

"Police evidence," he said, although he wasn't sure that it was.

The villagers, singly and in pairs, peered at the skull and debated as to whether it was Roger Murray. The general consensus was that it was. Each remembered a particular feature that marked the skull as belonging to Roger. None of it was scientific, but Finn began to have an image of the man. Finn was a talented amateur artist, and, when everyone had left, sketched out a picture of a man based on the structure of the skull and people's descriptions.

"To the life," Gus judged it. "To the very life. Only thing's missin' is the tooth."

But it wasn't. Not for much longer.

Finn and Hy took the skull home. They weren't sure if they were supposed to move it – Jamieson hadn't issued any specific instructions – but so many people had been to see it at Gus's, they didn't want to leave it there. Besides, Finn would have more time to examine it at Hy's.

They stuck it on the table near Hy's laptop when they got home, and opened a bottle of wine. Without meaning to, they polished off that bottle and another.

"Aren't you supposed to be examining the skull?"

"Time enough," said Finn.

"You're picking up the local dialect."

Finn grinned.

"Happen I am."

Hy threw a pillow at him.

It wasn't long before both fell asleep – Finn in the armchair; Hy on the couch.

Sometime in the middle of the night, Hy woke.

There were two eerie green eyes pulsing at her from across the room. For a moment, she was frozen.

Pulse. Green. Pulse. Green. Eyes alive with malevolence. Whacky? No. Whacky was at her feet. She could feel the warm purr of her.

Then who? What?

She pushed herself into a sitting position.

The pulsing green light had shifted. A grinning mouth.

The skull. Her laptop light pulsing into it and animating it.

Hy got up and blundered in the dark to the table to shift the skull. She knocked it over.

From deep in the arch of the skull came a glint. Hy stood without moving, staring at the spot. The light pulsed again. Again, the glint. She was afraid to move and lose sight of what she thought might be…

It wouldn't be going anywhere. She switched on the overhead light and Finn groaned. She grabbed the skull and peered in through the gap in the mouth.

Nothing.

Finn groaned again and stretched his arms. Hy grabbed a flashlight from beside the front door.

"What's up?" Finn called over, voice thick with sleep. He rubbed his eyes against the harsh overhead light. Hy trained the flashlight inside the skull and stuck her eye in the hole in the mouth.

A glint. A gold glint. Roger Murray – if it were he – may well have hung on to his tooth.

"I think it's the tooth."

"What?" Finn jumped up, wide awake. Hy handed him the skull and the flashlight.

"Look in. Look deep. Stick the flashlight in the right eyehole and twist it upwards. There's something there. Something gold."

"You're right. I think you're right. Lodged in the cranium."

It was late – almost midnight – but they decided to phone Jamieson. There was no answer on her landline, but there was on her cell phone.

"We've found the tooth." That's all he said. And she knew right away.

"The gold tooth? *The* gold tooth?"

"The same." Confidence suffused Finn's soft voice, with its drawling Boston inflection.

While Finn talked, Hy looked out the window to Ian's light on Shipwreck Hill. Flickering light in the living room. Computer light? TV? Candlelight? *Was Jamieson with Ian? This late at night?*

She was. And the candlelight had been flickering before she arrived. It had attracted her. She thought maybe he was giving her a signal. But he wasn't. Not to her. She was disappointed when he opened the door to her. He looked disappointed, too. She was just trying to bury her embarrassment and leave when Finn called.

"I'll be right there."

"I'm coming, too." Ian wanted in on this. He still felt sulky that Hy hadn't told him about the skull. He wanted to show her that his being with Jamieson at this time of night meant nothing. Nothing. She had just showed up. He wouldn't have done anything. He regretted those kisses the other night. Yes, he'd been interested, but not serious.

Jamieson seemed to get the message. She was all business as they jumped into the police cruiser. They were at Hy's in minutes.

"Show me." She burst through the door, surprising Hy. Jamieson was always tentative about the local custom of entering a house without knocking.

Ian entered in her wake.

So she had been with him.

Finn beckoned Jamieson over. He tilted the skull and shone a small flashlight into the main cavity. There was a glint. He directed the light more carefully and held it where it shone brightest on the gold.

A gold tooth. Lodged in the skull. So placed that only chance, not intent, could find it.

"How – ?" Hy, Jamieson and Ian spoke in unison.

"Good question." Finn put the skull right side up and trained a pocket magnifying glass on the tooth.

"With a magnifying glass, you can see that the tooth has taken an impact. Something drove it through the brain and lodged it in the skull. Perhaps you can see if you look closely." He held the skull out to Jamieson. She took hold of it and peered into it.

"A bullet?" Hy suggested.

"That's what I think," said Finn.

"So there were two bullets. One through the temple and…?"

"From the angle, I'd say through the mouth."

"What could that mean?" Jamieson handed the skull and flashlight over to Hy.

"Well, the one that hit the tooth presumably came from a

231

shot in the mouth. Suicide maybe. Or someone trying to make it look like suicide."

"Someone shot him in the mouth, and when that didn't work – maybe the tooth saved him somehow – shot him in the head." Finn stuck a finger into one hole in the skull and then into the other one, and swung it back and forth.

"Or he killed him with the first shot, and shot again for the hell of it."

Jamieson found it disconcerting. Hy found it funny when she told Gus the next day. Gus was not surprised.

"That Orwell allus was a nasty bit of business." Gus looked with satisfaction at the square of the crazy quilt she'd just completed. Her first one, done right.

Worth its weight in gold, she thought.

Chapter Thirty-Four

Jamieson had to conclude that, if the skull belonged to Roger Murray, he'd been killed with his own gun. Then thrown overboard. Hard to say which had claimed him first – drowning or the gunshot wounds, but probably the latter. The two men had been alone in the boat together. Orwell had returned alive. Since neither was here to speak for himself, she had to conclude Orwell killed Roger.

And tossed the gun into the brink after the body.

Case closed.

Or was it?

Moira's ad, "teepee" and all, turned out to be wildly successful. The bookings were flooding in for August, heritage month, and had an overcapacity for the last week of the celebrations. She gave up the double bedroom she and Frank shared, made up a cot for herself in the front room and a cot for Frank in the kitchen.

She thought, as she tucked in the sheets, that at least she would be spared his presence in bed.

It made for a happier, brighter Moira, who now actually glowed like a new bride.

Most people assumed that they'd finally "done it."

They hadn't. Not until Frank cooked up his grand plan.

"It's a great idea, Moira. You'll have more guests than you can handle. And neither of us will have to sleep in the kitchen."

But he wouldn't tell her what his idea was, and she shrugged it off as "fine talk."

Frank went online, and then to town, coming home with parcels, not for others, but for his idea.

He was seen pacing the lot next to the house, a piece of land that, oddly, no one had claimed, but that was unofficially considered to belong to the Toombs. They mowed it. That alone was a claim to ownership.

A knock on the door was unusual, especially as it was the screen door.

Jared MacPherson was on the stoop.

Holding a gun.

Hy opened the door. It gave out the classic screen door squeak of reluctant compliance.

Gun in his fist pointing the way, Jared stomped inside, leaving cakes of clay in the shape of his boot tread on the kitchen tiles.

The door slammed behind him.

Hy was stunned. Not quite afraid, but almost.

Jared grabbed the gun in both hands.

Hy stepped back. Okay. Afraid.

He poked the gun at her.

"What do you suppose I could get for this?"

She opened her mouth. Closed it. Opened it again. Closed it. Unable to speak.

"Well, that Mountie. She was interested. How interested, d'you think? You know her. She's in and out of here all the time."

Still Hy said nothing. She wished Jamieson had prepared her for this, because she had no idea what was going on.

If only Finn were here. But he was out scouring the shore, trying to find more clues to an ancient death.

"Something's been stirred up on the ocean floor," he'd said. "It may wash up more of this mystery." He'd tossed shovels and rakes and buckets into the back of her truck and sped off to the shore.

"This here's the gun kilt Roger Murray."

Jared grinned, revealing teeth stained with nicotine and decay.

Roger has better teeth than he does, she thought.

But she was instantly alert, her interest heightened. *The gun that killed Roger Murray?*

"How do you know?"

"They was all s'posed to be mine. All of Roger's guns. He was my uncle. Mother's brother. Left me twelve guns. They sold the rifles – eleven of them. But this one handgun, they kep' this one because they knew it come back on the boat with Orwell. Without Roger Murray. They was suspicious, I guess. I don't know, but they kep' it and always said it was the gun kilt Roger Murray. That Orwell had slipped it back with the others after the boat ride."

The gun was at Jared's side. He lifted it again and pointed it directly at Hy.

"So whaddya say? What's it worth?"

"What's it worth, to who?"

"You, mebbe. That copper?"

The screen door squeaked. Ian popped his head into the room. He'd come to square things with Hy over Jamieson. Surprise passed across his features at the sight of someone else in the room. Double surprise, laced with shock, when he saw Jared there. A step back when he saw the gun Jared had just pointed at him.

He held up his hands.

"Whoa now, what's all this about?"

"The gun that killed Roger Murray." Hy was relieved that Ian had showed up.

"Really?"

Ian eyed the weapon with interest.

"So he says."

"Can I see?" Ian put a hand forward. Jared pulled back.

"I think I can tell you something about it."

Jared hesitated and then gave up the gun.

Ian turned it over in his hands, stroked the long wood of the handle. Unmistakable.

"If I'm not mistaken, it's an Astral 600. Made by the Spanish for the Germans in World War Two. They did a good job, because they were making them for the Germans. Produced about fifty thousand but only delivered around ten thousand. Sold some more to German police in the 1950s, and a number must have got into civilian hands."

Hy's jaw had dropped.

"How do you know all this? I didn't think you were that interested in firearms."

Jared was eyeing Ian with respect.

"I'm not. But I am interested in World War Two history. You come across a lot of trivial information. And…" Ian's finger stabbed at his head a few times. "It sticks."

"So what's it worth?"

"I don't know. A bit maybe. I'd have to Google it." He sat down at Hy's laptop and, impatient at the slowness of her connection, finally got on the internet. He soon had the answer.

"About six or seven hundred dollars, if you have the holster and the magazines."

"I don't read magazines."

"No, the magazine that holds the cartridges for the gun."

Jared shook his head. "Don't think so."

"Well then, maybe five hundred."

"Not bad."

"Except," Hy drew the word out. "That may be evidence in a crime. A murder."

"Who cares about that anymore?" Jared looked sullen.

"Jamieson, for one."

"I'll help you sell it online if you want." Ian was seeking out potential sites on the laptop.

Greed lit up Jared's eyes.

"But only once you've cleared it with Jamieson," Hy warned.

"Jeez! Why should I clear it with her? She weren't around."

"You've got to clear it with her – and give it to her. I'll have it back to you within an hour," she lied.

Jared stood stubbornly silent, looking at the gun on the table from the sides of his eyes.

His hand came down on it.

"Don't even think of it. If you grab it and run, I'll just tell Jamieson."

Somewhat reluctantly, he handed the gun over to Hy.

He hauled open the squeaky screen door and left. Ian followed, having lost the opportunity to say what he meant to about Jamieson. She was attractive, yes, but she wasn't Hy. Surely Hy knew that.

Shortly after Ian left, Finn came in.

"So did you find anything more down there?"

Finn shook his head.

"No. Nothing. Looked everywhere in the site where we found the skull. Things like this will often come up in multiples – but no. Nothing," he repeated.

All Finn had come back with was a bucket of shells he'd found fascinating.

Just what I need. Hy eyed the bowls filled with shells around the room. Any receptacle soon filled with shells and rocks and driftwood. And now here was Finn adding to the collection.

"Nothing," he said again, shrugged his shoulders and put a kettle on to boil. "So what's the story on that?" Finn was pointing at the gun lying on the harvest table.

"The gun that killed Roger Murray."

"Really?"

Hy smiled, victorious. She picked up the gun.

"Could be. Belonged to Roger. Some people say Orwell shot him with it."

"Where'd you get it?"

"Jared Macpherson." Hy gestured in the general direction of Jared's house. "Local scumbag. Inherited it. Roger Murray was his uncle. Left him twelve guns, including this one."

Hy told him about the bargain she'd struck with Jared.

Finn looked at the clock.

"When was this?"

Hy smiled. "Oh, about half an hour ago."

"Hadn't you better get it back?"

"Jared can't tell time."

Hy's smile grew broader. "Besides, it's not going back to him. Jamieson is bound to keep it for a while. Have a look at it, Finn. Could it actually be the gun that killed Roger Murray?"

Finn sat down and examined the gun.

"Firearms never were my specialty, but I know enough to say this gun is of the right vintage. Other than that, there are too many variables, including the age of the skull, to say anything definitive. Could a gun like this make a hole like that in the skull? Could it have driven the tooth to lodge in the cranium? The answer is yes, to both questions."

Hy looked triumphant.

Finn caught the look. "To say it could have doesn't mean it did. We'd have to have much more specific evidence than we have that it was this gun, and not some other gun similar to it, that caused the wound. We're a long way from having anything conclusive – ever, I'm afraid."

Hy frowned. "What's the point of being a forensic anthropologist if you can't say things conclusively?"

Finn smiled, a small smile. "Exactly my point. I got fed up with the lack of certainty."

Hy hadn't given Cyril much thought. She felt guilty, but what could she do until the forensic evidence came in? And with so much going on? She took the gun up to the police house later and told Jamieson everything she knew about it – what Jared had said, what Finn had said. In turn, Jamieson told Hy about her search of Orwell's things in Wally Fraser's shed.

"Anything interesting?"

"Nothing. Clothes. Dishes. Fishing tackle. Oh, yes, some threatening notes from Roger Murray." Jamieson pointed to some crumpled papers on her desk. Whitey was worrying them with her claws. Jamieson shooed her off the desk. A few of the papers went fluttering down with her.

"Other than that, a box of papers, bills, a few photos. The contents of a junk drawer, really."

She should have known better than to tell Hy anything at all about her visit to the shed. Hy left the police house itching to have a look at Orwell's stuff herself. Maybe she could find what Jamieson might have missed.

All the way down from Shipwreck Hill and onto The Island Way, Hy was scheming as to how she might get Wally to let her in his shed. Padding along behind her was Whacky, a catnip mouse in her mouth. She was trying to give Hy the idea that you feed those you care for. So far, Hy had been annoyingly stubborn about refusing to feed her. The woman seemed to think that because she had two homes already, she didn't need a third.

Chapter Thirty-Five

www.theshores200.com
There have been some strange habitations built at The Shores over the years. One of the strangest – now just a circle of scorched ground on the cape – was a dome that went up overnight – quite a shock to the villagers when they looked out their windows one morning. They didn't like it, not one bit. Until they found out it was one of a very few in North America. It was supposed to last five hundred years. It didn't make five.

Frank had outlined six large circles, with generous amounts of space between them. One after another, around the perimeter of each circle, he erected metal poles, leaning inward.

He ripped open boxes of parachute silk to drape over his structures.

Hy had stopped on her way to Frasers', trying to come up with a way to poke about their shed, but fascinated by whatever it was that Frank was up to. She'd slipped into Gus's, and was watching from the window that had a perfect view of Moira's house and adjacent property. Finn and Dot and Gus were all watching Frank at work, too.

They'd been watching for nearly an hour, wondering what he was doing. Now it was clear.

"Wigwams," said Dot, suddenly realizing.

"Wigwams," Hy repeated the word, realization dawning for her, too, as she said it.

Gus had the same thought at the same time. "Wigwams," she whispered, and, so impressed was she by how unusual this was, she actually stood up and went over to the window to have a closer look.

She was just in time to see the main event – Frank becoming wrapped like a cocoon in the fabric by the breeze blowing across the cape. He struggled, fell, rolled over, and was rescued by big Billy Pride, come to see Madeline. Frank flailed about as Billy struggled to find the end of the fabric, and finally managed to unroll him. Frank bunched up the cloth in disgust, stuffed it in the box, and stood gazing at his wigwam skeletons and the metal rattling in the wind. He scratched his head, jumped in his van, and drove to town.

Hy left shortly after, still intent on getting a look at Orwell's belongings. Whacky and her catnip mouse linked up with her, still intent on teaching her the bring-a-friend-a-mouse philosophy.

Hy was in luck. Wally was standing at the side of his shed, the shed hiding him from the house. He was having a cigarette. When he saw Hy, he looked guilty, furtive, and as if he were about to toss it away. She gave him a gesture not to worry, and he gratefully took another haul.

She knew then that she had him in her power.

"Jamieson asked me to have a look at Orwell's stuff. In case she missed something. Second pair of eyes."

Wally's eyes narrowed. Did he believe her? He looked down at his cigarette. Back at her.

"Sure," he said. "Long as you don't tell the missus."

He meant about the cigarette, not the shed visit. They both knew that.

Wally pulled a set of keys out of his pocket, and unlocked the shed. He motioned her in, and Whacky skittered in ahead of her. Wally followed, suddenly taking a fit of hacking, the sound of phlegm harsh in his cough. A big gob of snot-filled spit narrowly missed Hy's foot. She shivered in disgust. It made Whacky jump up onto a shelf and hunker down, a suspicious cast to her eyes.

"Orwell's things," said Wally, gesturing at the trunk and boxes.

"Don't know why I kep' 'em, but…family, you know. There's Annie Crane's stuff – his mother." He pointed at a shelf above. "And Mary and Henry Fraser, up there. And I got… I got…" He looked around a bit bewildered at the possessions that had accumulated of deceased family members. The only thing that seemed to be his was the ride-on.

The heritage shed.

"I'll leave you to it."

"No, wait, I'm just looking for one thing."

Hy ignored the trunk, and opened box after box, until she found the one that was a junk drawer. If there were anything to be found, she was sure it would be there.

"Ah, yes. Here it is. The one Jamieson wants to look through. Mind if I take it to her?"

"Go ahead. Take it all, for all I care." It had only just occurred to Wally that his shed was a mausoleum. That he was rapidly getting buried under his relatives' lost lives.

It made him want another cigarette, and he lit up, blowing puffs of smoke behind him for Hy to gulp down. They emerged from the shed, both coughing and wheezing, like high school kids who'd smoked a joint in back of the school.

Whacky followed at a distance, her mouse forgotten, her eyes on Hy and the box.

Gladys could see Wally now, and she watched with a grim face as he made his way to the back door. Smoking again. She didn't have to see it.

She could smell it on him.

Frank returned with a van full of wood and fence posts, and began erecting a wind barrier along the bottom edge of the lot.

He soon had help. Billy rolled up his sleeves. Finn, bored by Hy's perusal of a bunch of old bills, and propelled by the environmental possibilities of Frank's project, got into the action. Wally, looking down from his house, was shamed into shrugging on his work clothes – at least he looked the part – and lending his somewhat useless support. Murdo ambled up from April's house on The Shore Lane and put his shoulder to it. Nathan stopped by at the end of the day, along with his dad, big Ben Mack, and mother Annabelle.

By the time the sun set and darkness fell, the wind barrier was up. Because of the rise and tilt of the land and the direction of the prevailing wind, it didn't obscure the rolling hills and the shore. Each one of the wigwams would have a view.

"A womb with a view," said Annabelle, envisioning what the wigwams would look like once complete.

"Worlds unto themselves," said Finn.

And they were. The work crew, inspired by Frank's vision, showed up the next day to envelope the skeletons in fabric. More metal poles were applied to the exterior to hold the fabric down. There was a "smoke hole" in the top of each wigwam, traditionally the opening to let smoke from the fire funnel out. Now it was a peephole to the stars.

When all the fabric was up and secured in place, Frank opened his last box. Battery-operated candle lanterns to hang in each of the wigwams. The effect was magical. Six cones of light-filled fabric, glowing warmly at the core.

"They've got a soul now." Lili had come to pick up Nathan to join his parents for dinner.

Perhaps only Lili could have said that without someone snickering. But no one did. The group stood in awe at what they – what Frank – had created.

Paper by painstaking paper, Hy scoured every bit of the box, her hands getting grubby from the grease of ages. Just as Jamieson and Finn had both thought. It was boring and useless.

She had emptied the box. She peered inside it. She turned it upside down.

She'd done her job. And there was nothing to show for it.

She was about to toss all the papers back in when Finn came through the door. He held out a hand.

"Come. You've got to see this. It is amazing."

Hy put the box down, and grabbed Finn's hand. The squeaky screen door slammed behind them.

Whacky jumped into the box, and began worrying the bottom of it with her claws as if there were something important there.

There was. But Hy had missed it.

Whacky worked and worked and worked at it, until the tiny corner of a slip of paper was visible.

If the woman would only bother to look at it.

Moira, who had ignored the proceedings as a fool's business, now emerged from the house. Tears jumped into her eyes at the sight.

It was magical.

So much beauty. So easily made.

The workers drifted off, throwing glances behind them at the wigwams, at what they had created, at the beauty that existed where none had before.

Frank walked over to Moira, and took her hand. She wiped her eyes with her apron. Frank led her to the nearest wigwam.

He opened the flap and led her inside. She circled the wigwam in wonder. He doused the lantern and directed her gaze upward.

The stars. Millions of stars, no exaggeration, dusted the sky.

Moira's eyes were fixed on the pinhole at the top of the wigwam.

"The Big Dipper," she said. "I only ever know the Big Dipper."

He doused the lantern.

"There's Orion's belt," he pointed.

The next wigwam: "And Cassiopeia."

Finn and Hy watched the trail of extinguishing lights, until there was only one wigwam that glowed with light – and life, it seemed like. Then they turned and left Moira and Frank to their very public privacy.

Chapter Thirty-Six

To whoever is looking at this, I hope you don't misjudge me. Mebbe I shouldn't even be writing it, but the truth should be set down somewhere, and if someone is reading this, then I guess they are meant to be reading this.

I killed Roger Murray...

"A confession!" Hy's eyes lit up.

"Keep reading."

Finn had encouraged her to keep looking when they got home to the pile of papers on the table. Hy began to go through them again as Finn made tea. He brought the pot and some mugs to the table. Whacky was purring, asleep in the bottom of the box. Hy had begun to toss the papers back in after giving each a second look, back and front, not bothering about the cat, knowing she would jump out as soon as she felt inconvenienced.

Instead, Whacky rose up out of the box on her hind legs and began batting the papers back at Hy. It became quite a game. Hy tired of it sooner than the cat.

"Okay, Whacky." She grabbed the cat around the chest to pull her out.

Whacky stuck her hind legs stubbornly up against the box and dug her claws in. Hy stood up, holding a cat and a box. She shook the cat, but Whacky hung on. Finally, Hy gave up, and put them both down on the table.

Finn reached forward and stroked the cat's whiskers. Whacky started to purr, and jumped out of the box to nuzzle Finn.

"Maybe she's trying to tell you something. Let's check the box again."

While Whacky snaked her way, purring loudly, around Finn's neck, he removed the few papers in the box. And saw it. The tiny corner of a piece of paper stuck in the bottom folds. He pulled it out. Gave it to her. That's what she was reading.

I killed Roger Murray...
I had to. I had no choice. He forced me to do it.

Hy was reading aloud. She looked up at Finn. He raised an eyebrow.

"Forced?"

"That's what it says."

Frank led Moira to the wigwam with the best view of the shore. The one where he had prepared a comfortable bed for them.

"You did this for me?" There was something inexpressible in Moira's face. Frank couldn't tell if she was happy or sad. She remained silent as she absorbed every loving detail.

The beautiful white sheets.

The fat goose down duvet.

The dozens of candle lanterns glowing.

No one had ever done anything like this for her.

Moira melted. She melted into Frank's arms as he had hoped she would. She began to shiver as the cold left her. The cold that had been inside her always. It came out in waves, in shudders. It scared Frank. But slowly it ebbed and Moira slipped down onto the bed. Frank sat down beside her. The cold was gone, and she was ready to let the warmth in.

By morning, Moira would be glowing like the bride she was.

And Frank would be resolved to stop fooling around with his customers, no matter how willing.

He had Moira now. Finally.

And Moira well and truly had Frank. And The Wigwam Village Bed and Breakfast, destined to become the most popular tourist home in The Shores – and one of the top ten on Red Island.

Run by a lovely couple. That's what their guests said.

A lovely couple.

We was out in the boat. The waves was high. I wanted to turn back, but he said we hadn't done what he brought me out for. I thought mebbe it was some kind of peacemaking – or to kill me. Nothing in between if it were Roger. He pulled out his gun. Had it tucked away in his pants. Instead of aiming it at me, as I expected, he turned it on hisself.

Again Hy looked up. Again Finn raised an eyebrow.

He said he was full of cancer. That's how the doctor had put it. He was full of cancer. It made me shiver. I could see the cancer eatin' up his bones, swellin' his organs and heart. His black heart.

"Not, strictly speaking, anatomically correct." There was a grim smile on Finn's face. "Any of that."

"He's not a doctor, Jim, he's a murderer."

"We'll see. Read on."

I come out here to kill myself, he says, and pin you with the murder. He had the gun pointed at his mouth. I leaped up and grabbed for it, and when I did, it went off, cause he had his finger on the trigger.

"Accidental death? Manslaughter?"

"Don't jump to conclusions until we've heard the whole story. There's a lot more writing there."

It tore into his head, but I never saw it come out the other side. Didn't see much blood, neither.

"The tooth lodged in the skull," said Finn. "The shot didn't kill him."

"Then what did?"

Finn smiled. So did Hy. "Read on."

Then he was groaning and thrashing about. Blood spurted out of his mouth. He was my enemy, but I couldn't let him die like that, a slow awful death. You wouldn't do it to an animal. The gun had fallen to the bottom of the boat. I picked it up, aimed it at his temple and shot him through the head.

Hy reeled back as if she'd been shot. Or had seen it happen, so vivid was the image the words conveyed.

"Murder? Manslaughter?"

"Maybe murder," said Finn. "Would depend on the criminal justice system – and your lawyer."

I knew I was in trouble. No one would believe I hadn't kilt him apurpose. So I threw him over the side. Well, I didn't eggsackly throw him. He was heavy, in spite of being all eat up by that cancer. Got him over the side, then sent the gun after him.

"But the gun – ""Read on."

Was almost two of us dead that dirty day. The waves comin' up high over the gunwales. I couldn't bucket and row at the same time. Thought I would sink, but I couldn't abandon ship cause I couldn't swim.

"What, a fisherman, and he couldn't swim?"
"Most of them can't."
"That's just nuts."
"Most of them will tell you there's no point in knowing how to swim – the cold water will kill you anyway."

Near didn't make it to shore. I kept looking back out to sea, expecting him to be chasing me. I thought I saw him floating out there, coming after me. I finally got to shore and pulled the dory up with the last of my strength. I collapsed right there in the sand at the edge of the water. Conked out in the pouring rain.
  When I came to, the boat was gone – slipped out into the water. Looking for Roger, mebbe.
  The boat was gone, but the gun was there, in hand's reach. It had washed ashore right alongside me. What a fright that gave me. I grabbed it and concealed it in my jacket. Just in time.

Someone had spotted me on the shore. That turned out lucky. Everyone assumed Roger had gone down with the boat and I'd been swept to shore. I didn't tell them any different.

I sneaked into Roger's that night and put the gun with his others, so it wouldn't be missed. And I prayed every day that his body wouldn't wash up on shore.

"I bet it got stuck in Six Fathom Hole or Nine Fathom Hole or Mack's Hole," said Hy. They were names of deep holes in the ocean floor just off shore.

"And just got unstuck recently."

Hy and Finn looked up, startled, to see Jamieson standing in the kitchen. She'd somehow managed to come in the screen door without it squeaking. She'd listened, silently, to most of the tale of Orwell's journey back to shore.

Jamieson held out her hand to retrieve the paper.

"Something I missed," she said. "I guess I have to thank you for this, but you know – "

"You should charge me for this."

Jamieson's refrain.

Strictly speaking, Hy had permission from Wally, but not from Jamieson.

Jamieson smiled.

"You'd need to verify the handwriting for that to be useful evidence." Finn had his hands folded on top of a few scraps of paper.

"There are other samples in there." Jamieson gestured impatiently at the pile beside the empty box.

Finn lifted his hands.

"The samples are here. Precious few. A word here. A phrase there. Just notes quickly scribbled. Not really enough to go on. Nothing definitive."

Jamieson frowned. She'd always found these forensic types a pain in the ass. Even if you had a confession in your hands, they could put a hole in it. As big and effective as the one in Roger Murray's skull.

"We can't say he wrote this without a doubt, especially as they taught handwriting so rigorously fifty years ago. Everyone was supposed to write the same. The same loops and curves they had to practice over and over again. It was like a brand. You might plant a footmark in the clay of a well-known brand of shoe, and the criminal might have that kind of shoe, but there would have to be specific marks – of wear, of a flaw or damage – something peculiar to that shoe alone, to say it was his shoe. Same with the handwriting."

"But we could surmise – "

"Surmise all you want, but I bet two different handwriting experts could come up with two different answers on this. And, even if they agreed, defence could argue he wrote it under duress. Who's to prove or disprove that?"

"You'd need other evidence to even suggest there was coercion."

"You would, but you would also need more evidence than you're willing to go on to prove your theory."

"You don't know my theory. I don't know my theory."

"True."

"Give me a minute." Jamieson sat down, clutching the paper. She scanned Orwell's confession. She looked up, straight at Finn.

"And my theory is?"

"That Orwell Crane murdered Roger Murray, and confessed to the crime."

"Possibly manslaughter."

"Possibly manslaughter."

"But it was fifty years ago." Hy got up to refresh the teapot. "Are you really going to open it up?"

"Yes," said Jamieson. "And close it."

As it happened, that occurred only in her mind. Budgetary restraints being what they were, detachment wasn't interested in a fifty-year-old case that had never been on the books. No one had reported Roger missing or dead. They hadn't thought to do it. The Shores was cut off from the main island now, and it most certainly was fifty years before, when transportation in winter was by horse and sled. The village had had to be self-sufficient, and the villagers took care of their business on their own.

"Drownded or kilt by Orwell Crane, both men were dead, so what good did it do bringing in the po-lees from away?" Gus spoke for the entire village on that point.

In fact, Roger Murray's entire existence was a question mark, detachment had pointed out. There was no certificate of birth. His parents – non-believers – had never had him baptized or entered in the parish records.

Even the confession didn't impress. Scratches on paper by an author unknown. No witness to the document.

Jamieson found herself having to deal with Superintendent Constable, who'd made The Shores his special beat since he'd first got involved in a case there the year before.

The Superintendent's last name had always been a problem and may have been responsible for his rise through the ranks because it was silly referring to Constable Constable. He had always been incompetent. Now that he was a superintendent he'd been put out to pasture with this assignment on Red

Island.

Put out to golf, more like, thought Jamieson.

The Superintendent was more often found on the links than in his office, and he'd picked The Shores as his special turf because, well, such a small village, how busy could it be?

He had very little interest in current crime. He certainly had none in a case over fifty years old. Not even murder.

"Not going to open it up. It's closed to begin with," he told Jamieson.

"But I have a confession."

"Murderer alive today?"

"No. Dead but…"

"The victim?"

"The victim?" *What was he asking?*

"Still alive?"

"Dead, obviously."

"This confession…"

"A written confession."

The superintendent glanced impatiently at his watch. He was going to be late for tee off.

"Not worth the paper it's written on. It is written on paper?"

"Yes."

"You have a skull?"

"Yes."

"A gun?"

"Yes."

"Well…"

A long pause suggested the superintendent was thinking. Hope rose in Jamieson.

"A confession. A skull, with bullet holes. A gun."

"Yes. Yes. And yes."

Again a long silence.

"Not enough. Sorry, my dear. Simply not enough. It all goes back to the victim. No proof he ever existed. If we tried to make a case of it, we'd be a laughingstock."

Jamieson was furious. But he was her superior officer. What could she say? Do? Other than return the evidence and close the case.

A case she'd never opened.

Chapter Thirty-Seven

Jamieson soon had other more important and more immediate matters to occupy her. Unknown to her, they were sitting in Hy's mailbox when she passed by on her morning rounds.

Hy didn't go down to the mailbox until later and excitement surged through her when she saw the Massachusetts postmark. Finn's friend in Boston. In spite of eagerness that made her hands shake, she didn't open it. Finn deserved the honour.

She hopped on her bicycle, and, with envelope clutched in one hand, sped down to The Shore Lane.

Finn had more or less moved into Gus's house. Gus didn't mind. There was plenty of room. But she did stipulate separate bedrooms. She had no idea if Finn and Dot obeyed. Gus didn't go upstairs anymore. The bedroom she shared with Abel was downstairs.

Hy stumbled over her feet in her rush to get up the stairs. She scraped a shin and twisted an ankle. Still, she had a big grin when she burst into the house. It was eleven o'clock. They were eating lunch. Or dinner. Or whatever. Gus, Dot and Finn were seated at the dining room table. Dottie was in her high chair.

Hy charged in, shoved the envelope at Finn and grabbed a seat, her eyes shining with expectation.

He picked up a knife, slit the envelope open neatly, and spent far too long, in Hy's view, scanning the contents.

"Well?" she said impatiently.

"Well," he said. "Pretty conclusive." He paused, on purpose, teasing them all.

"Arsenic. Lots of it."

"Is that what it says?"

"That's what it means." He flashed the paper, with its columns and numbers and scientific terms.

"Arsenic where?"

"In the hair, in the water. Not in the Jello crystals."

"Just what we thought." Hy jumped up. "If I show this to Jamieson, will she understand it?"

"She will, if I go with you."

Marlene and Gladys Fraser had joined forces to object to Frank's building of the Wigwam Village. Heritage, in Marlene's mind, was European, the only kind to which the province should be giving its stamp of approval.

Marlene insisted that the department of tourism would not countenance these temporary structures as part of the heritage landscape.

"Heritage landscape," growled Frank when Marlene tried to make her point to him one morning. He dumped the plate of poached eggs and toast on the table in front of her.

"Heritage landscape," he growled again, scanning his creation through the window. The light fabric was billowing on the sea breeze and the wigwams appeared to be dancing. His face

Bodies and Sole

softened. "And maybe it is," he said. "Fitting. Very fitting." He slipped out of the room and headed for the computer.

The next day, Marlene's "anti tipi" campaign began. She'd enlisted the aid of W.I. president Gladys Fraser. Gladys had agreed to throw her weight around to force Frank and Moira to dismantle the village.

The two women mounted a door-to-door campaign to protest and gather support. In spite of the set-to with Frank, they started at Moira's own door. Frank had said one thing, but Moira might say something else entirely.

They could have taken a clue from the wedding necklace Moira was wearing.

She wore it everywhere, with everything, even with her apron, although it looked ridiculous, the fabulous creation with her plain brown housedress. She listened with a grim frown as the two women raised their objections to the First Nations Village, as she liked to think of it. More dignified than Wigwam.

"It's Frank's heritage project. Right at the heart of the celebrations."

"But it has nothing to do with The Shores. It's The Shores celebration, not some indigenous affair."

Moira didn't know what indigenous meant, but Frank rescued her. He came to the door and put his arm around his wife. He had done his homework.

"It has everything to do with The Shores. This was a summer camp for the Mi'kmaq. They travelled here with their wigwams and fished from the shore and the pond, until they moved in the fall and winter to get away from the fierce north shore winds. There would have been wigwams dotting the landscape here long before there were any fields."

Marlene just stood there with her mouth open, unable to think of a comeback. Gladys frowned. Gladys always frowned.

"Can we offer you some tea?" Moira asked brightly.

"No," said the women in unison, and Marlene, forgetting she was staying there, marched off with Gladys. They soon tired of their mission and gave it up.

Jamieson stared at the paper Hy had thrust into her hands. It didn't make a lot of sense to her, but she was willing to believe what Finn told her. She wasn't so willing to accept how the evidence had been gathered.

Under dark of night. From the well, without the owner's permission. Could you steal well water? Certainly you could trespass on someone's property. But no one had made an accusation.

It wasn't the first time Jamieson had been forced to turn a blind eye to Hy's activities.

She sighed. Worse than the water was the hair. True, she'd told Jamieson that she'd been in the house, but now she was asking her to accept as evidence something that had been gained illegally, and by illegal entry.

"I can't use this," Jamieson said, poking at the reference to the arsenic content in the hair.

"But it's proof. Proof she murdered him…them. Probably."

"No," said Jamieson. "It's only proof that he ingested arsenic." Jamieson had been hit by the forensic bug, thought Hy. What good were forensics if they didn't confirm for you what common sense said was so?

Hy appealed to Finn. Before she could say a word, he was shaking his head. "She's right, Hy. We know there was arsenic in his system, but we have no idea, no proof, only speculation, of how it got in there."

"Then there's Moira and Cyril. Both ill from eating Jello made with that water. Aren't they our proof? The well water. Loaded with arsenic."

Finn smiled. "Not quite loaded."

"But enough to kill someone?"

"Over time, yes."

It was a line of investigation Jamieson preferred to pursue.

"I could get a legal sample of the water," she said. "But first I'm going to check with the provincial testing people to see what their records show."

"Right." Hy brightened. "Vera must have had the water tested to purchase the house, and the department's records would show what was in it."

"It might be arsenic, in which case, why did she use the well, or it might be clean…"

"In which case it could mean she put it there."

"We'll cross that bridge when we get to it. In the meantime…" Jamieson gestured at Finn. "I'll keep these if you don't mind. And let's keep quiet about this."

"You better move fast. There's a man at risk."

"Cyril?"

"Yes."

"I'm on it."

Jamieson didn't like to be told what to do, but she knew Hy could be right. It would have been better, perhaps, if she'd listened to her before now.

No sooner was Jamieson's door shut behind them than Hy was jumping up and down.

"She killed them. She killed them all." Then her glee abated.

"She's killing him. Cyril. I hope Jamieson moves her ass."

Jamieson was already on the phone to the provincial water-testing unit.

It wasn't long before, extension by extension, she reached the man who was able to divulge to her the contents of the analysis of the well at the Sullivan house, and the letter that had been sent to the new proprietor about dangerous arsenic levels caused likely by years of pesticide use in the neighbouring fields.

So she knew.

Vera knew there was arsenic in her water. If they only knew, it had clinched the deal on the house.

Moira and Hy knew there was a lot of bottled water in her fridge.

Never used to make Jello.

Hy's FB Status: You can turn your late love into a pencil. Correction... 240 pencils. A body makes a box. If the box has a sharpener built in, you can write with his remains.

Likes: 3

Comments: Who uses pencils anymore?
            And you can erase 'er. LOL.

With the exception of Marlene and Gladys, everyone liked the Wigwam Village. Island videographer Lester Joudry came out to document it and the rest of the media soon followed.

Marlene was in PR heaven, taking the credit with the tourism department, for the "buzz" she claimed to have created.

Time Was hit the stands and sold out on the island in twenty-four hours. Fortunately, several boxes had been reserved for the village. Each villager, right down to Dottie, got a free copy.

Hy had guided editing of the book all the way, refusing any

corrections in spelling and grammar or changes to content, written and photographic. She insisted it be published just as Gus had made it, including the story of the man who grew a bean sprout out of his forehead after a fall in a field in the spring. It was illustrated by Dot at age six.

It wasn't a lot different than many of the type of book that communities on the island had self-published over the years, but Gus's profound knowledge and wit took it over the top, all carefully recorded and transcribed by her daughter Dot. Gus's YouTube presence, achieved with a few pointers from Lester Joudry, had the media flocking to her door. She was the hottest media favourite on Red Island and beyond – and the grandmother everyone wished they'd had.

She did play hard to get, though.

"Well, they'll have to come here. I don't go all the way into Charlottetown except to the doctor and to the Exhibition if I've got a quilt in." There was a gleam in Gus's eye.

"They've made me a senior now, you know. That means there's less competition. Most of them my age aren't living anymore."

And so the media came to Gus Mack, and she presided on her throne – the purple rocker recliner now showing signs of wear on the arms. CBC radio and TV combined to do their interview, so as not to tire the old lady. Hy and Dot were there. To support her? No, to watch the show.

"Bin lookin' out this window more than sixty years," she said when asked where her knowledge of the community came from.

And the thing that surprised her most in all those years? The interviewer's eyes were slightly glazed, prepared to be bored by the stories of this old lady.

"My husband Abel flying out of the General Store when a

propane tank exploded. Landed not too far from here. Abel. Not the tank. On his feet. Not a hair on his head harmed. Just in time for lunch."

The reporters knew then that they had a live one, and she didn't disappoint. Told stories that made them laugh. One that made the hardened interviewer tearful.

"...died for love, Albert did. Hanged himself, he did, in the barn. Abel found him and cut him down. Shouldna, I guess, but he couldn't stand to see him up there one more moment. Kilt himself for love, Albert did. Forty years he waited for that woman to come back from the Boston States. She never did. Guess he just couldn't wait any more."

"She wowed them," Hy told Ian later. "She was really on form. Top form."

The entire village huddled in front of the TV that night to watch Gus on CBC Compass.

The opening shot showed Gus holding Dottie, with superimposed script reading "Great-Grandmother Gives Birth."

The shot dissolved into Gus, in exactly the same position, but now holding *Time Was: 200 Years at The Shores*.

Gus was shocked by the headline. "So help me Hannah. I'm just a grandma." But she was tickled to see the cover of *Time Was*, designed like a crazy quilt.

"Not an artist, mind." She rocked the chair back and forth. "No, never was an artist, but I'd say that was pretty good."

The media attention caught public attention. Soon Gus and her book were all over the Internet. The CBC TV clip about Abel with vintage photos of the old store went viral, the first edition of *Time Was* sold out across the country, and the publisher rushed a second edition into print.

A while later, Gus showed Hy a letter she'd received from

the publisher.

"Wants to know how to disburse the funds."

"They're yours."

"Not rightly. Those aren't my stories. They belong to The Shores."

"Then give the money to the hall. The Women's Institute will never have to worry about its upkeep again."

Gus nodded and rocked.

"Yes. I like that. We'll set a bit aside for Dottie, mind, being as she doesn't have a father."

"I'm sure there will be plenty to go around."

There was. The book was a steady seller at the hall and tourists weren't shy to come knocking at Gus's door to get an autograph. She sold quite a few from the comfort of her rocking chair. Especially when she hinted at her family connection to the island's iconic authoress, Lucy Maud Montgomery. The Campbells of Cavendish? No, it would have been on the mother's side, the armchair genealogists speculated.

Chapter Thirty-Eight

Vera Gloom's sour face greeted Jamieson at the door. She stood, a block of inhospitality, smack in the opening, her every gesture and facial expression unwelcoming, designed to send her visitor away.

Jamieson. In full uniform. With serious intent.

No niceties.

"Vera Gloom?"

"You know I'm Vera Gloom. Now get on with it."

"Vera Gloom, I am arresting you on suspicion of murder and attempted murder."

Jamieson had her handcuffs with her. Did you use handcuffs on an old lady? She'd never arrested a senior before.

"Don't be ridiculous."

"I should warn you of your right to remain silent until you have a lawyer."

"Lawyer? For what? Nursing old men in their final days? Is that a crime?"

"It could be. Especially nursing them, marrying them and killing them."

"Every one of them would tell you…will tell you…that I have been a blessing in his life." Vera's expression softened for a moment, the glimmer of a smile passed across her mouth.

"A blessing, yes, that is what I have been, a blessing."

Her eyes hardened, the smile turned into a thin line of hate.

"Come. Let's go ask them. They'll tell you."

Vera whirled around and began to march up the stairs.

Jamieson hadn't moved, trying to digest what Vera had said, what Vera apparently believed. That the men upstairs were alive.

"They can't tell me anything. They're dead, Mrs. Gloom. That's why I'm here. I have a warrant for your arrest on suspicion of murdering all three of your ex…late…husbands, and attempting to murder the one downstairs."

"Why would I do that?"

"Money. Investments. Pensions."

Vera turned.

"What grounds have you?"

"For one thing, arsenic in your well water. Of which you were aware. Contaminated water used to make Jello for your husband."

Vera's eyes opened in wide innocence.

"But the water was boiled."

"That doesn't remove arsenic."

Vera's eyes opened wider.

"It doesn't?"

"I think you know that."

Vera's resolve appeared to be coming undone. The grim line of hate was unbuckling, the expression in her eyes had become difficult to read because they were darting about wildly, focusing in no particular direction.

"Well, are you coming? They'll be waiting. They don't like me to keep them waiting."

Vera's hands clenched together. Her fingers were fussing with her rings. She looked down at them. She focused on the largest, bluest diamond.

"Willard." She was speaking to the ring. "Where are you when I need you, my darling. I have carried you with me all these years. We have never been apart."

Her attention shifted to the ring beside it – also a blue diamond, slightly smaller.

"And Archie, you and I have travelled a long road together." She lifted her hand and kissed the ring.

Jamieson thought it odd, but not unusual. Hy would have been fascinated because of what she knew about the blue diamonds. All Jamieson could conclude was that there had been perhaps two more husbands.

Dead husbands.

But she couldn't know they'd become diamonds.

Vera held out her hand. She flashed the rings in front of Jamieson, twirled them around.

"Meet my husbands, Willard and Archie." She stroked the rings, and tears slid from her eyes.

Mad. She's mad. This added new complications to the arrest. She might have to use handcuffs on this senior.

"But come. Come and meet the other boys."

Jamieson stepped forward, took hold of the banister and began to climb the stairs. Vera turned and went ahead.

And then stopped. Climbed a few more steps. Stopped.

Jamieson had almost caught up with her. Vera reached the last step. Turned to face Jamieson with that same uncompromising expression. An expression that became a grimace. Vera clutched at the banister. Doubled over. Looked up at Jamieson, an appeal in her eyes, agony etched across her face.

Jamieson flew the two steps between them, and caught Vera just as she lost her grip on the rail and fell forward. Vera wasn't heavy, but she hit Jamieson like a dead weight.

For a moment Jamieson hesitated between carrying Vera upstairs – the landing was closer – or downstairs. She picked her up and took her downstairs. She carried her into the room where Cyril was living and dying, and laid her on the couch.

She felt for a pulse. In the wrist. On the neck. No pulse. She placed a hand in front of Vera's open mouth. She felt no breath. She pulled her onto the floor and began to administer CPR. At the same time, she fumbled in her pocket for her cell phone and put in a call to Nathan. She knew she'd get a far more immediate response from him than calling 911, miles away in Winterside.

He arrived minutes later.

"Vera. Vera." He kept saying her name as he administered CPR. He used the defibrillator, worked on her for nearly an hour, as if she were a precious member of his family, not a nasty old bag of bones and a murderess.

Finally, he looked up at Jamieson, and shook his head. He closed Vera's eyes and went to back up his van right to the front door. He and Jamieson carried Vera out on a stretcher. It wasn't difficult. She weighed very little. As they lifted the stretcher to put her in the van, one of her arms fell to the side.

Her body was cold, and the cold and the jarring made the rings on her fingers loosen. Two blue diamond rings fell to the ground and rolled into a corner of the doorjamb. Neither Nathan nor Jamieson noticed.

With a grim look, Nathan secured the stretcher in the back

of the van and was just about to take off when Jamieson stopped him.

"You better take him, too."

"Him?"

Jamieson jerked her head toward the house. "Lover boy. You transported him out here, didn't you?"

Nathan jumped down from the cab of the van.

"Oh, him."

"He can't look after himself. He's probably dying." *Poisoned?*

"We better get him some care."

Cyril lay in the front room, where he had been spending his last days. He had slept through the drama with Vera, and he continued to sleep as they transported him out on the second stretcher and slid him inside the van next to Vera. His wife. In name and bank account only.

So it was that a scant few weeks after Nathan had delivered the new Mr. and Mrs. to The Shores, he was taking them away. One to the morgue. The other to the hospital. But likely not long for this world either.

United in life…reunited in death? Hubby didn't look as if he would make it all the way to Winterside.

He didn't.

Murder? Maybe. But what did it really matter anymore? No one would swing for it. Startled, Jamieson realized what that actually meant. At one time, Vera could have been hanged for her crimes. Now, if she'd lived to face justice, she might not even have spent the rest of her life in jail. Canada's hangman had been pensioned off before Vera was born. Otherwise, she might have picked him for her next husband, Jamieson thought.

It preyed upon Jamieson, the deaths of Vera Gloom and her husband Cyril. Had she caused Vera's death by shocking her with the arrest? That's what it had seemed like. And could she have prevented Cyril's? Perhaps, if she had listened to Hy sooner, but there had been no legal basis on which to make a move. Still, it nagged at her.

When she wasn't chewing on those worries, Jamieson was wondering what to do with the bodies. They couldn't continue to occupy the house. They couldn't stay at The Shores. Jamieson had no idea what to do with them. Would murder charges be laid against an old woman now dead? They should be. But what about evidence? Where would the bodies be stored?

The detachment had no interest in storing the cadavers. There simply wasn't space in the evidence room, and even if they could be squeezed in, they'd be constantly in the way and be damaged, get bits nicked off them. Lose an arm like the Venus de Milo?

The dilemma had been considered at the highest levels.

Jamieson finally got a call from Superintendent Constable. He was going to come out to inspect the situation.

He came the following day. The last time he'd been to The Shores, he'd been chased away by the unusual phenomenon of snakes falling from the sky. Terrified, he'd ordered Jamieson to take care of it, jumped in his car and sped off. This time, he darted several cautionary glances skyward as he sprinted from his car into the Sullivan house.

When Jamieson took him up to the second floor, he was appalled. He had been curious, but the superintendent was squeamish. He only got as far as Blair before losing the battle with his own terrified sense of mortality.

"I've seen enough," he managed through a wave of nausea.

"You'll have to leave them where they are for now," he decreed.

He had nothing more to offer before he scuttled back to his car, took off with a vehemence that suggested the plastic beings might be pursuing him, and ignored the speed limit in his haste to get back to the relative safety of his office and paperwork, too dull to kill a man.

Chapter Thirty-Nine

Jamieson shifted her obsession with her possible responsibility in the deaths of Vera and Cyril to the continued presence of the bodies just down the hill. She wasn't a religious woman, but she was a superstitious one, and she felt something should be done. What, she didn't know. Why, she didn't know that either.

She burst into Gus's kitchen when she could no longer stand her own thoughts about the bodies. As often was the case, Hy, Finn and Dot were having tea with Gus.

"What are we going to do about those bodies?"

"What do you think, on display at the hall, maybe?" Hy suggested. Dot grinned. So did Gus.

"I could curate it," said Finn.

"Perfect."

"I'm serious."

"Well, if you're serious, I'd get Lili to take a look at them."

"Lili? What could she do?"

"Calm your mind."

Hy was right, thought Jamieson. She needed to calm her mind. She went looking for Lili.

No one except Nathan had noticed that Lili had not gone by

the Sullivan house all summer. She took the county line road out of the village and back along a rutty red clay road – halfway to Winterside and back – just to get to the hall.

She had never liked the house, and she liked it less now.

"I sense the aura of evil."

The aura of evil, thought Hy, who had come along for the "exorcism."

There were bodies, but were there souls?

Lili claimed if there were she could sense them.

Jamieson had scoffed at the idea.

But then Jamieson had also scoffed at the idea that Lili could move objects with her mind. Until she had moved a wooden table with a thought. Played the piano by just thinking about it – and helped to solve a case of mind over murder a few years back.

Could Lili sense souls? And what if she could?

Did it matter if these bodies had souls?

It did to Lili. And maybe it did to Jamieson, too, though she'd never have admitted it.

Lili was pale, paler than usual, and she was shaking as they entered the house. But she knew she must do this.

One at a time, she went room to room.

First, to Blair. She stood, with the others behind her, in complete silence. Her glance darted around the room. She closed her eyes, and her arms lifted involuntarily. She stood unmoving for several minutes, like one in a trance.

She opened her eyes and moved forward. Touched Blair on the head. Closed her eyes again. Stayed in the position for some minutes, while the others, standing back in the hallway, became twitchy with impatience. Then she opened her eyes, moved slowly backward out of the room, her gaze sweeping the entire space again.

Next, she went into Charlie's room, repeating the entire performance. Eyes sweeping the room. The touch on the corpse's head. The backward move away and out of the room.

Then Hank. Same thing. No one said anything during this time, hardly daring to breathe, not wanting to crack Lili's concentration.

She backed out of Hank's room.

She turned to Hy and Jamieson.

"There are no souls here."

Her words were chilling.

"How do you know?" It came from Jamieson as a whisper.

"There is no lingering scent."

"Scent?" Hy's voice rose on a squeak.

"Souls have a scent. A sweet, lingering scent. But there is no soul lingering here. No scent. No sight. No small pocket of haze in the air. No sense, when I touch, no vibration. No doubt." Lili's voice was firm.

"There are bodies here, that you can see. But their souls have long gone somewhere better."

For Hy, this absence of the souls made the bodies creepier, more dead, if that were possible.

"Deader than dead," she said.

A small smile from Lili. "Yes. More dead than dead."

"So the…souls…" Jamieson choked out the word. She couldn't believe that she was having this conversation. "The souls have gone? The souls don't care what happens to the bodies?"

"No. They're not using them. They have abandoned them long ago. Only we care what happens to the bodies."

"Which is how they end up like this. Plastic."

"I imagine that's when the souls left. It was not possible for them to live in that environment. In plastic. They were driven out. Driven away."

"To where?" Jamieson.

"I don't know. I don't know where souls go. I don't know where they live in the body. Some say the mind. But where is the mind? We don't know that either. They used to say the soul lived in the heart, or spleen. Or liver, because that's the best-looking organ." Lili shook her head. "But a soul doesn't need to be good-looking. When the body departs, the soul leaves the body, and goes somewhere better."

Anywhere would be better than where these bodies were, this house they were in, this house that had evil built in. Was the house itself evil, did it need death and deception to fuel its own existence? It seemed that way, because nothing good had ever happened here. There was an evil that, unlike the souls, would not leave.

The souls were gone. Now the bodies would follow.

Perhaps also to a better place.

The house? It would sit on this spot, as it always had, through decay and transformation, always managing to lure someone else through its doors.

Was it leeching evil into the ground beneath it, from its tainted foundation?

Was this its heritage?

"Evil," said Lili as they left. "There's only one way to rid it of evil." She turned back toward the house, looked up and said one word, one word Hy strained to hear, but it was lost on the wind.

Chapter Forty

The word drummed through Lili's head all night and kept her awake.

Finally, she got out of bed, so as not to disturb Nathan, though he was snoring happily in a deep sleep.

It was that house she could see as a dim, dark outline from her bedroom window. That was keeping her awake. That house and its contents, no longer wanted by anybody, not even by their original occupants.

She pulled the shawl off the back of the white wicker chair, wrapped it around her over her cotton nightgown and sat down, eyes fixed on the Sullivan house. Wild Rose Cottage. An evocative but deceptive name. It sounded beautiful. But it was ugly to its bones.

Her eyes narrowed as she thought of the evil that had happened there. Brother killing brother. Twice over. And something more. She was sure there was something more. Evil in its beginnings, laid with the foundation. Lili's pure mind could entertain the idea of evil only so long. Soon it began to drift to happier thoughts—of her garden plans for the following year and the beautiful tablecloth she was embroidering for Ben and Annabelle's twenty-fifth wedding anniversary in the fall.

Nathan's snoring sometimes had the effect of lulling her to sleep, and it did now, combining with these happy thoughts to bring her ease of mind. Her eyes drooped shut and her head fell to one side. Her hands that had been clinging to the shawl fell open and her arms dropped to the sides.

And so they stayed for some hours, Nathan sawing away, occasionally grunting and flipping over, but asleep. Lili slept, but not as deeply, ready to be awoken by the tiniest unusual sensation.

It was a warm light playing on her eyelids that tickled her into semi-consciousness. Slowly she opened them, only half-open, staring into the golden sliver of dawn as it slid in a thin line above the horizon. Shots of orange and yellow light streaked across the water and sky and poured in the window. She stood, not yet fully awake. Up on the hill, the light surrounded the big house, a glow shimmering all around it, a terrifying beauty. The image dazzled her.

She moved as if in a trance, dragged her dressing gown off the chair and slipped into it, white cotton like her nightdress. She slid her feet into her slippers, and lit a candle to guide her downstairs, preferring a gentle entrance into the day rather than the harsh electric lights.

She floated down the stairs, her feet not seeming to touch the treads, her white nightgown and robe billowing around her, catching the draft from the hall window left slightly open to let in the cool night air.

She blew out the candle and opened the front door. It squeaked as she stepped out into the early morning. The damp air had swollen it in its frame. A wave of chill air startled her, and she stopped moving for a moment, looking around her, puzzled, as if wondering why she had come outside.

Her eyes fixed on the big house, still bathed in the glow of the sunrise. The sun was rising in each window, orange globe after orange globe shimmering on the dark glass.

The images impelled her forward, as if she had no will of her own.

She glided up the hill toward the house.

The evil house.

Its contents of no consequence to themselves or anyone else anymore.

She looked like a wraith herself, her white cotton nightclothes drifting around her in the light morning breeze, catching the glow of the morning sun.

The glow that encircled the house moved higher on the horizon.

The house. Her trance became a purpose, a purpose of which she was sure, although she didn't know where the idea had come from. She felt no power to go against it, to control it.

She tripped toward the house, hands buried in the pockets of her dressing gown, clutching, clutching…what? The fabric. To keep her perennially cold fingers warm. She stumbled, partly from speed, partly from anxiety, a haste of the mind. A haste to be done this morning's task.

The house must be stopped.

She pulled her hands from her pockets. Rubbed them together. Blew on them. And then she noticed her feet. In slippers. Bunny slippers.

If anyone came across her, they would think she was mad. Was she?

She felt odd, not in command of herself, as if some other force were guiding her actions.

The sun had let go of the house. Its brilliance no longer bathed the huge building in its glow. It was now dark and gloomy.

Lili, without a thought, followed her feet where they were determined to go.

The bunny slippers, quickly turning from white to red from the island clay, didn't hesitate in pattering around to the back of the house.

The cellar hatch. The only entrance into the cellar of the house, in spite of all the grand renovations, were two large doors angled on the ground, tucked up against the house. Lili grabbed the handle of the right-hand door. It pulled back against her. It was heavy, maybe too heavy for Lili. She lacked leverage, because she had to stretch almost her full length to grab hold of the handle.

After a few attempts, she was ready to give up, when suddenly the door cooperated, and flung her back as it came open. She landed on her back, now covered in red clay.

But she had opened the door. And she would close it behind her – so that no one would interrupt her in her purpose.

The cellar was lined with massive island stone, carved out of the capes, chiseled, the marks of man evident in every stone. Every damp, musty stone. Some owners clung to these foundations with pride. They were heritage after all. Most were crumbling or sliding in, tired of the long years of the weight, the burden of the house they carried.

She stepped down onto one of the massive stones, used to create a stairway. She held the door above her as she went. Another step. And then another. When she was far enough down, she let go the door. It creaked and slammed shut.

A hook on the one door spun around, and looped itself into the waiting metal eye on the other door. She turned, briefly, at the sound, saw the latch had closed itself, and, unbothered, continued into the musty dark.

She didn't worry about how she would get out.

This was a woman who could move objects with her mind.

She followed the smell of oil to the furnace.

The oil tank was there. New rules. At one time, you could put an oil tank in the cellar. Then you couldn't. Now you could again.

It suited her purposes.

She dipped a hand into her pocket for the box of matches she'd used to light the candle. Had she known all along? Some part of her had, drawn here by the morning sun, by its image of the house aflame with light.

Aflame.

She pulled out the matches, looked around her with eyes now accustomed to the light, found the light switch – and her way.

The area was littered with recycling boxes of paper and cardboard. There were paint cans and solvents of various kinds. Stuff left behind by a careless contractor. No one to account to anymore.

No half measures. It must go up this time. Twice before, the house had conquered fire.

Not this time, thought Lily. Not this time. She lit the papers. She lit the cardboard. The papers and the cardboard smoldered, turning brown, but were not catching. Not catching. She used every match. She hoped that it would work. She prayed, as only Lili could pray.

Prayers that could shift reality.

The fire responded, took life, blazed out at her and she turned and ran. She had a moment of panic at seeing the cellar door shut.

She shoved up on it. Heavy. Too heavy.

She could hear the roar of the flames behind her.

She pushed. Nothing. Pushed again.

Then she remembered. The hook and eye. The door had shut itself. The house was evil, trying to kill her as she was trying to kill it.

Tit for tat. What else could she expect?

She reached for the hook.

It was beyond her grasp.

The cellar was filling with smoke. It was billowing up behind her, coming for her, rising up and over her, curling and circling around her.

She must not panic.

Calm, Lili, calm. In spite of the smoke, she took a deep breath. And another.

Too much. She began to cough. She couldn't stop the hacking, the burning that sliced her lungs – as if the fire itself were searing through her body.

Calm, Lili, calm.

She could feel the heat of the fire behind her.

To many it might seem an odd time to be invoking yogic mind techniques, but that's just what she was doing. Ignoring the smoke, the heat, the roar of the inferno behind her. The flames coming closer.

A deep breath. Suppress the coughing. A deep breath. Harness that inner strength, and –

Stretch.

The tip of her finger touched the hook, but couldn't take hold of it.

The smoke swirled around her, intoxicating, inviting her to come with it, to forget her labours, to slip into sleep and become one with the flame.

Chapter Forty-One

Jamieson was standing outside the police house at the top of the hill, looking toward the shore, in the golden glow of the still-rising sun, the black, light-tipped waters, and the sand turning golden with the approaching day.

Something made Jamieson turn. Did she see, hear, smell fire coming from the Sullivan house? The southwest wind that morning favoured it.

She should have smelled it. She probably should have heard the roar. By this time, surely she could have seen the flames leaping out of the building. She'd saved this house once before when fire broke out. She'd wondered then why she'd bothered.

And she was wondering why she should bother now.

Best be rid of it. Let it go. Delay the call. At the very least, the volunteer firefighters should not be called into this. Risk men's lives for that…that…she was beginning to agree with Lili that the house was evil. Jamieson had read once that all spaces retain all the sounds ever made in them, if scientists could figure out a way to retrieve them. Surely that must stand for actions, too. Evil actions contained within the house, touching everyone who had touched it.

Every contact leaves a trace.

The Sullivan house had heard the crackling of fire three times. Would this be the last? Should it be?

Jamieson's gaze turned from the shore and the sun licking fire across the water. She was looking down on the flames leaping out of the Sullivan house.

Good riddance.

Lili slid down to the bottom step, her strength giving out. It was a good thing she did, because close to the floor, there was still oxygen, oxygen that she gulped down and kept in reserve. Her yogic training gave her lungs maximum efficiency. Breath after breath.

Calm, Lili, calm.

She slowed her breathing. The smoke swirled around her. The flames leaped at her, coming close enough almost to light her cotton nightgown on fire. From deep within the cellar, the roar of the fire took shape.

Soon, she knew, there would be an explosion, bright light, and then – ?

Lili's faith did not comfort her. She lost consciousness.

Hy was just heading out for her morning run when she saw Jamieson standing at the top of Shipwreck Hill. Looking, not toward the shore, but inland, down the back of the hill toward the Sullivan house.

Unmoving, in spite of the smoke billowing from below.

When Hy got to Jamieson, she appeared to be in something of a trance.

Hy knew Jamieson didn't like to be touched, but she had to shake her.

"Jamieson. The Sullivan house is on fire."

"Let it burn."

"What? What if someone's in there?"

"There's no one in there. Remember what Lili said: 'no souls there.'"

Lili. Lili had also said, "There's only one way to rid it of evil." And then that one word, lost on the wind. That one lost word. *Fire.* That was it. Lili had said fire.

Had Lili set the place on fire?

Hardly the sort of thing that a gentle soul like Lili would do. *Still…*

Hy grabbed Jamieson by the sleeve.

"Lili might be in there."

"What? How do you know?"

"I don't know. But there's a chance. Come." She dragged at Jamieson's sleeve.

The two women ran down the hill toward the house, stumbling clumsily as they went. Hy fell once and Jamieson hauled her up.

They headed directly for the thickest smoke, billowing out of the cellar hatch.

Hy hauled on the hatch. No give.

Jamieson moved in beside her, and they both yanked at the doors.

No give.

"It's secured from the inside." Hy gave Jamieson a look of despair.

"That means there's someone in there."

"Lili?"

Inside, through a fog of semi-consciousness, Lili's ears ached with the sound of a hammer. *A hammer? No. Pounding. Pound-*

ing of some kind. Where?

She came to. Heard her name:

"Lili. Lili." Hy kept repeating it, more desperate each time. If not Lili, someone had to be in there, with the hatch secured from the inside.

As the smoke whirled around her, suffocating her, Lili struggled up the stairs again, on all fours.

She still couldn't reach the hook, but she pushed.

She pushed and Hy and Jamieson pulled.

Push. Pull. Push. Pull. Push again.

And it came loose, the hook from the door.

Lili fell forward as the door gave way.

She stared up in shock, smoke engulfing the three of them. Jamieson and Hy grabbed onto her and pulled her out.

Her legs were like jelly. Fear. Fear of the fire – and fear of the law.

When Lili was safely out, Jamieson slammed the cellar doors shut to the roar of the inferno. They moved back from the burning building.

"Shall we call the firefighters?" Hy appealed to Jamieson. It wasn't the question she wanted to ask. She wanted to quiz Lili on what had happened, but that was Jamieson's job.

Jamieson said nothing, just stared up at the building.

"Shall we?"

Jamieson shook her head. She prayed that it would all go up in smoke.

Lili was thinking the same thing. She looked up to the second floor.

She was thinking about them. The bodies. The boys.

Plastic. Would they burn, or would they melt?

Melt, probably. But they would be somewhere better. Somewhere they belonged. In that life, not in this one. And the evil that was in this house she hoped would perish in the fire, or she had taken the risk for nothing.

On the second floor, three men were finally being allowed to rest in peace. It wasn't a graceful way to go, but none of them are.

At first Blair, Charlie and Hank looked as if they were very, very sad, their faces dissolving into a long liquid unhappiness. Their limbs, their torsos, every part of them plastic, began to run. Just from the heat. The three were unrecognizable even before the flames roared into their rooms and licked at what was left of them, puddles of plastic on the floor until there was no floor.

They were never found of course. There was a whole house on top of them. That was their grave. The Sullivan house. Wild Rose Cottage.

"You're not going to put in a call?" Hy felt she was missing something. Jamieson had changed in the last year, but such a brazen neglect of duty? And she hadn't said anything to Lili.

Suddenly, Lili remembered. The oil tank.

"Get away," she called to Jamieson and Hy. "The oil tank. The oil tank."

The three women chased through the rose shrubs, ripping at their garments, to get away from the burning building.

The explosion sent some of the island stone foundation flying out into the garden, one massive block landing close to them. Lili just narrowly escaped being hit by it. Her heart was heaving in her chest. There was sweat on her forehead and her chest. But her hands were still cold. Cold as death.

Two small objects hit the stone with a "ping." The flames

glinted off them.

"Her rings." Hy snatched them up and held her hand open so Jamieson could see.

Blue diamonds.

"She spoke to them," said Jamieson.

"I'm not surprised. Husbands four and five. Here." Hy gave one of the rings to Jamieson. Then she heaved hers into the burning building. Thousands of dollars worth of gem. Jamieson did the same.

"May they rest in peace," said Hy.

The flames were now leaping up to the roof, hungrily consuming the cedar shingles.

"I'm not going to risk men's lives. Not for that." Jamieson turned to Lili. "You were very foolish to go in there and try to put it out."

Both Lili and Hy were silent.

Did Jamieson really believe…?

"You could have killed yourself."

How nearly she had.

"Whatever made you do it, I don't know," Hy chimed in, wanting to support Jamieson in this road she'd decided to follow. The road of Lili's innocence. Hy looked down at Lili's bunny slippers.

How could someone who wore bunny slippers possibly be guilty of arson? Dirty red-stained bunny slippers and a smudge of smoke across her face that made her look like a third-grade tomboy.

Only Lili was silent, not knowing whether to confess or accept this gift, this absolution.

What she had done was right, the right thing to do, she knew, and so she kept silent. They all did. They never mentioned it again.

Jamieson did not make a call until she and Hy saw Lili safely home, gave a brief sketch of the circumstances to Nathan, and left Lili in his arms. She and Hy returned past the house and Jamieson paused for a moment to inspect it, the flames leaping out of the roof, all the windows broken, revealing the charred insides.

Gone. It was gone now. Too far gone to be saved.

By the time Hy and Jamieson got back to the police house, the fire was most certainly too far gone to be fought, on its way to being reduced to rubble. Jamieson made the call – to tell the volunteer firefighters to stay away.

She never questioned Lili. Never considered a charge. Convinced herself that Lili had not been there to set the fire, but to stop it. It was clear that Jamieson simply didn't care about the loss of the house. She would report it as a fire, undetected until it was well out of control and not worth the risk of human life.

She got away with it. And Lili did, too. And the authorities in Charlottetown never questioned her. For one thing, they weren't willing to share precious resources with The Shores. They allowed Jamieson to be a law unto herself. As long as she sent in believable reports and didn't ask for anything.

It would be a long time before the rubble was removed and anyone thought of building there again.

A long time.

Lili would be around to warn people off, and Jamieson was inclined to fall in with her.

If she'd been questioned about it, and if she'd been honest, she'd have said it was a good thing the house was destroyed, and that the bodies in it were finally at rest.

Souls or no souls.

Chapter Forty-Two

Gus thought the skull should be buried, and the tooth along with it.

"It's a curse," she told Dot and Finn anytime they would listen.

"It was Roger's great-great…well, I don't know how many greats…grandfather who built that Sullivan house. Built the evil right in. Brother murdered brother twice over in that house." The whole village knew that. Now the rest of the world was learning those stories in *Time Was*.

"Never was any good to anyone, that house. And him and his tooth showing up and that house burning to the ground at the same time. It's a sign, I tell ya. A sign."

"A sign of what?" Hy asked, popping in on Gus's monologue one day.

"A sign it were never meant to be. Evil built right in," she repeated.

"How was it built in?"

"There was a killin' as it was goin' up. Blood spilled on the foundation stones."

"A murder?" Hy was intrigued.

"Mebbe. Mebbe not."

"The young wife. Roger's ancestor made a play for her. Or she may have been foolin' around with him. Mebbe they had a lovers' quarrel. Mebbe that's how she fell down the stone steps into the cellar and bled all over the sandstone, dead before anyone found her. No one to say what happened. That house was built on the blood of a bride."

"You didn't tell this story in the book."

"No." Gus shook her head. "I didn't like the taste of it. It wouldn't be fittin'. Sides, no one knows what really happened."

Hy grinned. "That didn't stop you from telling a lot of other stories."

Gus smiled. "Happen it didn't. But the ones I told, if they ain't true, they're at least folklore."

Hy noticed there was no dish down for Blacky. It occurred to her that there hadn't been the last time she was here.

"What's happened with Blacky?"

"Gorn somewhere else, I guess."

Did Gus know she'd been sharing the cat with Jamieson?

"Dottie here was helping herself to the cat food, so I put it up on the warshing machine, in there." Gus pointed to the laundry room. "Blacky didn't fancy that. Wouldn't eat anything up there, not even my good table scraps. Circled and circled around the place I useta put the dish, but I was just as stubborn. Hasn't been back in a few days. I hope she's all right."

"I'm sure she is. I'll let you know if I see her."

That gave Hy two reasons to speed up to Jamieson's. She couldn't keep the Sullivan house story she'd heard from Gus to herself, and she was curious, a bit concerned, about Whacky.

Those fears were put to rest as she cycled up to the front door, where Jamieson was putting down a saucer of fish, purring along with the cat.

"Whitey's eating."

Jamieson looked up and flushed. She was so focused on the cat and purring so loudly, she hadn't heard Hy approach.

"I've finally managed to get her to eat."

"What's she got there?"

"She's got sole."

Hy laughed. "I bet she does."

Jamieson smiled one of her rare smiles.

"That's all she'll eat. Sole. She's here almost all the time now."

So Jamieson had won the battle of Whacky. Hy approved. Gus had no need of a cat, but Jamieson… Jamieson needed something. A bit of light companionship. Perfect. It might keep her mind off Ian.

Something else was on Jamieson's mind, though. Hy knew she was struggling with the fact that she'd let that fire go out of control. She told her Gus's take on the building of Sullivan house.

It did seem to help.

"Evil built in?" Jamieson repeated Hy's words. Gus's words.

Jamieson had thought it, too. She'd also thought the idea was fanciful, and shoved it aside, but The Shores had seeped into Jamieson's way of thinking, and this idea of evil being set down with the island stone foundation made sense to her. She was thinking in a Red Island way.

Evil built in. And now purged with fire.

And what of the skull?

Should it be buried, as Gus recommended, or could it be turned to good?

Bodies and Sole

The whole village knew that Roger Murray's gold tooth was lodged in his skull. And the whole village had decided something must be done about it. Jamieson had not been able to open a case and therefore the skull was not police evidence anymore. It was anyone's to have.

Jamieson called a meeting in the hall. Everyone came. All agreed, unhappily, that Jared MacPherson had the best claim to the tooth. He was, as far as anyone knew, Roger's nearest, if not only, next of kin.

Jared was whining that it should be his. Witness the guns. Roger's most valuable possessions had been left to him, so the skull should be his as well.

But Roger, like Jared, had debts. He owed the Frasers. He owed the Macks. He owed the Joudrys. In fact, he owed just about everyone in the village. Perhaps not the full amount that gold tooth had climbed to in fifty years, but certainly the original amount and more.

The hall was in an uproar, everyone staking a claim to the tooth.

Jamieson couldn't bear the thought that whoever might get the skull would smash it to pieces in order to get at it. Vera's bodies had given her a greater respect for the remains of the dead.

Then she had her idea. She held up a hand to bring the crowd to order and let them know her decision.

They left, subdued and shaking their heads at her crazy pronouncement.

Hy's Facebook Status: On the Oscars red carpet, the question is "Who are you wearing?" In The Shores this Heritage Week, it's "When are you wearing?" Or, possibly, "OMG! WHAT are you wearing?"
Likes: 7

Comments:　No one.
　　　　　　Never.
　　　　　　Nothing.

Heritage Homecoming Week had arrived, and the village was dressing in period costume, the only idea they'd agreed on with Marlene.

Sort of.

"I'm wearing 'right now,'" said Gus. That is, what she "allus" wore: her housedress and an apron. Sensible lace-up black shoes.

The Shores began to look more like Woodstock than an east coast fishing village. The decision to allow costumes representing any time period of the past two hundred years had made for a mish-mash of eras and a wide range of ability in costuming. Since long skirts abounded, even in the heat of late August, along with flowered and lace blouses, it looked both like the 1960s and 1860s.

A number of the younger villagers were dressed as hippies. Jared MacPherson designated himself as the official heritage dealer.

He'd dug out some of his father's clothing from half a century before – a dashiki, beads and sandals – and paraded around the village in a cloud of sweet-smelling smoke, always managing to keep a few steps ahead of Jamieson.

He gathered a following of young people, dressed like him, deep with admiration for someone they thought had been a genuine hippie, who, in his own words, "might of gone to Woodstock." He hadn't even been born then.

Jared found the number of his admirers constantly changing,

as the Frasers or Joudrys saw their grandkids through the haze of smoke that surrounded him, and hauled them out by the ear or hair or shirtsleeve. They soon bounded back, tagged onto his shirttails and breathed in deeply, not the fragrant air of The Shores, but of Jared's homegrown.

When it wasn't looking like Woodstock, the village rather resembled Frontier Town. Most of the women, unwilling to put a lot of effort into dressing up men who would only resent it, had opted for a fifties look. Not 1850s, but 1950s. They were wearing Levi jeans and checkered shirts rolled up at the sleeves. Those who smoked, like Wally Fraser, had a pack of smokes tucked in their sleeves or front pockets.

Moira, meantime, brought the wild west thundering into The Shores. Rejecting the unlucky fish costuming, she, with the help of the Sears catalogue, had put together an Indian princess outfit to beat them all. Unrelenting embroidery of eagles and birds, beading to beat the band, rows of necklaces, moccasins on her feet, and yes, sad to say, a feathered headdress. She tried to make Frank wear one, too, but caved in and let him wear a cowboy hat and boots.

Ian had opted for that look and Hy had, too. The checkered shirts and Levis, that is. Not the cowboy hat. Finn just kept wearing head-to-toe black and Dot hadn't decided what to do.

"You wouldn't get me in one of them rigs." Gus pointed to Annabelle and April Dewey who were "gussied up," as Gus put it, in pretty authentic-looking dresses of the 1800s. Both were whizzes with a needle. They'd become the poster girls of the celebration, with April's six kids clustered around and all in appropriate costume. Murdo was in hiding, in the comfort of April's nineteenth-century kitchen. That was costume enough for him.

He could have hidden behind his police uniform, but he wasn't sure where it was. He hadn't worn it, or done anything official in it, in more than a year. It was no longer expected – by anyone, not even Jamieson.

Jamieson had decided to dress up for the week, too. Why should she be left out? She was hoping, though barely admitting it to herself, to turn Ian's eye her way again. And so, hair down and flowing, she wore the silk blouse that had seemed to have such a positive effect on him that night he kissed her.

But he hardly even glanced at her. Other men did. Frank. Wally Fraser. Jared MacPherson. A couple of seasonal residents who'd never bothered to look at Jamieson before. Now they were stimulated by the thought of tumbling a local girl, and a police officer to boot. Not exactly a cavalcade of Romeos, but Jamieson stirred some male interest in that silk blouse.

Just not Ian's.

Bessie and Jessie, Moira's two maiden aunts from New Brunswick, had missed her wedding, but were excited to visit and take part in the celebration – as long as Moira didn't put them up in a wigwam. They didn't have to worry about dressing up. They'd arrived, dressed for the part. Long skirts, frilly blouses and old lady lace-up boots were what they wore every day.

Marlene had decided to opt out, saying to anyone who might look at her critically: "Someone has to maintain an official presence." So there she was, in the stinking heat, in a navy suit, white cotton shirt and her service badge, adding to the hodgepodge of centuries and cultures, almost all of which had nothing to do with The Shores.

Marlene took photographs selectively, isolating the compliant April Dewey and her horde, and a few others who appeared to have plucked their heritage from this place in another time. People like Bessie and Jessie. From Tatamagouche. Not The Shores. But much more suitable.

A truer picture would be recorded by Lester Joudry. In his video, The Shores seemed lost in time and place, at the mercy of gangs of aging would-be James Deans and flower children.

Chapter Forty-Three

www.theshores200.com
It's Heritage Day at The Shores, the village's 200th birthday. This whole summer has been leading up to this day. Still time to join us and celebrate.
Likes: 21
Comment: Will there be fireworks…with dead people in them?

"Ssh. Listen to that."

Hy and Ian were up on the widow's walk on the roof of his house, the best view in The Shores.

"What?" He handed her a coffee. He kept a Keurig on the roof.

"That."

"That? I don't hear anything."

"That's exactly it. You hear nothing."

"Correct."

"No ride-ons."

"Of course. Nice."

"Um-hm."

They were on the walk to get a bird's eye view of the day's events.

Moira had generously donated one wigwam as a heritage

museum designed by local high school students. She had devoted another to Mi'kmaw heritage, most especially her own. She'd retrieved the wedding outfit from the compost bin, and laid it out facing front, the damage to the back concealed.

Also concealed from Moira at the moment was Bessie and Jessie's wedding present to her. They had actually given up in despair of her ever getting married, and a year before had sent her the multiple-place setting of dishes they'd collected over the years with stamps earned for purchases at the Tatamagouche grocery store. They were plastic ware with little flowers on them, a knockoff of Corning Ware.

Not ungrateful, Moira had deemed them "too good to use" and put them away with other such family treasures.

Bessie and Jessie decided this was the appropriate occasion to bring them out. They would be perfect for refreshments being served to dignitaries in the hall. They rooted around Moira's when she was out the day before – she was spending quite a bit of time with Frank in the wigwam – and found them in cha cupboard in the kitchen.

Their eyes twinkled. They smiled. Nodded in harmony.

"Too good to use," said Bessie.

"Too good to use," said Jessie.

They were delighted. Their niece had found their gift too good to use. In the Toombs family, that was the highest accolade.

But sometimes sacrifices had to be made.

Box after box, they brought them out.

They covered the kitchen floor. Now what?

They were lucky that Billy showed up to see Madeline, because they never could have transported them over to the hall themselves, even though the dishes were only plastic.

They twittered along beside him, back and forth to the hall, until the dishes were all safely stacked in the W.I. kitchen.

Then they began to wash them.

Marlene had woken from an afternoon nap at Moira's and seen the activity from one back door to the other. She got up and went over to see what was going on.

"Oh, they're lovely." Marlene stroked the pretty floral pattern on one of the dishes. "Simply lovely."

Bessie and Jessie smiled.

"Aren't they?" said Bessie.

"Aren't they?" said Jessie.

They were relieved when Moira showed up.

"What a good idea," she said. This was a new Moira, softened by Frank's caresses, able to give credit where it was due. She'd thought about offering up the set for the official ceremonies in the hall, but had hesitated, so engrained was it in her nature to save, put aside, treasure.

But the Premier would be eating brownies here. And several MLAs, many of them ministers in the provincial government. Eating off her plates. She swelled with pride at the thought.

But the occasion did not cure Moira of her ways.

When they were finished with the plates at the hall, she would wrap them all up again – with Bessie and Jessie's help and approval – and store them in the cupboard in the kitchen. Who knows when they would see the light of day again.

In the meantime, she made sure that Frank took lots of photographs with his cell phone of all the dignitaries eating off her dishes. She later hung several of them in her front hall.

For lesser mortals not partaking of the goodies served up on Moira's plates, Nathan, Billy and Finn had constructed a model size "hall" outside as a refreshment stand. All the official business would take place inside the hall, while, outside, the whole common area was a flea market.

At one table sat the skull of Roger Murphy. It was the centre of Jamieson's "sword in the stone" event. For a toonie, anyone could have one try at removing the gold tooth from the skull. The tooth would go to the winner and proceeds would go to the county hospital.

Jamieson's stipulation was that no damage could be done to the skull in any way.

But no one could do it. No one could get a hand or fingers into any aperture in the skull to get a chance at the gold.

Jared didn't have a hope. His great big mitts came nowhere near being able to penetrate the skull. He skulked around while others tried, hoping to put them off and win by default. He was seriously considering knocking the skull off the table and smashing it "accidentally."

Gladys Fraser had the smallest hands of any woman in The Shores, and proud of it, but even she could only get the ends of four fingers, up to the knuckles, into Roger's gap-toothed grin. She tried so hard, she threatened to dislodge some of the other teeth.

Finally, Dottie waddled up to the booth, took the skull in her arms, and stuck a baby fist in through the bullet hole. The tooth came out in her hand. She immediately began to chew on it, until Dot, seeing her, rescued the toddler and her prize.

"First visit from the tooth fairy," said Dot, holding the gold tooth high so it glinted in the sun.

"She didn't pay her toonie," Jared mumbled after the fact. He had thrown a slug into the jar.

"For her education," decreed Gus. "Fittin'."

Roger remained on display beside a large replica skull and, for a loonie a toss, people could win a prize. Proceeds also went to the county hospital. Finn was giving a forensic talk about the skull and pointing out to a group of bloodthirsty youngsters – most of them Deweys – what the marks on it might mean.

Sticking his finger in the hole – always a fun party trick – he'd outline the possibilities.

"This is almost certainly a bullet hole, though it's changed somewhat in size and shape since the incident occurred more than fifty years ago. Smoothed for one thing. It's the approximate size of a bullet discharged by a gun in Constable Jamieson's possession, but we don't know any more than that. The hole's too worn by time to give us any specific information. Not the brand, and we can't say that a particular person with a specific gun shot Roger. Though it's a safe bet that the guy in the boat with him did."

Ben was offering tourists a taste of "heritage farming." He had a barn full of old equipment – the Macks never gave anything away. He'd oiled it up and got it going and he and Nathan and a couple of the local lads were giving educational rides through his fields.

Gladys Fraser had command of Wally's shed. The Women's Institute had stuck up a sign:

Heritage Shed Circa 1962.

"Genuine metal do-it-yourselfer," Wally would slap the siding. "First of its kind."

The women had opened up the insides – all the boxes of people's lives over a hundred and fifty years. They'd combed through them for artifacts now on display: hair combs, suspenders, love letters, irons, corsets, all neatly laid out and identified as the W.I. heritage project. The Cranes – Gladys's family – were on one side; the Frasers on the other. Interesting mementos and photos decorated the boxes and trunks, and so fertile were the two families, it amounted to a history of the village.

They thought it might make another book. Hy agreed.

Wally and his beloved John Deere had been banished from the shed, but he didn't care. He had a "building," bigger than a shed, and this one contained not just Wally's new tractor, but every ride-on he'd ever owned, going back fifty years. It was a museum in itself. Wally had spent the last weeks polishing and servicing every one of the vehicles, all of which were in working order. They were just waiting for the "turfew" to be over to exit the building on parade, each driven by a Fraser man or boy.

Wally had spent many happy hours in the building, playing with his toys.

And smoking.

There was a "heritage moment of silence" at noon so people could hear what The Shores sounded like before there were ride-ons. And there was the much-anticipated draw for the winner of the John Deere machine.

The entries were stuffed into a brand-new gas can, shaken, and Dottie stuck a tiny hand in to pull out the winner, with as much dispatch as she had taken hold of the gold tooth.

"Billy Pride," Marlene called out.

Billy flushed bright red, and ran up to accept the keys, held them up high and yelled:

"Wheels."

Because, for Billy, it was more than just a ride-on. It was his way of making a living, and his way of getting around the village. He didn't have a car.

He grabbed one of the five filled gas cans that were part of the prize, filled up the tractor, hoisted tiny girlfriend Madeline on the back, and drove off, if not into the sunset, into the noonday sun.

That was Wally's cue to fire up his heritage ride-ons, with the help of his extended family of grandchildren. The Frasers rode their vehicles from Wally's, past Gus Mack's, up The Shore Lane and around the hall. They did it once. They did it twice. They did it three times. And kept on going.

Marlene could do nothing but open and shut her mouth, and guide the dignitaries into the hall where refreshments awaited them – as well as a concert and stepdancing by the local children.

If asked, the dignitaries would have said they preferred to listen to the ride-ons.

Wally was fully aware that the villagers had promised to keep their mowers silent for the whole day.

"But, in my opinion," he said later, explaining himself, "them ride-ons is heritage, too, and meant to be part of the day. And, anyway, wasn't Billy riding his?"

Wally was envious of Billy's win – and him with shameful little around his house to mow. Though his own John Deere was just a year old, Wally was already having unfaithful thoughts about replacing it. How to get it past Gladys was the problem.

For now, The Shores was filled with the sound of tractors mowing.

"Just as it should be," said Wally.

"Wouldn't know it was summer otherwise," said Harold MacLean.

"Hyuup," he punctuated the statement after a brief pause.

Abel Mack was nowhere to be found to venture his opinion, but Gus was at a table giving a workshop called "Ancient and Crazy Quilts." She was also signing and selling copies of her bestseller.

Cat moved up from Big Bay for the day with his clothing line, including a number of fine items made of sole.

"It's my new line," he told Hy later in the day. "It ain't easy. Very delicate. Very hard to do.

"I've named it specially for The Shores." He flipped over a cardboard sign and propped it up behind the dainties:

It read:

Don't Tell a Sole.

Hy sifted through the merchandise. All made of sole. A bit racy for the Shores. Camisoles. Lacy panties, short short slips. Well maybe some of the tourists would go for them. They did. By the end of the day, Cat put up another sign:

Soled out.

As night fell on a long day of celebration, the villagers walked down The Shore Lane, candles in glass containers lighting their way to the water.

Behind them the six golden cones of light lit up the village centre outside Moira's house.

Frank and the village boys had organized a fireworks display on the beach. Soon rockets and roman candles were banging and whizzing and throwing balls of light into the night sky.

Jamieson was back in uniform, in case of trouble. There was drinking going on, to which she turned a blind eye. One of the drinkers was her police partner Murdo.

Three star shells went off in sequence, showering dazzling

light on the shore.

"That could be one of Vera's boys." Hy grinned and nuzzled into Ian's chest.

"What do you mean?"

"Well, you can have your ashes mixed with firecracker powder…"

"And go out with a bang?"

"Exactly. People do it."

"They do this, too," he tilted her chin.

He kissed her.

And then he did it again.

Jamieson turned her head away. Whitey abandoned a fish carcass she'd been batting around and came to wind herself around Jamieson's ankles. Jamieson nudged her away. The cat kept coming back, until finally Jamieson picked her up, and held her warm body close, against the chill.

Acknowledgements

I'm grateful for the hard work of the talented people at The Acorn Press: Terrilee Bulger, Sherie Hodds, Laurie Brinklow and Matt Reid. I'm honoured to be in their company.

Many thanks to my early readers for pointing out the gaping holes and errors in usage: The possibly prejudiced Kirsten MacLeod, my daughter and great supporter. My good friend, JoAnne Wilson, of the excellent editorial eye and generous spirit. Margo MacNaughton, to whom this book is dedicated, for her superior command of the English language, the comma, in particular, and her ability to keep me straight on critical plot points. Thanks to Nancy and to Frances for the delicious and well-orchestrated launches.